Secret Passages
Nothing Ever Happens in Tuttlebury

JOHNNA ANNE GURR

authorHOUSE

AuthorHouse™
1663 Liberty Drive
Bloomington, IN 47403
www.authorhouse.com
Phone: 833-262-8899

Published by AuthorHouse 06/14/2022

ISBN: 978-1-6655-5870-9 (sc)
ISBN: 978-1-6655-5869-3 (e)

Library of Congress Control Number: 2022908271

Print information available on the last page.

Interior Image Credit: Samuel Gurr and Johnna Anne Gurr

This book is printed on acid-free paper.

Contents

Dedication

I wish to honor my four grown children. In their earlier years, they commandeered a refrigerator carton, creating and exploring.

I am grateful for the privilege to teach middle school students; they taught me as well.

To Lucian, his devotion to writing children's books inspired this story.

A special dedication to Bianca Page, a resourceful high school student, who assisted in editing this book.

And to my very supportive husband.

"Hope is the thing with feathers that perches in the soul. And sings the tune without words. And never stops at all."
Emily Dickinson

Introduction

*Y*ou may be shaking your head wondering how this book came to be. Actually, it was quite by accident. The original intent was to pen a story thar focused on motherhood and children—that is, my life with a brood of kids. Words of wisdom would arise from their interesting happenings, spotlighted for all to see. Each would be gazed upon like the singular goldfish swimming in a bathroom cup. Of course, I would ask them first and being of good nature, they would shake their heads affirmatively. But their crooked smile would wish this effort a fading mist in the sky. So, they were hoping.

As I sat with pad and pencil—usually this stirs creative juices which a blue screen chokes—the story took a form beyond the boundaries of home sweet home. This accounting would involve another ample sized family; a fictional one, although fodder from personal experience would very likely surface. As a family of six and two more on the way, they were traveling to a new home, new friends and a new life. Everyday circumstances would blend with spine tingling drama of the unexpected and the fantastical.

The age of the children hovers in middle to early high school years. Having taught middle schoolers and raised them myself, I have decided to profile this stage of life.

Incorporated is a view of today's world with all its advantages and pitfalls; challenging young people to become responsible, successful adults. There is a plethora of distractions and difficulties as well as the heralding of major achievements and advancements. But hasn't life on planet Earth always been so? In my time, I can remember witnessing the tragic coverage of the death of President Kennedy as well the thrill of seeing the Apollo moon landing in my own living room.

Today's world is encumbered with many complications arising from the explosion of technology. Informational and communicative equipment is embraced with fingers gliding over keyboards of computers, cell phones, and other gadgetry. Peer pressure has driven young people—and other ages as well—into welcoming forms of social media that transcends from that same living room to a global outreach. Even more challenging is the constant media coverage of events involving issues such as the worldwide pandemic, various kinds of criminal activity and efforts for social justice.

To grow up, there is so much to consider.

Yet the everyday is lived in the most ordinary of daily things. From the early morning yawn to nightfall's droopy eyelids, there are endless decisions and tasks to complete and hotdogs and hamburgers to grill. There is much to contemplate especially when you're a young adult whose brain circuitry and bodily form is undergoing major overhaul—fledging to become fully formed adults.

Sometimes to go forward, you need to step backward. This story takes place in the now of modern technology but eases into a simpler time of farm life where everyday realities resist and sometimes collide.

And serendipitous surprises happen.

Prologue

It was a steamy hot day and it was only early April. Grandpa Norfeld always liked them that way. But today's tidal wave of sweat was getting out of hand. He had already drenched his worn plaid shirt and was wiping his neck with an old red handkerchief. He would endure.

Definitely he believed old school thinking and ways of doing things ... he wouldn't let his son destroy the house with that fancy stuff, what was it called; central air? He had finally given in to a couple of those wall boxes that pumped out smelly ice cube air. He refused to turn them on, that is, unless his son's family was paying a visit. He was an old man and could do what he darn well pleased.

Grandpa walked to the kitchen window, holding his huge cup of black coffee. He pushed the worn café curtains aside and looked outside. Dried out grass covered a portion of the backyard but looking beyond was an acreage of fallow ground. Hard, and now unused, nature had seeded it with flower, trees, and every sort of weed. He blinked and imagined as it had been, an abundant farm yielding corn and tomato as well as his beloved strawberry. The livestock barn was to the right filled with the happy mooing of cows and scent of manure. How he loved those animals! He would rise at four in the morning for the first milking and return to the kitchen by nine to enjoy a second breakfast with his dear wife. She often made pancakes with blueberries and warmed real maple syrup. Life couldn't get much better.

But now his wonderful wife and the blueberry pancakes and the farm were gone. A cherished memory in his heart.

Grandpa took a gulp of his coffee and nodded sadly. They had been a happy family. All he learned about farming he had gladly taught his daughter and son. He wanted them to know how to manage a farm. Because like many a father would hope; the children would carry on the business. He had done so for his dad. But it wasn't to be. His son refused and even his daughter who had shown interest had left to become a nurse. He sold off most of the property and maintained a small crop with the use of hired help. Stepping into his eighty-fifth year, he didn't have the strength to farm this place anymore. He had tried hard, with sleeves pulled up to his taunt upper muscles. Still the kids always hollered at him. He finally realized he had to slow down.

Grabbing his cup, Grandpa Norfeld went out to the porch. Days like this reminded him of his youth when the family worked as a team to turn over the soil and ready it for planting. He was given responsibility for the strawberry crop. This was alright with him; the anticipation of strawberry shortcake and handfuls of berry sweetness in his mouth would ease up any aches and pains. With his rough hand, he rubbed his unshaven face and grunted. Perhaps he could do a little, just plant a row or two of those wonderful seedlings. He could buy then over at Rosetta's today. The ground was softening from the winter frost, he could dig a little bit. Couldn't he?

Draining the last sip of goodness from his stained coffee mug, he threw on his dirt crusted work boots. Walking through the generous yard, he passed the dilapidated swing set, the weatherworn red barn, the chicken coups and rusty barbed wire that had established old property lines. He had a particular shovel in mind and he believed it was in the great shed. The sun burrowed a hole in his balding head—at least he had a few strands left—and the damp air sat heavy in his lungs. Sweat was rolling down his neck, soaking his back. Maybe he should turn back to the house. His wife words pounded in his mind. "Stop always being so stubborn and use common sense."

But he had to do this.

Grandpa stood before the weathered shed, it's once smooth paint now peels of gray and white; the padlock rusted over. He reached into his pocket for the ring of farm keys. Now he knew there were two, the shiny master and the grimy copy. Could he have lost it? Or maybe he had purposely misplaced this key because the last time … He decided to search his other dungaree pocket. There it was! He gingerly eased in the dirty key and as the padlock fell open, he quickly tossed the key under the dingy mat.

Stale, musty air poured over him as the creaky door opened. There was the smell of dank wood and something putrid; perhaps a field mouse had broken in and couldn't get out. Grandpa was not dissuaded as he stepped into the forbidding gloom. Fumbling for the chain to the ceiling light, he tripped over odd objects. Lurching for it again, the worn chain broke away from the dusty light bulb. Darkness filled every cranny, only a solitary sunbeam from the doorway attempted to pierce through. He blinked several times, his eyes slowly acclimating. He could make out large forms, looming and awkward. Some were covered, others thrown about. So much for the once tidy shed, he had kept. But as far as he remembered, the farm implements, especially the favored shovel, should be on the far wall. Grandpa carefully took a few more steps.

And stopped.

Suddenly he couldn't move. Flashes of blue, red and yellow folded and swirled into intense shades of violet and aquamarine. Grandpa shuttered and grabbed his head. Was he imagining or was this really happening? His stomach lurched, the sensation of lifting and spinning was terrifying. The next moment he was resting in a calm of soft white light, like being in the eye of the storm. Strong images filled his vision of things he did not understand. There were torrential rains, unsettled voices, trees falling and family as he not known them; wrinkled and seasoned with life. There was movement as he was pushed sideways and then he floated upwards and peered down at the red checkerboard tablecloth and his steaming mug of morning coffee. In a flash, Grandpa was jerked backwards, like the sudden sensation of an amusement park ride. His eyes were filled with varying tones of sepia. Nostalgic. Photographs of life before. His lap was full of young children—giggling, excited little ones. Grandpa laughed and at the same time his heart filled with longing. There was a desire to return to those times, dreaming he could once again see his loved ones.

Suddenly Grandpa grabbed his chest, the rapid thumping making him dizzy. Seated in the carriage of a roller coaster, he went up and up, halted in mid-air, then plunged downward. "No!" He threw his arms forward to stop the ride. He now remembered why he had avoided the shed. *This had happened before.* He began to tremble uncontrollably. How could he get out? His heart was pounding, pounding, pounding. Willfully he stepped back towards the door. Sweat was flowing down his face; a hard smirk lifted his chin. With superhero strength he rushed out the creaky door, sliding unto the grass.

Stunned he lay there, his body so heavy, so full of pain.

He looked up and saw a misty figure of someone that was otherworldly. This womanly form was wearing a familiar strawberry apron. She gestured to him in a welcoming manner. The mist ebbed a bit; as he recognized his dear wife, Emma. Grandpa relaxed. His heart was now peaceful. Gentle symphonic tones were playing as a dazzling radiance beaconed.

Grandpa Norfeld eased himself to his feet and followed.

Grab a Box and Go!

Sleep wouldn't come. Robert sat up, tossed his black hair and then mashed his face into the pillow. Already early morning light was peeking through the crooked blinds. He had emptied his model rocketry box trying to jumpstart sleep, as he counted the space ships he had created. He breathed deeply, trying to free fall to dreamland. But cameo photos of the last few days replayed in his head.

Yesterday was the worst, and the best. Robert had finished his final project and went to visit his high school science teacher, Mr. Elliot. He wanted to leave his report and bolt out of there. But so much for that, as the teacher waved him to a chair. Standing firmly in place, Mr. Elliot thumbed slowly through the pages. He stroked every hair of his beard, as he hummed to himself. Apprehension crept into every chalky corner of the classroom.

1

"Robert, from what I reviewed here, you appear to have covered your topic surprisingly well, and for a freshman you have developed some feasible possibilities. This report should help bring up your grade this semester. Also, your contribution to the science fair was engaging with the self-made model rockets, and the film launching them." Mr. Elliot went over to where Robert was sitting, making eye contact. "I believe if you continue putting effort in all your subjects, your overall average will improve." Shaking Robert's hand, he turned and abruptly left the room.

In a flash, Robert was out of there. His cell phone had shut off so he had to get to his girlfriend's locker and leave her a message about the party. It was supposed to be a surprise for him and he wanted to make sure she knew. The lock gave way as he expertly entered the numbers. Leaving the scribbled note, he glanced about the silent hall hoping that she would show up. No sign of the pretty girl with the long dark hair. But she rarely stayed late because she was responsible for the daily upkeep of her golden retriever. How she loved that dog! Sometimes he wondered if he was playing the starter band in her life.

She came to the party! They danced for a long time in the midst of a full house swaying with deafening music and voices. It was the most awesome party ever. All his friends came, the pizza was the way he liked it with creamy mozzarella and olives. One guy had brought a karaoke machine and was singing—well, mostly yelling and annoying all the guests. But the best part was when the girl with the long black hair tucked herself into his arms and their lips met in a long kiss. A kiss that could he played over and over in his mind. So amazing was this girl named Jessica.

"Robert, Robert, this is the second time I've called you," yelled his father. "The next time I'm coming up to your room! Hey, your brother and sisters were up early doing their share. Where are you, the big brother who's supposed to set an example!"

Robert moaned and yanked the summer blankets up around his long, lean body. Ugh. Just when he was falling asleep. Besides the pinging in his head, his stomach was flopping like a striper on a hook. The chaos in the house had escalated as heavy footsteps pounded the staircase. Grunts and groans harmonized like a bad concert as the family pulled and yanked. His father was shouting orders like a referee at a game. Robert hugged both pillows to his ear. Not working.

Abruptly the bedroom door crashed open. Startled, Robert sat board straight, the blue plaid sheets falling to the floor.

"Get up and get dressed young man! Grab some boxes and head down to the moving van. You can get some breakfast on the folding table which your mother picked up this morning. The pancakes may be cold, but that's what happens when you stay in bed too long."

Robert stared at the door as it slammed open. There was a terrible ache in his gut. The last thing he wanted was greasy fast food. As he pulled on jeans, a soiled tee shirt and strong work boots, he wondered how this was really happening and hoped it was an awful nightmare.

He stood, and peered into his reflection from the mirror he taken down from the bureau last night. He was a wreck. But he didn't much care. He kind of liked this messy look, fingering his black snarly hair, which hung down his neck. But his remarkably dark eyes were another thing; very red and swollen from all that tossing and turning. Dad would be in his face about his appearance, blame it on the party last night and say how he hated the hair. Robert rooted for an elastic band in his pocket and quickly knotted a pony tail.

Stacking boxes in his arms, he realized he had forgotten a very important one; his stash of model rockets and starter robotics projects. Carrying this load with caution, he joined the stomping parade down the steep staircase, through the long hallway to the ample sized living room door, out to the giant moving truck. Some friends and neighbors were helping as well. Mrs. Norfeld commandeered the helm. Even though many months pregnant, she stood confident, shouting orders where to place everything. The professional movers shrugged then gave in, racing about like squirrels gathering acorns. She had an eye for this sort of thing; how to snug furniture and crates just right so nothing would fall or break. Everything was in perfect order so that unpacking would flow smoothly into their new home, not dumped into a mound in the living room.

Robert piled boxes to the side and wiped the sweat from his neck. He peered sadly down the street. There was the rounded cul-de-sac where he learned to roller skate, ride a bike and master the skateboard; although one crazy stunt put him in the emergency room. His eyes wandered down the paved driveway to the coolest basketball hoop ever. This was the practice zone. Here with his good friends, Dewayne, George and Jamal, he would prepare for the next basketball game. His friends were decent players and Robert tried to be as good as them. Often, it was Jamal who would bring home those great basket shots.

He turned towards the old Colonial which he had called home. What had once seemed so grand now appeared small. And so sad. Even the uneven gray and white shutters seemed like distressed eyebrows. Dad had mowed the lawn one last time but the golf green perfection would no longer please them but await others. Robert looked away, swiping a tear off his cheek.

Following his father's lead, the family headed into the house for a final look-over. There were a few items here and there which were quickly disposed. Total emptiness remained; the stark weird echo of open spaces. Gone were the rainbow colors of fresh flowers on the table, the mouth-watering smells of baking chicken with potatoes and the constant boom from the television. All gone. It was like they had never lived here. Yet they had. All those memories pressed down in his heart.

Soon the movers climbed into their truck and the family crammed into their trusty salmon tinted station wagon with the third seat. No one looked back, Robert thought, until he noticed his father. Mr. Norfeld was watching out the rearview mirror his eyes puffed and wet. Suddenly he jumped from the car seat and raced towards the backyard porch. In moments he returned, his treasured bird-watching binoculars in his hand. "I can't leave without these. You never know what kind of birds I'll find. Maybe even see my favorite singing grosbeak."

Finally, they were on their way. The ride was tedious and sweaty. With little air conditioning, all the windows were open wide, the swishing of surrounding cars noisy and hypnotic. Mr. Norfeld was at the wheel and for a while his wife chatted on and on. Then things quieted. His sisters were snoring in the way-back third seat and his brother had managed to cram in a library of genres, his head buried in the pages.

Pushing the hard covered books aside, Robert fell into the left corner of the back seat, his hand holding on to the cell phone. His fingers efficiently danced out text messages to all his friends. He would rather have spoken to them, especially to Dewayne, but not here, not in this jammed car. But he was not able to reach his girlfriend and his phone was running out of power. Why was she not responding? He had to talk to her; that last kiss had been the best, strong yet tender. Way better than her light pecks on the side of his mouth. Had he done anything wrong? Maybe he had said something stupid again but he had no idea what it was. Frustrated he tried once more as his cell battery turned off.

The station wagon began slowing down: the roadway food signs were calling.

"Come on gang. I'm tired of driving and need a break and a burger. We've driven five hours and only a few more to go. I know your mother really needs to walk around and also find a lady's room. Expecting twins is like that. Have this be a good pit stop; I want to keep making excellent time so we get there when the moving truck does. Or even a little before. I know your mother marked where things go; she really wants to direct the unloading." Dad grinned and winked at his wife.

Parking the station wagon, everyone piled out.

* * *

The rest of the way Robert was annoyed by everything. He was especially bothered by all the change in the car. Mrs. Norfeld had rearranged her seating to the back seat so she could have a grow-up talk with his older sister, Danielle, which was alright with him. Paul had to pick up armfuls of books and move to the way-back joining his younger sister Natalie. That left him in the front passenger seat right next to his father, which was not alright with him.

Mr. Norfeld broke the silence. "So, Robert, you've been awfully quiet all the way up. Still tired?"

Robert shrugged. He didn't feel like talking. He leaned over and twisted the radio dial, trying to find a familiar channel. But all he found were country tunes. How appropriate. He yanked up the volume and looked over at his father. Mr. Norfeld was singing, his hand tapping notes on the steering wheel. How could he be so happy, and not notice that his son's life had been pulled like a skateboard leaving him flat on his face? Heck, it was early June and he was going on sixteen, but Robert felt like his life was over.

"You know Robert, I think you'll really like living at the old farm. When I was younger, I used to help your grandpa with milking the cows, planting corn, feeding chickens. There were even pigs which I hated because they smelled so bad, but the bacon was the best. We had horses too but we really didn't need them because we had the tractor, but Grandpa kept them for us …"

"Dad, I've heard this story over and over. Can't we change the subject?"

"Robert, you interrupted me!" Frustrated, Mr. Norfeld tousled his graying hair. "I want you to be pleased with this move. Getting grandpa's house is a special opportunity. Remember I told you that our old house was a getting too small? Well, it was also too expensive. This farmhouse will be affordable and big enough for all of us. We will have a good life there. You know, Grandpa would have been glad to see us now."

"You're talking like you're glad Grandpa died."

Dad turned and gave Robert a long, forlorn look. "Mind your manners, young man! You're the oldest and things are going to change. You're growing up and you've finished your first year of high school. You did alright but you could do better, anyway that's what the principal said. I agree. You could also do better at home. Be more responsible. I'll be

7

counting on you to take charge of things. Help us settle, help your mother carry things, especially since the babies will be coming soon and I will be working a lot getting used to this new job." Dad paused as he took a difficult lane change.

Robert squirmed in his seat; his innards volcanic lava ready to erupt. Take charge! Hadn't he done enough already! What about his brother with his nose in the books or his sisters who were always playing softball or violin? What about his life? What about his friends, especially his new girlfriend, Jessica? He was now in high school and had a life!

"Robert, will you be able to help?"

Robert turned his head and saw his reflection in the window. His face was tight and hostile looking. Eyebrows arched like a villain over eyes that were pools of ink. Bitterness was snaking through his veins, as he clenched his hands together. Taking a deep breath Robert looked into his lap and said, "Yeah."

"I knew I could depend on you," replied his father he turned up the music.

2

Cheese Danish with Attitude

The bowl was overflowing with his favorite sugared wheat flakes as Paul generously poured the milk. He hungrily dug in, not caring that a puddle was forming on the tablecloth. He looked up at the clock. Again, he was the early bird. For the past few days, he had been the first one up. Everyone else was still dreaming under their sheets. That is, except for his father who had left hours ago for his new job. Yeah, it was a transfer, but was still new for him.

Mom was always up with the sunrise, but the move had really made her tired. Usually, she was determined to arrange the house just so; her marching orders never let up. Sometimes she could be like an army sergeant. He was glad she wasn't up yet to yell at him for eating too much. Still hungry, he poured himself a heaping second of cereal. He was getting worried; Mom was losing that rosy glow. With the twins coming soon, he was glad she was sleeping in. Hmm … his sister wouldn't be the youngest anymore. But he would always be the younger, short brother. Maybe. Now they had to make room for two more kids.

Paul glanced around the kitchen peering into a portion of the living room and dining room. For only moving a few weeks ago, most everything was settled—like they had been here for years. But it was also awkward. Sure, he was used to this house, he had loved visiting his grandparents, but it was weird being here without them, almost like they had stolen this place. He really missed them. He could almost hear his grandpa's jovial laugher and feel those heartening pats on his back. Grandma was always baking; he really stuffed down those fresh baked strawberry rhubarb pies. Paul left his spoon in the cereal bowl. He sniffled into a tissue, his nose red, his eyes swollen and teary. No, he wasn't crying. It was only his allergies. That's all.

"Good morning! Paul, you're really the early this morning. Enjoying that cereal, I see," said Mrs. Norfeld as she winked at her son.

"Yeah. I didn't want to wake you so I helped myself to breakfast." Paul stood and offered her a seat. "Hey Mom, please sit down with me. I can make you something good to eat. What do you think?"

"Paul, you're so kind. I only want coffee and some leftover Danish cheese pastry, but I'll sit with you."

"Okay. But sometime you have to let me cook," Paul said as he leaned over and handed her the pastry box. "You know I like to eat and I would surprise you."

"I would enjoy that very much, Paul. Perhaps tonight …"

"Morning you guys. C'mon, leave some breakfast for me," said Robert as he tore off a piece of the coffee cake and grabbed the package of cereal and a bowl. The table shook as he leaned over the table for the milk carton, tipping it sideways.

"Wow! Robert what a mess you've made! There's milk everywhere. On me and on mom! And on my favorite shorts. You had better clean this up!" Paul jumped up, drying himself with a napkin.

"It's only a little spilled milk," said Robert, "you're making such a big deal." He frowned at Paul and gathered his breakfast for a quick getaway.

"Just where do you think you're going young man," said Mr. Norfeld as she grabbed Robert's shoulder. She was now standing; all six feet of her, the flowing housecoat accentuating the greatness of her pregnant form.

Robert threw down his coffeecake and ran to get paper towels. Glancing over his shoulder, he shouted, "Paul, c'mon you can help too, you're always getting out of stuff!"

"What, you want me to clean! But I didn't make this mess. Mom, please tell him to shut up or …"

"What's with all the noise," said Danielle—Danie for short including everyone except her brothers—as she entered the room and surveyed the chaos.

Natalie, their younger sister trailed in, silently unwrapped a roll of paper towels and began cleaning the floor. She even wiped under the table, emerging with crumbs sprinkled in her curly auburn hair.

"What are you doing, that's Robert's job," shouted Paul.

"Well, you guys are fighting and I'm not letting mom go under a table. Dad said we need to be a team and you're very bad examples."

Quiet filled the room like a pause button had been pushed.

Mrs. Norfeld brushed stray hairs from her face as she sat on the kitchen stool, leaning back on the counter. "I have another box of cheese pastry we can share once the milk is wiped up."

Activity fluttered as she continued, "I know you all would have done a good job cleaning even if I didn't throw in the bribe. Oh, Natalie, don't pout; you took the lead and I appreciate it." From the refrigerator, she pulled out the other coffee cake and poured herself another cup of coffee.

"These past two weeks everyone has been a great help to me with unpacking and fixing this house. You've moved out the old furniture, taking trips to the dump. Even the repainting of the bedrooms is almost finished. Decorating comes next. Please not too many nails when you hang the posters. Find those sticky pads." She took a sip from the large mug and swiped her forehead. "There is still so much left to do. The twins will be coming soon and the nursery needs a lot of work."

"But Mom, this is summer," began Danielle, "Our summer vacation. All we do is work and work. We came here from miles away, I don't know anyone, and I don't want to work all my time away!"

"Yeah," said Robert. You and Dad dragged us here and now what? In a few weeks I will start in another high school with perfect strangers! I miss my old friends, especially Dewayne." He slammed his hand on the kitchen table. "And all I get is the corner bedroom with him!" Robert angrily waved his hand in Paul's direction.

The last bite of a third piece of pastry caught in Paul's throat. He coughed rigorously. "Yep, my sisters get all the good stuff," he choked out staring hard at Danielle and Natalie.

"You got that right! How come the girls get the biggest and nicest room?" shouted Robert. "I have to listen to Paul's snoring all night and my stuff is so crowded. And he has way too many books!" Robert took a breath and scratched his head. "In case you forgot, I'm the oldest and I should get that privilege."

Mrs. Norfeld again stood. She put on that no-nonsense parental face, with the tight pressed lips. "Enough! We've discussed this over and over. We had to move! The farm was here. So together we can make this work. Right now!"

Suddenly the phone rang.

A hush. Who could be calling them? Mrs. Norfeld reached for the land phone, cradling it on her shoulder. "Hello, this is the Norfeld residence," she said in halting tones, trying to switch up from annoyed mom to television mother. "Yes, this is Nancy Norfeld. And you're Mrs. Tuttle? Yes, I remember talking with you. Hmm. We've just moved in. Need help? Well, we're doing okay. You're right, I'm expecting twins, the due date is coming up. Yes, we're growing. It's almost like having a second family since I had the other children when I was younger. What's that? Yes, I'm feeling fine. What? A picnic at four this afternoon? Sounds delightful. Well, I'm not sure. I'll talk with my husband and get back with you. A present? Why, that's very nice. I appreciate your thoughtfulness. Yes, you too, have a wonderful day."

"Well?" asked Paul.

Robert, Danielle and Natalie leaned in to hear. Mrs. Norfeld's face was oddly flushed but her good nature had returned. "That was Mrs. Tuttle from down the road. They're having a big barbecue tonight and invited us. They also bought a special house warming gift. I know this is last minute but it sounds like a good time. We could meet some of the neighbors and not worry about supper. I have to talk to your father."

"What about asking us," asked Natalie. "I don't know any of those people and I would rather fix the nursery."

Robert nodded. "Or pick on your stupid violin. You know you haven't any talent at all." Robert's mouth twisted into an ugly scowl.

"What! That's not a nice thing for a brother to say!" Natalie's plump cheeks turned fiery red. "You know my violin makes me happy. You're the most miserable person in the whole world!"

"Robert, that comment was totally unacceptable! Standing within a breath's distance, Mrs. Norfeld stared hard at her son. "You had better apologize to your sister!"

Robert squirmed in his seat. "Ok, ok, Natalie that was my bad, let's be all good. Hey, I agree with you. I really don't care about these farm people; they seem strange to me."

"Come on, this could be fun and that's what you all want," said Mrs. Norfeld, nodding at everyone especially Danielle.

Danielle angrily rubbed her face with her fingertips. She finally spoke. "First of all, I think that Natalie plays great for only being nine well, almost ten years old. She can be a bit repetitive, but I think she'll give concerts one day. As for me, I'm tired of all this housework. I want some real fun, like playing softball in a summer league. You know I had to quit the other team and I'm aching to get up at bat. But a picnic? I really don't want to. Sorry Mom. Love you."

Then came a yawning creak and a crash of the screen door. In stormed Mr. Norfeld. He was grinning as he hauled in several grocery bags.

"I'm home for lunch. Or a late breakfast since you're all still in your pajamas?" He dumped the contents of his shopping treasures on the table. Piled high was a fresh baked strawberry rhubarb pie, applesauce, milk, picture hangers, computer paper, and toothpaste. "I also stopped by this place that has fresh donuts and bought us a dozen." He popped open the box, the mouth-watering sweetness floating in the air.

Hands with no napkins dove into the confections.

"Before I forget there is also this." From a thick brown bag Dad pulled a large can and several brushes. "Since grandpa used to always paint outside but is no longer with us, we'll pick up a brush."

Abruptly mouths stopped chewing, crumbs hanging off their lips. Everyone froze in some weird mime pose, wondering what to do next. Mr. Norfeld reached for his favorite raspberry filled donut and ate half in one bite. "Like I was saying, we'll paint the house so nice grandpa would be proud. I was thinking that since the gray paint is dark and shabby looking, why don't we perk it up by painting it a creamy yellow? Then we can find a nice evergreen for the trim. You know I decided to work the rest of the day at home but we can at least start today. Maybe test the paint on the back porch.

"You know hon—Mrs. Norfeld's loving name for her husband— there are other things going on today. A few minutes ago, there was a phone call."

"Darn, I almost forgot. When I was at the donut shop, there was a nice man there, a Mr. Tuttle. He invited us all to a picnic tonight. Mrs. Tuttle said we didn't have to bring anything. And guess what? They have some kind of present for us, not sure what that's all about. But let's go!" He waved his hands excitedly, giving his wife a large toothy smile.

Everyone knew tonight was a done deal. But first they had to get dressed and ready the nursery for the twins.

They filed out solemnly, no longer wanting to discuss the upcoming evening.

* * *

All except Paul. He sat on his bed and fumed. His father was in the den, hovering over the computer, his mother and sisters were fixing the nursery, and Robert had taken off on his bike to who knows where? What's up with his brother? How dare Robert talk bad about him! He thought they were good bros but obviously not. Was there something wrong with him or had Robert changed? It seemed like everyone was different somehow. He didn't like it.

Paul repositioned himself on fluffy pillows, eyeing stacks of books in the floor to ceiling case and piled everywhere around him. How he wanted to read but since the move his concentration was off, and he hadn't been able to finish anything. Besides this was old stuff since he couldn't get to the library. It was so far away. He couldn't wait until he got his license but being only in middle school, sixteen was a long way off. Heck, he was too young and stupid. He could have prepared a great breakfast if his mother had let him. And Dad hardly paid attention to him; it was always Robert this and Robert that. Paul took a deep breath and pushed away the opened books.

Well, he would show them a thing or two!

Paul marched himself into the kitchen. Now where had his father left it? He grabbed a honey dipped donut as he searched. There it was hiding in the corner—the brand-new can of yellow paint. What was it his father had said? It was something about painting the porch first. Paul picked up the can and read; for external use only. Hmm, so this was only for outside. He turned the label to the directions and soaked it all in. He had never done this before, but he had watched his sisters' paint and he had read books about this. How hard could this really be?

Thinking logically, he tucked a pile of newspaper under his arm, picked up one of the fresh new brushes, a special can opener and grabbed the paint by its handle. A man on a mission, he headed for the porch and went out the screen door. Efficiently he threw newspapers down, covering the slate terrace that surrounded the porch. He went to pry open the can and halted. Something was missing. Yes, he still needed rags. But there was something else … how had grandpa done this? He closed his eyes and then looked up. In his memory there was his grandfather and he wasn't painting. With a plaid clad arm, he maneuvered a metal implement; he was scraping the house! Paul squinted again. Grandpa was gone but a badly weathered porch wall stared back, its tangled peels a horrific design. This was going to take longer than he thought.

Like his grandfather used to do, he tied a red bandana around his thick crew cut, pieces of hair sticking out. Then steadying a stepladder, thank goodness it was only a single story high, he scraped away, careful not to cause deep gauges. Sweat soaked through his clothes. Although his arms ached, Paul kept working until he finally finished. Looking down, he saw the newspaper had become a swarm of deep gray curlicues. Now to paint. He stirred the paint until smooth and dipped his brush. Immediately satisfaction flowed with the initial swipes of glowing yellow. The repulsive dark gray was gone! Confidence surged, his arm slapping paint. So focused, he didn't smell the baking chocolate chip cookies. Nor did he notice that his father had swiped a few of the confections and stood behind him. Munching. Watching.

Paul just kept dipping the brush.

3

The Barbeque

Mr. Norfeld stood by the back door, keys impatiently twirling in his fingers. "Where is everyone? C'mon Nancy, you've made enough cookies for the entire town! Throw them in a bag and grab your purse. I'm anxious to meet these people."

"Hon, I need a couple of minutes to get ready. The cookies are already on a special plate. Why don't you do me a favor and carry them out to the car. Put them on the front seat so I can perch them on my lap."

"Oh, what lap?"

"What did you say?"

"Nothing. I'll take the chocolate chippers out and get the car warmed up," said Dad as he quickly lifted the plastic wrap and snatched a couple of the cookies.

"There you go warming the car when it's a hundred degrees out!"

"Can't hear you Nance," shouted Mr. Norfeld as the door banged behind him.

"Let's go kids! Your father's getting jumpy and so am I. Where are you?"

Suddenly Paul rushed into the kitchen. "Mom, I'm ready. I had to finish a project I started. Well, I really didn't finish; but I had to clean everything up. Including myself."

"Paul, what on earth are you talking about?" With a serious stare, Mrs. Norfeld took in his appearance from head to foot, noticing specks of yellow paint accenting his coffee-colored hair. Nodding, she smiled. "You look clean to me; in fact, you look very nice in that shirt. But tell me, how did you get dirty?"

"I'll show you when we get home."

"Mom, sorry we're late getting ready. Natalie wouldn't stop playing her violin. She plays even more when she gets upset. We'll head right out to the car," said Danielle as the door slammed for the second time.

"But wait a minute. I want to see how you both look." By the time she got to the door, the station wagon had already swooped up her two daughters. "Paul, go get Robert so we can go."

Paul's eyes twitched nervously. "Umm ... Robert's not here. He took off on his bike a while ago, said he didn't want to go to a stupid picnic."

"Robert did what?" Mrs. Norfeld's bright hazel eyes grew large.

Both of them startled. Outside the cacophony of the car horn blared angrily. Mrs. Norfeld looked over at Paul. "Get in the way-back seat and say nothing about this to dad. I'll handle it."

Quickly Paul lifted the back hatch of the station wagon and hopped in. Approaching the passenger seat, Mrs. Norfeld gathered her floral maternity dress and sat, settling a huge plate of chocolate confections on her lap. "We're ready," she said.

Mr. Norfeld nodded; his head down as he swirled the knob to an upbeat tune. Then he pushed hard on the pedal, kicking up the driveway pebbles.

* * *

Restless, Paul squirmed in his seat. His usual stash of books was piled in the middle, calling to him but he had absolutely no interest. All he could think about was how angry his father would be once he knew Robert wasn't here. But how could he not know; wasn't he watching when they came out of the house? His mother said to be quiet, but somehow, he would be in the middle of all this. When would they get there? Maybe he could hide under a tree. He stared out the window. Row after row of corn stalks. This was taking so long for just being a piece down the road. A piece—who talks like that and what does that mean anyhow?

Unexpectedly, a quick turn and a jerk lurched the digesting donuts in Paul's stomach. Dad parked the station wagon on the grass and Paul now had the best view from the oversized rear window. The scenario was cut and pasted right from a post card he had seen—a full-fledged farm maintained well with red paint and white trim and a herd of cows grazing off to the far side. What wasn't so idyllic was that the entire yard had been transformed into an improvised parking lot. Dad angled their car among a crowd of others. This was going to be some picnic.

"C'mon Paul," said Danielle as she lifted the handle of

22

the hatchback. Are you getting out or not? Where's Robert?" She eyed Paul suspiciously.

Paul shrugged, comfortable in the soft leather seat. "I have nothing to say, except I don't want to be at this picnic."

"Yeah, you don't want to go, I've heard that excuse before. Hey, I told mom I wasn't coming and she gave me that look. The look that keeps me doing all the stuff around the house. Paul, get out of the car!" Danielle pulled on her brother's sleeve.

"Alright, take your hands off my new shirt. I'll get out but I'm sitting under a tree over there." Paul pointed to a full silver maple way across the property.

"Then go. But I can already smell the food. You're going to miss out on some good eats, especially mom's great cookies." Danielle shut the hatch and watched her brother walk away. "You still haven't told me where Robert is!" Paul threw up his arms, quickening his pace. Danielle shrugged and turning, bumped into an elbow.

"Hi, I'm Sarah Tuttle. Are you from the new family that moved in?"

"Yeah, I'm Danielle Norfeld, Danie for short. We've been unpacking for days, and haven't met any neighbors yet. Until you, Sarah." She smiled; her eyes filled with expectation.

Sarah laughed, a big smile boasting a full set of braces. "Now you know where I live and you'll meet all the families from miles around. We have this picnic a couple times a year and it's a great time, but it's also a lot of work. She tossed her ponytail to her side. "But you know, I think I getting a little old for this, I really wanted to play softball today, but my dad said I had to help."

"Softball? You play? Tell me what field. I want to hit some balls or even see a game."

"Sarah, come help with the burgers, bring your friend

with you!" shouted a robust fellow outfitted in barbeque garb with the words, *Tuttle can Roast* written in black across his white apron. Mr. Tuttle. Next to him a very large woman with striking gray hair was shouting directions and waving her hands. With an angry smirk, she grabbed a box and shoved it to his side. She turned to leave, her apron boasting the same family logo.

Mrs. Tuttle, most likely. A scary, no-nonsense person.

A few minutes later, both girls were handed aprons and stood beside Sarah's father, Mr. Tuttle, learning to become short order cooks beginning with dishing out barbecue. As the savory smoke hung over the hunger crowd, Danielle filled dish after dish with juicy steaks, burgers and huge hot dogs hoping soon to fill up her own plate. She glanced over at Sarah who was covered with sweat and messy splashes of ketchup. Looking down on her soiled apron, she laughed, realizing what a good time she was having. This move wasn't going to be so bad after all.

As Danielle and Sarah plated the last of the barbecue, the crowd moved to tables offering tasty dishes like macaroni and cheese and baked beans. They finally feasted at the colorful paper lined tables. Danielle wiped the grease from her hands. Now she could eat. She reached for a plate and loaded on a burger and hot dog, drooling as she imagined the sides she would mound around them.

Suddenly the joviality of young male voices was heard as several young men approached. Mr. Tuttle laughed, making small talk. Sarah ogled them like she was at some pop concert. But Danielle halted, awkwardly pointing the serving fork with one hand and hiding her plate with the other. In the line stood a half dozen of high school guys, all quite handsome but wearing the attitude and the black gear that men with motorcycles flaunt. But one stood out among the rest. His clothing was a bit off, a lame effort to resemble the others. Danielle gasped—this was her brother! For only living in this town a short time, he had been pulled into this odd group. More like a gang. Nothing like the guys from the basketball team who were fun and not trouble makers. What was Robert getting into?

Robert looked away.

"Well, guys you're in luck, said Mr. Tuttle as he dug through the meat boxes. "We finished the steaks and my favorite fresh caught trout, but here's what's left of the burgers and I grill up the last of the dogs."

Sarah flung off her soiled apron and flashed them a radiant smile boasting a heavy layer of metal. "Hey, what took you guys so long to get your food? The best stuff is almost gone. I saw you hanging near the horse barn. What's so interesting there?" She then gazed her attention on the fellow with long blonde hair. He grinned back.

Danielle's questioning eyes were glued to her brother's. His spoke a warning—shut up, or you'll be sorry. She was taken aback by the anger and hostility. She had seen this side of Robert before, usually when he was upset with his brother or mom and dad. But he had never acted like this to her. They had an understanding. Correction. They had had an understanding. This person standing before her wasn't her brother. He was acting like someone else. And he stood very close to a short, muscular guy, who seemed older than the rest. They were acting like friends. Danielle thought she heard someone call him Alex.

Quickly the group of guys dressed in black, loaded their plates with sides and then herded to the other side of the barn. Except for the blond- haired guy. Sarah had her arm wrapped around his as they walked away, no longer interested in the picnic or her new friend. Danielle shrugged it off, looking around the yard for a familiar face. Just a lot of chattering strangers. Then she noticed her parents. Her mother was sitting with the twins and a group of women, her arms gesturing away as she recounted a story. Dad was standing by the porch smoking cigars with all the men as one by one they filed into the great white farmhouse. Where was Natalie? At that moment a group of young girls ran by her, shouting and giggling, including her sister. Natalie was really having a great time. Looking over at the huge maple tree, Danielle decided to enjoy this yummy lunch with her younger brother.

"Hi, Paul! I want to picnic with you."

"Ok, I guess. Since when would you choose me over Robert? Hey, I'm not even allowed to call you Danie."

A look of sadness swept over Danielle's face. "Umm … I'm sorry about that," she said nearly choking on a potato chip. "You're always busy reading."

"Well, I'm not busy now, only eating and thinking." Paul peeled the cupcake wrapper and took a generous bite. He grunted. "Still can't put the whole thing in my mouth like dad does. Neither can you, Danielle!"

Danielle's cheeks reddened. "Paul, please call me Danie from now on. I know I've been a jerk. Give me a chance to do better." She put on her most apologetic look but Paul had turned his head.

"Ok."

"What are you thinking about?"

"Paul wrinkled his nose and smirked. "Well, Danie, if you really want to know, I am a stranger here. I don't know these people and they seem so weird anyway. I really miss my friends at home."

"What friends?"

Paul gave his sister a disgusted glance and proceeded to

unwrap another cupcake. "There were some guys I used to hang with, not as many as you, but so what! That's how much you know about me."

"Alright, I'm sorry I said that. My bad. I remember Mike and Jerry. They seemed like good guys. I'm feeling down too. I miss my softball team and everyone at school."

"Yeah. I've been thinking how hard starting a new school is going to be. I know it's only June but this town is weird. Don't you think? I mean this family probably owns everything."

"Paul, you've lost me. What are you talking about?"

"Well, didn't you watch all the signage as we drove here?"

"No. I didn't, what of it?"

"Danie, there's Tuttlebury signs everywhere."

"Duh! We did move to Tuttlebury!"

"Yep. But don't you know the name of this family hosting this picnic?"

"Yes, I met some of the Tuttle family. Is this a trick question?"

"You were flipping burgers with Mr. Tuttle, who probably is one of the men in charge of this town.

"Well, I can't say. But it seems like you think this Tuttle family is up to something."

"Danie, look over there!"

Danielle was speechless as she also stared out across the corn fields.

They moved close to the maple as they watched the red barn. There was Robert and he was huddling with three gang members. As they broke apart, Robert wandered over to one boy who handed him something. They patted each other's backs as they parted. Grabbing his bike, Robert wheeled it to their vintage station wagon and loaded it up on the rack. Opening the hatchback, he took out his backpack, threw it over his over his shoulder and walked to the other side of the street. The rush of a motorcycle edged close and waited as Robert searched his pack and handed the driver a brown envelope. The bike skidded away, creating a huge dust bloom. He ran back to the family car and perched on the metal rim of the open hatchback, his long legs dangling over the edge.

"Oh no! I served burgers to these strange guys. Robert was there, dressed like them and acting weird. I was surprised but now, I'm blown away!"

Paul stared across the lot at his brother. "I've been really annoyed with Robert's nasty words and laziness. But hanging out with this gang can only bring more trouble for him and for us. He'd better watch out!"

"Let's go talk to him!" Danielle elbowed Paul as they headed for the station wagon.

They were too late. Their very tired mother was getting in the front seat, while Dad carried a huge basket with fun edibles covered with rainbow foil. He went to the way-back seat, and situated the bulky present near his irritable older son. 'Watch this basket doesn't fall. No nibbling!" He waved Danielle, Paul and Natalie to the back seat, as they sat very tight in birth order. They heard their father secure the back latch, then climb into the driver's seat. Not sensing the tension that surrounded them or deciding to ignore it, he hummed all the way home.

4

Special Delivery

Natalie sat up in her mound of pink mermaid sheets and rubbed the stardust from her eyes. The shower had been running and running like a giant waterfall. Why was everyone up and being so noisy? The bathroom door was open a little, probably Danie was getting ready. She rolled over and fell and into a light slumber where she kept thinking and thinking. She glanced over at her purple clock. It was almost noon. Enough of sleep! Walking into the hallway, she noticed that her brothers' door was shut tight and the special alcove to her parents' room was quiet as well. She was very hungry, so in her ballerina type slippers she ran down the long staircase her fingers flowing on the smooth mahogany railing. Happy thoughts flooded her mind—of living in this wonderful old house and of making new friends at the picnic. She turned the corner into the kitchen.

What a mess! Kitchen cabinets were flung open, the counter and sink filled with dirty pots and pans. There were crumbs from delicious coffee cakes and cold scrambled ham and eggs glued to plates. A full pot of coffee on the side of the table stood warmed and untouched. Mom was going be angry since she kept her kitchen like the pictures in the magazines found at the grocery check-out. Where was she anyway?

"Mom, where are you? Don't worry I'll help clean up." Natalie shouted.

"Will you please shut up!" said Paul as he slid into a kitchen chair.

"Well, smarty pants, do you know who made this mess?"

A yellow lined tablet with shaky handwriting, caught their attention. Insistent, they both grabbed, tearing it. "Now see what you did! It's a letter from mom and now you've ruined it!" Paul pushed his sister, snatching his portion and began reading to himself. He summarized aloud. "Natalie, she says that the babies are coming. She left for the hospital with Dad, Robert and Danielle. They will call and tell us how things are going."

Natalie walked behind her brother's chair and seized the letter. "Hey, why didn't you read it out loud? I'm not dumb. But you think so because you skipped a grade and have all those books. I'll read it to myself too." Huge tears streamed down her cheek.

Paul's brown eyes grew large and concerned. He stumbled over to Natalie and patted her on the back. "Don't be upset, mom will be home soon. She will be bringing us new twin brothers or sisters."

"No, it's not that, well it is. I won't be her little girl anymore. I won't be her favorite." Natalie sobbed as she choked out the words.

"What do you mean? I thought that by being the youngest boy …" Paul halted realizing how selfish and thoughtless he sounded. He stood by Natalie and awkwardly swept his arm around her. "I apologize for being a terrible person."

Natalie stared at Paul in disbelief. Such kindness had not happened before. Was this for real? Was he truly sorry or putting on an act? She shrugged from the embrace. "Please, I'm not a little girl anymore. In case you haven't noticed, I'm growing up."

Paul nodded meekly. "Really, I'm sorry. Sometimes I'm not a good brother but you're the best sister. I'm going to try harder. And you're growing up just fine." Paul patted Natalie on the shoulder.

Natalie wiped tears and smiled. "And Paul …"

Knocking over the trashcan, Robert rushed into the room.

"Robert!" exclaimed Natalie and Paul.

"Can't talk now. Dad is waiting outside. Have to grab his wallet and insurance card for the hospital. Mom is ok. Guess what? We have two new brothers. Sorry, Natalie, we'll outnumber you and Danielle," said Robert as ran out the back door.

Chuckling, Natalie righted the trash pail and stooping, refilled it. Paul quickly joined her. "Natalie, why are you laughing?"

"Because of a lot of things. That mom is okay. That the babies are okay." Natalie's happy eyes were gleaming. And because we have new brothers and I won't be left behind, since I'll still be the youngest daughter."

Paul gawked at his sister. Then he headed towards the refrigerator to hunt for a leftover. "Oh, no!"

"What's the matter Paul?"

They both stood before the open refrigerator, their socks

drenched. Water had formed pools not only on the floor but in every corner and bowl-shaped place.

Paul scratched his head. "Looks like condensation. Like mom always says, "Because it's so hot, keep the door shut or all the food will melt!"

Natalie stuck her head in the top freezer. "Hmm, I don't think so. No one probably touched the freezer this morning and all the stuff is wet and thawing out."

"We're in trouble, aren't we? When our parents get home with the new babies, there's going to be spoiled food and a lot of yelling!"

"Yes, you're right, the food is going bad and they will be upset. But we didn't do this. It's not only because of the heat, but because the refrigerator is old. I remember grandma putting leftovers in it. It was probably ready to break anyway. This hot summer doesn't help."

"Natalie, when did you get so smart?"

"Since you noticed that I'm becoming a big girl."

"Okay, you're growing up. But now, what are we supposed to do with all the sopping wet food?"

Natalie waved for him to follow as they hurried down to the basement. They filled their arms with mops, pails, rags and dragged an oversized cooler upstairs. They dried up the floor and the interior of the refrigerator.

"Now what," asked Paul. "All the food is somewhat dry, but it's going to rot."

"Now that's what this cooler is for. Let's fill it with as much stuff as possible. But leave the freezer alone. I'll put some masking tape across it, so the food will stay frozen a little longer."

"How to you know all this stuff? You're still a kid. Did mom tell you?"

"Hey, I have some common sense. And I watch when

things happen at my friends' houses. I also turn the TV to fix-it shows. I don't read as much as you but I'm still learning things. That's how."

Working as a team, Paul and Natalie stuffed the oversized cooler, continuously rearranging items to fit. Paul took one last look at all the cold edibles, especially the hamburger meat and the sausage. He looked up at Natalie and grinned.

"Paul, why do you have that silly smile on your face?"

"Well, I'm thinking that we can prepare a great supper with all this stuff; that is if everyone comes home by then. Probably mom will be in the hospital a little longer; she stayed two days when you were born. But Dad, Danielle and Robert will be hungry. How about a tomato sauce with some ziti and a salad? We can also make a dessert and use up the soft ice-cream. We could bake my favorite—chocolate cupcakes."

Natalie's mouth hung open and her eyes grew enormous. "But I don't know how to cook."

"That's okay, because I think I know how. I've been watching mom. We can also use her cookbooks and look up stuff on the computer. Want to try?"

"Hold on, it just took all this time to take care of the refrigerator. I haven't even had breakfast or showered and it's almost two in the afternoon!

"Yeah, you're right. Why don't we grab a quick snack, get washed up and start cooking about three?"

"Ok, I can do that," said Natalie as she filled a paper plate with coffee cake and grabbed a banana. She hurried upstairs.

Paul lingered, exploring the pantry for dry goods. He loaded the counter with bread crumbs for meatballs, parmesan cheese, a box of ziti, and a chocolate cake mix. Lastly, he found the cupcake liners and tossed them with the mix. "We'll be cooking soon! Hey Natalie, I'm coming up. Don't use up all the hot water!"

The gushing shower water suddenly stopped as other sounds drifted through the hallways. Violin strings of Beethoven's Ode to Joy and Bach's "Jesu, Joy of Man's Desiring," echoed off the walls. The violin was played with the elegance and flourish of someone far older than a nine soon to be ten-year old.

* * *

"What! You've started without me!" Annoyed, Paul looked over his sister's shoulder.

"I decided to do some mixing. I found the cupcake pan, liners and a can of French vanilla icing; mom's favorite flavor. I started because I did help her bake them up a couple of times. I've already preheated the oven." Natalie proudly picked up the cupcake pan, each liner evenly dispensed with batter, and popped then into the hot stove.

"I thought you didn't know how to cook!"

Natalie giggled. "I can't cook but I can bake a little, I think."

"Well, if you can learn to cook as well as you play that violin, you'll do fine. I didn't know you could play those hard pieces."

"When I had to leave my music teacher, I was so upset. But she gave me a lot of music to work on. I've been trying hard."

"You're doing great. Maybe once everything settles down, you can take lessons again."

"I hope so. So where do we start with dinner?"

"With the meatballs and sauce. I found mom's tasty

recipe in her special box; although I don't think she uses it anymore because she knows it by heart."

They both set to work. Soon a huge pan of garlicky tomato sauce was loaded to the top of the pan with over-sized meatballs. The spicy concoction had their eyes watering and stomachs growling. Paul tossed the salad and boiled water for the pasta while Natalie frosted the cooled cupcakes. Then they set the table extra nice with special plates from the China cabinet.

"What do we have here!" This time Dad burst through the door, Danielle and Robert right behind him. "Wow, I smelled garlic in the driveway!" He stood behind a very startled Paul and Natalie, and placing his large hands on their waists, drew them together in a loving bear hug.

"I've got a huge appetite and I wasn't sure what to do for supper. This day has been so exciting. It's one of the best days of my life; of all our lives! I held the babies right after they were born, two new sons! They were very handsome. Mr. Norfeld's smile was so big it seemed to wrap around his head. "Let's eat and celebrate!" He stepped over to the refrigerator, throwing it wide open.

And paused.

Natalie and Paul gasped. Danielle and Robert shook their heads.

The celebration was over.

Mr. Norfeld scratched his head as he stooped down into the fridge. "Um, now where is that bottle of wine I was saving ... where is everything?"

Natalie and Paul nodded bleakly to one another, each wishing to be swallowed up into the busy wallpaper.

"Did you two clean this refrigerator out?" He looked over his shoulder at his children.

Paul and Natalie mumbled a hushed and contrite, "Yes."

"I can't believe it! You two did it! I was worried that I would come home to a dripping mess to clean up." Dad stood up and although a bit perplexed, he was still grinning. "Show me where you put all the food so I can find the wine."

"It was me, Dad. I broke the refrigerator by keeping it open too long. But Natalie helped me clean up and put a seal on the freezer and stick all the rest in the cooler. Over there." Paul pointed a shaky finger to a far corner in the kitchen, relieved to have confessed.

"No, Dad, it was my fault," said Natalie. "I got up late last night to get a snack and must have forgotten to close the door."

Dad stood very still, his eyes roaming from one penitent face to another. "What are you two talking about?" He began to laugh and rub his chin. "When we left this morning this crazy refrigerator was a mess.

We cleaned it up best we could, but we had to get your mother to the hospital. She was all upset about it and I told her not to worry—that we would have a new one before she came home. I wasn't sure how to keep this promise but then I remembered Mr. Tuttle has a brother who sells appliances and he had told me that if we needed anything to give a holler. Well, after the twins were born, I gave him a call and wouldn't you know it, they offered me a great price on one. They can even deliver it tonight. How's that for a great day?" Mr. Norfled went over to the cooler and pulled out the inexpensive red wine. "Let's eat! I can't wait to taste what Paul and Natalie cooked up. If Paul cooks like he painted the porch, we're in for a treat."

Festivity filled the air like Christmas eve. Dad toasted with his favorite crystal glass, the four children with plastic cups filled with ginger ale as they enjoyed a tasty ziti dinner.

Across the table Paul winked at Natalie. They had done their mother proud.

Getting everyone's attention, Robert thumped the table, and then raised his glass of soda. "Here's to Mom and Dad and our new brothers, William and Joseph! Here's to all of us being together soon. And for our new refrigerator. We hope it comes tonight!"

All heads nodded in agreement as their glasses clanked.

Danielle broke in. She wasn't about to be left out this time. "While Dad and Robert stayed in the waiting room, I went in with mom and they put a hospital gown over me. From the back of the small labor room, I watched the entire delivery. It was awesome. I was scared and excited at the same time. The babies came very fast, first William and then Joseph. They were so tiny, so beautiful, and very noisy. After the nurse cleaned them up and swaddled them, which means wrapping them tight in a striped blanket, she gave them to mom to hold. But after a few minutes she let me hold Joseph. I've never held a newborn before!"

Everyone sat very still taking in all their sister had said.

Dad nodded at Danielle and smiled. "The doctor came out to tell us the good news and had us put on hospital gowns. I got to hold my new sons! Robert, you were so gentle as you held William."

Robert flashed a crooked grin as he nodded to everyone. "Awesome. It was great."

"Dessert is ready!" Natalie placed in front of them a tray of chocolate cupcakes decorated with thick vanilla frosting and chocolate shots. "I made them all myself!" She then rushed to the freezer and pulled off the packing tape. "And there's lots of ice cream to put on them."

"She really did bake them! There's a pot of decafe coffee as well," said Paul as he readied the cups and saucers.

Everyone was peeling cupcake wrappings and sipping coffee, except for Natalie who carefully wrapped three of the sugary creations. "They're for mom and the twins."

"What about you?" asked Danielle.

Natalie chucked. "Well, I kind of had my fill when I took them out of the oven. You see, every good baker has to taste to be sure it's good." She picked up the platter of remaining cupcakes. "Who wants another?"

Just then heavy footsteps resounded on the back steps followed by a huge rap on the door. The refrigerator had arrived.

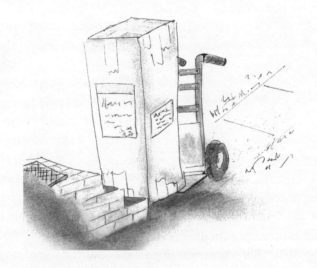

The Refrigerator Box

*P*aul perched himself on the front-porch steps and licked a double decker ice-cream cone. He had fixed it himself with the last waffle cone and heaping mounds of chocolate and pistachio. As his tongue swirled and caught every drip, he admired his paint job on the porch even though he still had the trim to do. Smiling, he remembered the great compliment about the pasta dinner dad had given him the day the twins were born. Then the refrigerator came and everyone burst into action. It was a happy and productive chaos. The bell had rung and there was Mr. George Tuttle accompanied by his brother. They were standing beside a transporter truck hauling the biggest box he had ever seen!

It was the refrigerator of their dreams. Especially for mom. She noticed it first thing when came home from the hospital. She charged over to the fridge leaving the babies in in the available arms of Danielle and Natalie. Mom inspected every possible inch. Most of all, she loved the silver color and black chrome as well as the ample storage for frozen goods. Paul had never seen her this pleased about an appliance. Mom looked ready to hug this giant behemoth, instead she flung open the door and fingered the shiny racks. Then she did something extremely annoying—she took all the food items out and began cleaning the entire inside. Again! They had already done this horrible job. Now they had a redo. Whatever. But Paul chuckled as he watched his mother polish the refrigerator happily singing Broadway tunes.

To him the refrigerator was just okay—he would have preferred a side by side like his friends with an attached ice-maker. Probably that style wasn't right for their growing family. Yet the bottom freezer was huge and would be great for all kinds of his favorite ice cream. But his assignment wasn't any fun since had to restack all the icy frozen goods in mom's special order. Even though it was boiling hot outside, his fingers had gone numb with cold. Ouch! At least the freezer was working fine.

But now the new-fangled appliance fit snug in a corner of the kitchen. As a family, except for Robert who took off, they had finally packed it a second time making mom happy. Then it was plugged in. It was alive and humming—do all these new models sing like this? They all hugged, feeling proud of themselves.

That had been a really awesome time and kind of scary.

Paul was ready to head to his room, a carton of defrosted pastry under his arm. Bang! Robert rushed by knocking into Paul, the strawberry crescents scattering on the floor. Paul waved his fists; ready to throw a punch. He restrained himself but angry tingles continued up his scalp. As Paul ran after Robert, he saw a flash of metal and grabbed his brother's arm. Robert squirmed away, revealing a box cutter. "Leave me alone," he said, "I have to tear up that box!"

"What box?" Paul shouted. Robert sneered as Paul realized what was going on. Robert was going to destroy it—that humongous refrigerator box. Heck no, this wasn't happening on his watch. The boys chased though the wallpapered halls, knocking over furniture along the way. They both charged the back door, running towards the garage where Dad had headed with the carton.

"But why?" shouted Paul as he tried to catch his breath. "It's a great box. It could be used for so many things. Like storing tools or old clothes. Maybe section it off and put paint supplies in it."

Robert abruptly stopped and yelled over his shoulder; his eyebrows arched in anger. "You just don't know do you? Those Tuttle people are weird. I don't want anything to do with them or that box!"

Robert ran faster as Paul tried to keep up. Abruptly two sets of sneakers halted in the dust.

Dad was already there, glaring at them. His girth and height stood firm; his arms folded assertively over his chest. "Sorry boys, the decision has already been made. It's a strong box, and we're keeping it. But there's no space for it in this garage. Stop arguing and both of you haul it off to the shed. I'll help by opening the door and clearing a space."

Remembering this incident was curdling the ice cream in Paul's stomach. Paul hadn't meant to be mean to his brother. But Robert had been so determined. Paul was single-minded as well—that box shouldn't be ruined. Why had Robert felt so strongly about destroying it? He figured the Tuttle's were notable people around this town. But why bother with a cardboard box? He hadn't a clue.

Paul finished the ice-cream and wiped the sticky

41

chocolate from his chin. The delivery of both the twins and the refrigerator had been something else. He jumped up and headed to the shed. It was a decent walk from the house. June was ebbing and so was the lush green yard as he stomped through browning grass and bare spots. Glancing over at the tattered chicken coop, he remembered summer days when he gathered enough eggs for his grandmother to fry up a scrumptious omelet with ham and cheese. The red and blue slide and swing set that had been great fun were horribly rusted. Paul's eyes rested upon the oversized hutch grandpa had built for their rabbits. Paul swiped a tear and wondered why he was getting so down. It almost felt like Grandpa was walking beside him; he almost could see that great toothy smile, enjoy his robust laugh.

The shed door was ajar, what was he was hearing? It was the sound of strings, flutes—a grand orchestration with one violin distinct among the others. Was he imagining, or was this a chapter in a book he read?

No. It probably was Natalie; playing along with music from her cell phone. He had to admit, that as much as everyone complained and made fun of her, his sister was getting pretty good. And she would only be starting the fifth grade. Paul entered the shed expecting to see his sister, yet all was still. But hadn't he just heard her? Paul shook his head and glanced about the tidy space. Evidenced around him he thought was dad's handiwork. Maybe not. While the shed had been straightened out, and lawn chairs piled to one side, dad's cleaning solution wouldn't have touched the windows or the refrigerator carton. Because the moldy, tattered curtains had been removed and sparkling window panes yielded to the summer glow. And catching that glow was velvet drapery that was hung over the box, creating a makeshift entrance. Whew, so much fixing. Natalie must have been here … but where was she now?

Something moved.

Paul heard a loud thump. Glancing around the shed, his eyes again fell towards the far corner. To the grand carton. Its height and girth seemed magnified, the thickness of its constitution mean and strong; its presence ominous and creepy. But he would not be chased away. Hey, he was no coward, although Robert often called him a wuss. This noise was probably a flutter of newspaper or a little mouse. He had to find Natalie. Paul edged closer to the seeming alien monolith. He was now standing right beside it. Paul's heart was pounding a patriotic march and his mouth had gone dry. The dank, humid air pressed upon him, so he could hardly breathe. Should he run or stay? He had read about this situation and understood what fear can do. Real or imagined, it didn't matter. Fear is fear and he knew he was really afraid. He could leave. Right? The door wasn't that far away. Or show he had the guts to walk into this box. He could make that reasonable choice; after all he had brains. He had read all those articles. His breath shallow, and sweat running down his back, Paul moved his foot forward.

His body froze in place.

Suddenly he was shaking from head to toe.

There was a flash of light, edged in rainbow hues. His body was rocking as bouncing rays swept around him, the scent of fruity trees tickling his nose.

Then a slap on his shoulder.

It was Natalie. She was looking up at him with one of her know-it-all faces.

"Did you just see that? The firecracker burst of light? And where were you? Were you in the box?" said Paul.

"See what? I've been here awhile fixing this shed up.

There's a lot more to do but I got tired and decided to sit. I must have fallen asleep."

"But I heard you playing your violin. The best I ever heard."

For a long moment Natalie was silent, her nose twitching as it did when she was annoyed. "Paul, I don't know what you're talking about. I didn't bring my violin here, it's really a dirty place."

"But I heard you playing."

"After I cleaned, I got tired and took a nap, that's all."

It was now Paul who wore the puzzled frown. He rubbed his face like his father did when he tried to figure something. "Natalie, tell me one thing, did you take your nap in that box?"

Natalie shrugged, and walked to the door. "I'm done here for today. Besides it's almost supper. I'm going back to the house." She glanced over her shoulder and said, "Want to come?"

Paul gave his sister a long look as they sprinted from the shed.

* * *

Natalie wanted time to herself. Finally, supper plates were finished. Mom was out on the porch with the twins, watching the birds and the sunset. Dad was in the study finishing some work. Danielle was throwing softballs with one of the players and Robert ... well, he wasn't home. As for Paul, he was thumbing through a pile of books. Now for some alone time in her bedroom, thank-you.

Natalie went into the closet and removing a loose floor panel, she retrieved her special book. The cover was decorated with rainbows and stars all shiny with glitter.

Inside the pages were filled with copious long hand and detailed drawings. A diary it was not, since she only wrote when she really wanted to.

Today was one of those days.

Cradling the book, Natalie remembered when she had discovered this secret spot and was so happy to have found a hiding space. Finding it had been amazing. One day, she had finished writing and figured the best place to put the book was under the mattress. As she knelt on the floor and lifted, she heard a noise in the closet. Something had fallen; making funny clinking noises. She felt goosebumps rise up and down her back.

It was only a box of pens and pencils. She fell to her hands and knees and gathered them up but as she stood the floorboard creaked and loosened. She nudged the weathered board and it lifted it, to a dark space. Careful not to catch a splinter, her hand eased down into the open floor. She flushed with excitement. She had found a secret space and it was empty and waiting for her!

Today she wasn't scared either. For she had sat in the refrigerator box and played her violin and the box had played along with her. She had felt sleepy and closed her eyes. In a dream like sequence, she went back to days earlier, when she had visited the farmhouse and grandpa was telling his stories. While puffing his pipe, he often weaved curious tales, encircling her with clouds of cherry scent. She was laughing as she awakened, glad to have again heard grandpa's voice.

Natalie sat cross-legged on the shaggy rug, her back supported by thick comforters on the bed. She placed the journal on her lap, smoothing the delicate pages. Head down, soft curls circled her cheek; her tongue licked her upper lip as her hand sped along the page. Wanting to cite every detail, she didn't notice the whiff of pipe smoke. Instead, she focused on the incredible thing that happened to her in that box. Something so wonderful it had taken her breath away. No one would believe her, she hardly understood it herself. But here in this room, in this special journal, she let her nimble fingers cover page after page in lovely cursive.

The secret would be kept safe within the colorful binder. For now.

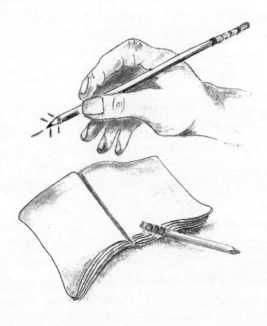

Fireworks!

*T*he smell of crackling of bacon and the sweet goodness of maple sugar pancakes stirred the four sleepy-eyed children. Except for the twins who cried all night despite mom's constant rocking and soothing ballads. Now they were out cold. Go figure. Robert, Paul, Natalie and Danielle rushed down the stairs to the kitchen. They were halted at the door by the sound of very irritated voices. This was eavesdropping at its best as each one hovered close enough to get an earful. Appetites had vanished as curiosity soared.

"You're blaming me for not getting any rest last night. I can't even remember what a full night's sleep is like!"

"Well, Nancy if you would only let me do my share. You know, I could go out and buy formula and bottles and then I could help with the night feedings."

"No way, Ted! As a nurse, I believe in the importance of

mother's milk because of the important nutrients that I only can give them. I also want to be close to the babies and bond by hugging and rocking them. I know I've only worked part-time and now, not at all. But I'm still a nurse!"

"Hon, you're working too hard! It's only been a few weeks since you came home from the hospital and you haven't stopped yet!" Ted's voice softened. "Look Nancy, I love you and the babies and I want to help. I'm not usually here during the day but I'm here at night."

"Yeah Ted, we'll see. Right now, you're helping with the breakfast. You can also give me a hand with preparing dessert for the fireworks gathering tonight. Later on, we can plan a light coffee brunch for after the welcoming at the church. "First we need to make some decisions."

"Church welcoming? Since when did this happen? I thought we're having a little party to celebrate the twins right here, at home. And why church? We haven't been in years and we don't belong to one!"

Nancy cleared her voice as she placed the remainder of the oily bacon on paper towels to drain. "It's like this. We live in your father's house and he had always hoped we would go to the church. With the birth of the twins, I was thinking it would be a good time to get some faith going. Here's the thing ... the Tuttle's have invited us to join their church and celebrate in their hall. It would be their gift to us. But I also like your father's parish since we visited it over the years. And joining there would honor your parents. Maybe we could attend both. What do you think?"

Ted stood still. His face was like a cartoon animation, flipping through emotions. Irritation flushed his cheeks, his eyes cloudy with confusion. He shook his head back and forth. "Nancy, I don't know about this. You mean we would go to grandpa's church, as well as the Tuttle church.

Both of them? If we're going to church, we should consider doing everything in one place; not all this running around. I suggest taking the Tuttle's up on their suggestion. The Tuttle family has been really good to us and being involved with them would be nice," said Ted, his eyes now hopeful.

Lost in thought, Nancy rubbed her fingertips together. "I figured you would say that. In many ways I feel uncomfortable as well. As you know, I've only been to church on occasion, so one parish is fine."

"Yes, I know, you left the kids at home for me to watch."

"And I appreciate all you've done. Last week I spoke to the pastor at grandpa's church and he suggested that we come to services and plan a discussion time. Why don't we at least try your family's church? I could be honest and tell Mrs. Tuttle that we need time to decide. For a little while we could visit both churches and then make a choice."

"Hmm. I'm glad that you'll give the Tuttle congregation a try. I know that grandpa and grandpa loved their church, and we can honor them by at least visiting." Ted stroked the stubble on his chin, and grinned sheepishly.

Nancy laughed. "Yes, from their heavenly places I can hear then clapping."

The old kitchen door creaked open.

Mrs. Norfeld's arched cheeks drooped, but her husband was hardly surprised, his lips broadening into a playful smile. "I know you've been out in the hall for a while. No use hollering anymore. Let's eat this special 4th of July pancake breakfast. We have a lot to talk about."

* * *

"Hey Danie, that was a great hit. We just have to hold them," said Sarah as she ran off to get her water bottle.

Danielle nodded; her cheeks etched with dirty sweat lines. For right now she was glad to sit on the bench. She snatched off her cap and shook out soggy braids. Gulping down tap water from her bottle, she let the warm breeze flow over her damp uniform. Darn. This day had to be the hottest on record. And in this heat, their team had been battling out this game. Up unto minutes ago, they were getting beat bad. Then the tide turned. Her team scored precious runs and she had proudly finished up the top of the ninth inning by hitting a home run. Danielle smiled to herself; she hadn't done that in a long time and it felt great.

Good to be back.

Now they were in the bottom of the last inning and like Sarah said they had to hold their lead. Danielle looked over at the field behind the dugout where the coach was throwing practice pitches to their ace closing pitcher. But they would all have to play extremely well so as to win this game and be done with it. Fancy exhibition game or not, she had no desire to play extra innings. Honestly, she wanted to go home to a cool shower and frosty drink.

Speaking of home, Danielle scanned the crowd looking for her family. She had ridden out on her bike with Robert; but where was he? He had promised to watch her game. Danielle shook her head and kicked the dirt. Robert was becoming more and more difficult. Sullen and out of it. Saying one thing, then doing another. She had always found him to be a decent brother. But not anymore. What was up? Maybe the move and leaving his new girlfriend had made him depressed. Danielle was trying to be a good sister but it wasn't working. Robert seemed more interested in these local guys he had met; his arms waving with excitement when they talked.

Eyes still roving, Danielle scouted for the rest of her

family. Probably Natalie stayed back because she wanted to frost baked brownies for tonight and Paul had been walking around with a paint can; whatever that was about. Yes, there was her mother sitting on the bleachers with a group of ladies, chatting away. They probably had not seen her home run. Disappointed, her eyes wandered the field hunting for her father. There he was! He was standing near a bench rocking the twins with one hand and watching the scoreboard. Had he seen her awesome home run? She hoped so. But no problem. Because she still felt that jolt of pride running down her spine.

She turned her gaze ever so slightly—what was that? A flurry of assorted tee shirts waved in the wind as a group of bicycle riders flew past her. Robert was tucked into the pack.

To finish the game, Danielle played a boring outfielder, not her favored short stop position. But being new, how could she really expect anything more? One home run wasn't going to win them over; she would have to be an all-around great player. But not today. No balls came her way and the other players were making lots of mistakes. Trying to play harder, their team was coming up short. But they weren't the only ones. The away team was actually playing worse than them; they couldn't seem to get a piece of the ball and when they did: they ran like elephants. Must be the heat. It had distressed both teams but incredibly they had won. Danielle drank deep from her water bottle and then poured the rest over her head. Sarah was going crazy celebrating with the girls, but she wasn't feeling it. It had been a very long, hot game and a cool shower was calling her. But home had to wait as she hopped on her bike to find Robert.

She hoped he would be at the Tuttle barn.

* * *

Even with the front gate thrown open, the heavy air and the smelly hay threatened to suffocate him. As he stood in a far corner, Robert eyes shifted around the huge barn, then to the guys who surrounded him, their faces full off contempt. Sweat oozed from every pore and Robert's heart beat wildly. He was the one being singled out. He needed help. Robert glanced over at Alex, his new friend. Or supposed friend, since Alex quickly lowered his head and hid behind another gang member.

"Robert, you know things about us, but we can't tell you anymore until we trust you," said the older youth with the tattoos on his muscled arms.

"But what do you mean? I've already done some stuff. You can trust me."

One of the members with long yellowish hair spoke. "Robert. Yeah, yeah, taking all those designer boots from the Johnson's store was nothing. It's like this. You have to do for us so we can do for you. See how far your loyalty goes—see if it's real or not."

Robert felt his parched mouth pucker up; his stomach tightened. "But I am loyal, tell me what else I need to do to prove it," he said attempting to sound courageous. Which he was not, as nervous sweat soaked through his clothing. He felt extremely lightheaded and steadied his shaking hands in his pockets.

No one said anything. Every eye pierced through him speaking a clear message. Just do it!

It was an aching long pause.

"Now it is time for your next step," said the young man with scary blue eyes. "The small stuff is done, now for a serious assignment."

The guys grouped in a huddle around Robert, some placing arms tightly across his back. So much of the conversation was inaudible except the three words; Sander Farm next.

* * *

Hiding near the farm tools Danielle stirred and knocked a heavy rake to the ground floor. She rushed out the side door nearly tripping over herself. Had they heard her? Hopefully not. Although she couldn't see everything, she had heard a lot. Robert was in terrible trouble. She had wanted to find out what that guy had given her brother at the barbecue. Yet she had found out even more. Scared, Danielle hustled to her bike, forcing the pedals as never before.

As Danielle walked through the back door, thoughts of a cool shower and writing a note to her brother were instantly changed. Laughing and snacking on plates of cheese and crackers were her parents and a group of strangers. There was a middle-aged man and woman sitting with two teenagers about her age. Mom was rushing about setting out fancy napkins and pouring iced tea. She looked up at Danielle. "It's good you finally got home. We have company; neighbors from back home. Wouldn't you know they have family in this county and since they were passing through, decided to drop by. Please meet Mr. and Mrs. Taylor; their son Jeff, and their daughter Jessica. Jessica is Robert's good friend.

Danielle nodded politely and smiled. But inside emotions were crashing like great tidal waves. This really shouldn't be happening. But it was.

* * *

As their family and the Taylor's sat together for the 4TH of July festivity, all eyes stared excitedly at the firework blaze in the night sky. Waves of wonderment flowed like young cornstalks in the wind along with lots of clapping. Accompaniment from the local high school band was well done although their violinist was not as a talented as Natalie. Yet her sister seemed not to care as she talked with her new friends. The townsfolk were having an exceedingly happy time. But not the rest of her family. Danielle caught frequent glances from her parents, Paul and the Taylor family. They were all acting funny, putting on the pretense of enjoying themselves with forced conversation and distracted faces. Jessica's head kept bobbing away as she scanned the crowd.

They were all awaiting Robert's arrival.

He never came.

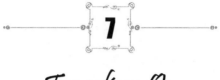

Traveling On

$\mathcal{P}$aul was sick of all of this. Supper was over and he had already done his part to clear up. Still sunny out, he grabbed up an armful of books and hastily ran out the back door. The atmosphere in the house was becoming toxic— nerves were on edge, everyone was picking fights with one another. Even the twins felt the tension and kept on crying and crying. He had to get out. He wished he had a license and a car so he could go far away. He could take his bike but he wasn't as good a rider as Danielle or Robert. Probably it was all the stuff he hauled causing him to lose balance. Paul headed toward the shed to find a lawn chair and then pick the best shade tree.

The back of Paul's neck tingled. This shed always gave him the creeps—even when grandpa was still here. Now it was much worse. He swallowed hard. "C'mon, time to be a man and not a wimp," he said aloud. Yet he knew something wasn't right the last time he'd gone into the shed and found Natalie there. Paul took a deep breath and threw open the door, letting the sunshine in. Inside the musty scent was nasty on his tongue, yet the overnight coolness was drying the sweat. He promised himself to be quick; grab a lawn chair and run! The chairs were hung on the back wall. Paul yanked one off its hook. "Now to get out of here," Paul spoke aloud. Then he halted. What was that? From the corner he saw something move. A mouse? The last bit of sunlight? Or his imagination—he had been reading more thrillers lately since raiding grandpa's dusty bookcase.

It happened again. Paul's stomach lurched and he felt dizzy. He wanted to get out. Instead, he looked toward the direction of the noise. "Hey, you're not going to scare me!" Paul moved swiftly to the entrance of the refrigerator box. Hanging was a shabby floor length curtain, a poor attempt at decoration probably the effort by one of his sisters. As he stared the velvet drape curtain lifted and blew outward! Paul's face tingled with fear. He edged closer and shouted, "Natalie, I know you're in there. Enough of these pranks. I'm coming in after you! He threw the lawn chair to the side. With the back of his hand, he parted the curtain and tightened his fists. He lowered his head and peeked in.

No Natalie.

Inside the usual dimension of the carton had changed—it had become a full-sized room.

Paul froze in place. His alert brain had become scrambled eggs. He knew what he was seeing couldn't be. But somehow was. He was standing in a study with bright area rugs and comfortable lounging furniture as well as a dark cherry desk. Books of every size and classification were stacked tight in floor to ceiling bookshelves. Dim light shrouded a masculine form sitting at a desk. The man's head was propped by a hairy arm, hung over a thick oversized volume. In the other was a large ham and cheese combo with a huge bite taken out. This figure was oddly familiar, reminding him of someone.

In the middle of the room, vivid white light danced in spotlighted fashion. Strings of violin resounded, playfully skipping around the walls and into his heart. Eyes closed tight; Paul swayed with every note. He was being soothed; like when his sister Natalie would play. But strains of this piece were far more complicated. Paul stepped closer to the delicate notes to the form of a young woman dressed in a dazzling sequined gown. Could that be? Not! He knew his mind was playing tricks on him.

Natalie sat before him. One arm held a violin under her chin, the other gently slid the bow.

How could this be happening? But there was his sister and she was all grown up and exceptionally beautiful.

Paul had to get out of here. Now. Tearing through the curtain, he crashed through the shed door and into their acreage of land. Finding soft grass under a full silver maple, Paul leaned against the trunk and stared into the sky. Where was he? What had he just seen? None of this was real—it was a nightmare during the day. He could forget any of this happened. Or he could march into the house and demand that everyone come out and see. Ugh. Yes, he could. But like the books he read, once the witnesses show up the evidence is gone. All gone. Then he would look like a stupid kid making up stuff. Who knows, maybe he was.

Paul felt he was losing it. Since the move there was a lot to be worried about. He was very angry about everything; like leaving his home and friends. Even thinking about a new school this Fall gave him a headache. No new friends had come his way, and he hadn't bothered looking. Books were his best friends but he could hardly get to the library. His mind continued to wander … his eyelids, like window shades, were pulling shut as he fell into a sound sleep.

"Paul, Paul", shouted Danielle. "There you are. I didn't know where you went. Sleeping like nothing's happening. Wake-up!"

Danielle shook her brother's shoulder. "Robert is up to something at the Sander farm!

Paul jolted up from his sleepy haze. "What did you say?"

"Here, look!" Danielle opened to a text message on her cell phone and handed it to Paul.

His mind full of cobwebs, Paul was baffled from the message. Morse code would have been better understood. It seemed like a yell for help and somehow Robert was involved.

"Paul, what's the matter with you! You keep reading it so slow and you're the speed reader!" She went to grab the phone but Paul swiftly moved.

"Let me see it. Again." He scrolled to the top of the chaotic message and read it aloud.

Danielle, I am going to the Sander's farm I really didn't want things to go this far have to get away from here will be home late Don't tell mom dad or Natalie definitely not Paul leave me some clean clothes and towel near backyard hose. Loosen the screen in my bedroom window See you later Robert.

Paul's passive stare met Danielle's frightened eyes. "Don't you get it? Robert has put himself in a very bad spot and he's in deep. I think he's been bullied by that gang into doing awful stuff and I wouldn't be surprised if they asked him to do more. We have to help him and not say a word to anyone."

"Well, I'm not sure. Maybe we should go to the police.

Or at least tell mom and dad." Paul gave his sister a pleading look.

"And put Robert in serious danger! That's why Robert didn't want you to know, you're crazy honest. Our brother is depending on us." Danielle grabbed Paul's shoulder and held tight. "You have to promise not to tell our parents. We need to help Robert," said Danielle with the strength of a lion, although she felt as weak as newborn kitty.

Paul's mouth went dry and he choked on the repeating vapors of supper. "Yeah," was all he could say.

* * *

Robert rode his bike hard as if involved in a race for his life, which he was. The details of what happened swirled around like a cyclone in his head. What he had been commanded to do; what he wanted to do. A drastic clash of conscience that was smashing into headstrong bullies. He couldn't believe it; he was becoming one of the them—the Tuttle gang. He wished he had power over them; that would feel good. Right now, his sweating body reeked of the tires he had slashed. Worst was the manure pile he had fallen into as he chased the cows from the barn. Now he was covered in all that muck. Serves him right. He wanted life to be the way things once were … wishing he could crawl into the childhood covers. But he knew he couldn't go back. Things had changed. He had become a different person.

With the slyness of a panther, Robert found the hose in the back of his house. "Yikes!" The jet spray hit him like icy needles. He washed and toweled the filth and sweat, easing his aching body into the fresh clothing that Danielle had left. His plan was to play it dumb for a couple of days and then leave home. Hopefully no one would tell on him. He then threw the smelly clothing into a black garbage bag, burying it deep in the trash can.

The morning sky was brightening. Robert headed toward the house and climbed up to the second level. Quietly the window screen was pushed aside as he hauled himself into the bedroom. Pulling the sheets over his head, he fell into a dead sleep.

* * *

It was mid-morning; anxiety levels were exploding in the kitchen. Mrs. Norfeld was hopping between two screaming babies, ringing phones and strawberry jam that was simmering on the stove. The kitchen shutter door hesitantly opened. She a gave a wary look to Danielle and Paul, her voice edgy. "Well, it's about time you both got up for breakfast. Please help me with this jam. Where's Natalie and Robert? Honestly that boy is turning into a good for nothing around here! Your father waited for you to go with him to the Sanders house but he rushed there himself. Turns out the tires of the farm vehicles and cars were slashed. The barn was broken into and the cows ran off. Mrs. Sanders must be terrified. You know, I chatted with her at the fireworks. This is terrible. It's too soon to know how it happened. I think it was those awful boys who speed around with motorcycles, knocking us off the road." She picked up one of the fussy twins and began rocking away, helping calm the baby and herself.

Avoiding her mother's gaze, Danielle stooped over and picked up baby William.

Paul was standing there like a garden scarecrow.

Mrs. Norfeld kissed little Joseph on the forehead and set him in the infant seat. "Paul, are going to stand there doing nothing! How about stirring down the strawberry jam before it flies out of the pan to the ceiling!"

"Come on, Mom. Doesn't Natalie like to cook this stuff?" Paul picked up wooden spoon and instantly the heat of the angry concoction met with the humidity of the day. He had to catch his breath.

Mrs. Norfeld stopped cutting berries and looked irritably at her son.

The testy look on Paul's face dissolved, his eyes becoming apologetic.

"Sorry mom. The jam is thick now and has white crud floating."

"Turn off the burner and wash these other berries." She went to the stove. "You've done a good job. Now I'll spoon off that scum and bottle the rest into those hot jars. Then it can thicken, as they say, "set up.""

"Mom, I love your jam … can I sample it when it cools?"

"Morning, Danie. You missed all the fun Paul and I had boiling it up. In a few minutes you can try some jam on toast. But first call Natalie down; can't have her sleeping all day."

But there was no need. Sounding like a herd of horses, in came Natalie and Robert.

Like a mime in true freeze position, everyone halted. Even the babies quieted. Natalie was a sight with hair tossed like hay and eyes swollen and red. Robert was freshly dressed in a neat tee shirt and washed pants. He looked himself but his affect seemed odd, like he was acting in a play.

Mrs. Norfeld's' face flushed in surprise. "Why, I didn't know you both were upstairs all this time. Robert, I had looked for you earlier and didn't see you around," she said looking at her son with suspicion.

"I can smell that strawberry jam all the way upstairs. I came down to help out. What would you like me to do?" His words sounded calm but his moved stiffly. His eyes looked downward, eyes that were large and hollow.

The back door swung open and in came Mr. Norfeld. His face was tight, his hands shaky. He threw full grocery bags on the counter and began slamming kitchen cabinets. "What's the matter with you people, never shutting anything! What, do you think we live in a barn? Well, I guess we do." He waved to the bags he had thrown down. "Here's the groceries you asked for earlier, forgot to take them out of the car before I went to see Sanders. Some food might have spoiled."

"Don't worry Dad," said Natalie as she unloaded the bags. "Please tell us what you found out." She went over to her father and patted his shoulder.

Dad's face softened as he took in Natalie's kind demeanor. But forehead lines hardened as he noted rebellion on Robert's face. "Well, I couldn't get very close with the police rushing around. I saw the damaged barn door and the cut tires. The cows looked okay and were being rounded-up."

"Did you talk to the Sanders … hope my new friend Katie is alright," said Natalie, her eyes hopeful.

"Dad, how bad were the tires cut?"

"Why would someone do this? The Sanders are such nice people, said Mrs. Norfeld, her eyes teary.

"How's Mrs. Sanders, did you get to talk to her? Or at least see her?"

I've heard that the Sander's don't get along with the Tuttle's. Do you think this was a kind of hate crime?"

Stomping his work boots, Mr. Norfeld, "Hold on here, you're all yelling at once! Let me talk!" He then folded his arms to his chest in a no-nonsense pose. The room became pin quiet. "That's better. There was a lot of commotion, so I didn't talk to the family. But the neighbors were okay, which must be true since the police didn't rush anyone out. Lots of rumors about how all this happened, no one is saying. Supposedly their experts will figure that out. As for a hate crime—can't say for sure. This town has been good to us, they seem to be kind people. Maybe it was weird pranksters from somewhere else. As far as I know, the Sanders need to fix their vehicles; but their home, family and livestock are fine. And that's good enough for me." Mr. Norfeld stepped over to the refrigerator to pour a glass of milk and grab a cookie.

"But, Dad," said Danielle, we want to know more. If you don't tell us, I'm riding over there myself!"

Natalie and Paul confirmed their sister's concern and stood by her.

Robert moved to a far corner.

"If any of you go over there now, then all of you will be grounded for the rest of the summer," said Mr. Norfeld as he took a snack and went to the den.

The buzz in the kitchen silenced. The four siblings scattered to various nooks of the old farmhouse. Paul roamed off to read out on the porch, Danielle cleaned her softball equipment in the garage and Robert went upstairs and crashed into bed. The twins babbled along with sound of clinking glass as Mrs. Norfeld finished packing the hot jars with the strawberry preserves.

Natalie retreated to her secret place in her bedroom closet. She pushed aside mismatched shoes, pulling out her decorated journal from beneath the wooden boards. Cradling the journal in her arms, she penned in deliberate strokes … *Robert messed up those tires and he will do other bad things if he is not stopped. The box showed me an awful future for my brother… of being arrested and going to jail. That is, if the mysterious rays in the box are telling of things that might happen or will happen.* Natalie swiped her eyes, but continued to write, the tears dampening and blurring the penned entry, as she hoped for the best but feared the worse.

Beyond the Cornfields

"*H*urry up!" shouted Mr. Norfeld waving his hands. I took this day off so we could do some things and have a little fun. Your mother wants to check out the Glendan Mall way down in Boenville so she can find the twins matching outfits for the church welcoming and a little something for us. As you know, we have been getting ready to join a church. We had thought of going to the one the Tuttle family attends, but mom and I are considering your grandparents' parish. I know that Natalie, Danielle and at times, Paul have come with us to church and have asked the pastor really great questions, especially you, Natalie. Paul, your comments always get the compliments. We're almost ready to join. Also, I thanked the Tuttle's for inviting us to use their hall, but we might have our own celebration! Well, once your mother and I decide everything, we'll tell you.

He glanced over his shoulder the kids. "Well, enough of all this. We're planning to make a fun lunch stop as well, so buckle up!"

Paul had stuffed himself into the back seat jammed between two baby car carriers filled with his cooing brothers. He placed books under his feet and tucked a little snack by his side. He was glad that at least Robert wasn't here since he was busy working for the Tuttlebury Country Store. Robert didn't like this job as a stock clerk, said he was working with those awful Tuttle people, who owned everything, and now owned him. That was his brother Robert, always complaining.

Paul stretched his legs in the tight seat. Enough of thinking about Robert. But he didn't like where he was either, on this stupid day trip. This had all been his father's idea as he replayed the long dialog in his head—of how this would be a nice family time. "Yeah, right," Paul thought aloud, his father could be very demanding. He would have liked to have stayed home and read under a nice shade tree with an ice-cream cone. If he felt like working, he could have started painting the side of the house. Paul had already finished the porch plus the trim and was proud of his work. Dad had praised him even though no one else seemed to notice. They were all busy with their cell phone friends, sports or the violin. Hmm. But really his father was okay. Maybe he could urge dad to buy a couple of books. This trip wasn't going to be so bad after all, if he didn't melt first. Paul wiped his forehead; he was sweating big-time.

"Hey Dad, could you turn on the air? We're all are roasting back here!

"Yeah, Dad. I'm soaking through my outfit and my nice hair is frizzing."

"Ok, you should feel an icy breeze."

"Hey, Paul are you feeling cool? Are the vents even open in the back seat?"

"The vents are wide open and the twins and I are getting hotter. In the way-back Danielle and Natalie probably can't breathe! I bet the air is not working! Again. Why do we have to drive in this rundown old Volvo?"

"Everyone calm down! I'm doing the best I can. Why don't you all read like your brother or call one of your friends? Your cell phones are glued to you." Dad's voice had become tense.

Then in mellow tone, Mrs. Norfled barged in. "Kids, we have a little problem. The air conditioner isn't up to par today. Please open all your windows so we can get comfortable. Look forward to our nice lunch. We're going to a very special place and you can order whatever you want." Mr. Norfeld put on a sour face but his wife appeared not to notice. "We can also dessert and coffee and Natalie you can have a sip."

Windows rolled down and the discontent quieted in the anticipation of a special lunch. Cell phones distracted as fingers danced along the keys.

Except for Paul. He rarely used his phone; he wasn't even sure where he had left it. Besides any so-called friends had been left behind in the old neighborhood. And he hadn't made any new ones yet. But phones were good for looking up stuff. He didn't feel like doing that or even reading. Instead, he decided to watch the view. Lines of early bright green cornstalks were stretching towards the sky, giving promise of tasty cooked ears dripping with salted butter. As he leaned his head out the window he sniffed in their sweet goodness. He loved corn; it was the best of all the veggies. Hay fields brushed by and seemed to sway in the wind reminding him of patriotic songs. An earthy smell filled his nose. Looking over the field he saw black and white cows grazing as well as corralled horses; their coats shiny as they stood proud and elegant.

They passed by a calendar ready farm that was decorated in shades of red and white. Then came fields of unfamiliar produce that was growing close to the ground. More corn. More wheat. Farm after farm after farm. One reminded him of the Tuttle's place. Paul eyes fluttered as he lulled into a nap. Dosing, he pictured the Tuttle farm and realized something he hadn't noticed of before. Way behind the grain silo was a large wooden cabin. High grasses hugged the weathered structure with tints of green and gray. He remembered something had caught his eye. But he had dismissed it. What could it have been? A reflection of sorts? Then he saw Robert, standing in front of him. He was looking all weird like he had done something that wasn't right. Did his brother have some connection with that that old building?

Paul's eyes popped open with curiosity. Had he been dreaming; was any of this real? It certainly felt like it was. Suddenly he wanted to fast forward the day, grab his bike and find this place; although really not sure where it was, but he had an idea.

First, he had a lot of eating and shopping to do.

* * *

The ride home was a flip side to the morning. Everyone was excited and animated. Their newly acquired treasures took the lead as they compared incredible markdowns. Paul included. He loved the books he found and wished he could open one, but the car was too noisy, the conversations interesting. A headliner was planning another trip to a new mall; an enormous one. It had an amusement park, a mini golf range and an art museum. Food was the next topic. With satisfied stomachs they recalled all the good eats at the lunch buffet and luscious dessert choices. It was great fun filling the plate over and over again. Once they finished, something strange happened, Mr. Norfeld broke them into two groups, and gave each kid cash to shop! Paul was excited even though at first, he thought it was a weird test. But he didn't think twice when he was paired with his sisters, Danielle and Natalie. This was very okay with him. His parents followed pushing the twins in their second-hand tandem stroller. If they lost sight of one another, a meeting place was decided, the ice-cream shop near the exit, which they all took advantage of. Awesome! Two desserts in one day! This had to be the best day ever.

They were almost home as dimming sunlight dotted the hills and dusk settled the valley. Now talked out and tired, the only sound was light jazz on the radio, another of dad's favorites. Paul was easing into another nap when he remembered his desire to ride out to that old cabin, he had dreamed about. With forlorn he studied the sky. Any minute the remnant of light would fade into a heavy dark drape of darkness—as the sky splashed with a wash of twinkling stars that you could almost touch.

* * *

Robert finished sweeping for the day and hung his blue striped apron in partitioned corner of the storage room. This space served as a break area, washroom, and a place to put all your stuff. As he sat on one of the worn chairs to change up his work boots, he heard the jangle of the door chime as Mrs. Tuttle came in.

"Hey, George are you still here?"

There was no answer.

"George, I need to talk to you … and I know you're here because I was watching outside, and you didn't lock up. C'mon out, you lazy good for nothing, before I smack you with a frying pan!"

Robert's facial muscles tensed as he inched over to a rack of musty coats and squatted to the side.

There was a crash. Then fast footsteps as the back door creaked open.

"Not so quick Mr. Tuttle." The thick end of the broom landed hard on the door as it shut tight.

"Elsa, you almost tripped me!"

"Yeah. Almost doesn't count." The hefty middle-aged woman dressed in grimy work jeans and boots, swiped errant gray hairs under her cap. "Come over to the register table. I've brought us some treats from town, two large cappuccinos and a claw donut especially for you."

George walked stubbornly to the counter and grunted. "Trying to butter me up?"

"You wish. We need to talk," said Elsa with pursed lips.

"A bit edgy I see. Well, I can play that game better than you!" George crashed his hand on the counter knocking the donut bag to the floor.

Elsa was not put off. "It goes like this. We hired this kid Robert, so you could keep an eye on him. Make him do what we say. Well, he failed and so have you. I've done my job trying to befriend his mother who is always tied up with those bratty twins. I've also done all the planning for the picnics and church events. But you were supposed to get your fellas to really pressure this kid to throw some flames around the Sanders farm, not just slash tires. What's the matter with you George; losing your nerve?"

Moving closer to the wall, thorough a decayed knot of wood, Robert witnessed the couple as their hostile words shook the store. Then he heard the word—fire! His face twisted in anger; his body trembled. The gang hadn't told him to torch anything. Hadn't he done enough with those silly cows and tires? What did they want with him?

"Woman, you had better shut up, if you know what is good!" Mr. Tuttle's arm angrily sliced through the air. Muttering, he picked up his coffee. "I don't have to answer to you!"

"You most certainly do! You would have nothing without me. This house, this land, this county belongs to me! It was called Lidleton after my family a whole lot longer than Tuttlebury. George, you would be living in a barn if you hadn't married me!"

"Yep. I've heard this all before. Woman, you know I'm sick of it. I've done a lot to keep this town going."

"And Mister, you're going to keep hearing it! We need to get rid of these traitor families and keep our land secure. And what do you do? You take your lousy time and mess around like an old dog."

"Hey, wait a minute. Didn't I clear out the dead wood families; like the Browns, the Madison's, the Lanton's and the Norfeld's?

"Stop there! Mr.and Mrs. Norfeld died all my themselves. Their son, Ted came back with his family. Now there is a new generation of them—they have to leave! Too goodie two shoes for me. You and Mr. Norfeld … what do you call him now George; your best friend forever? Sickening. And his son, Robert is so annoying; he complicates things by changing his mind all the time."

"Elsa, honey, I'm working on this situation. I'll have everything under control soon, real soon. No worries."

Mrs. Tuttle shoulders bristled as she grabbed her coffee and headed out. "Well, we'll see how things go. If you don't step up to the plate, then I certainly will! Ha! You'll find your bed will be the stinky couch in the garage." With the kick of her boot, she heaved the door shut, shaking the beams of the shop.

Robert watched silently, his breath shallow. Mr. Tuttle was in no hurry. He retrieved the bag from the floor, chumped noisily on the oversized glazed donut and slurped his coffee. Shaking his head, he got up and began to close the shop for the evening. He counted out the earnings from the register and put the cash in his pocket. He puttered around fixing this and shutting that, most of which was out of Robert's eye view. It seemed like forever before Robert heard the clicking of light switches and husky footsteps at the entrance as the dead bolt locked down.

Mr. Tuttle was gone.

Robert sat very still for a long, long time. His eyes pierced the darkness, ears hung on every hint of sound. Silence. It was time. Like a spy, he inched carefully through the store to the basement exit. Using the flashlight on his phone, he made his way down the uneven stairs, through the piles of stocked goods and out a window with the broken latch. This welcome escape could not have been appreciated more.

9

Two Brothers Grim

*I*t was Sunday morning, and no sausages were crackling in the pan or pancakes toasting golden brown and luscious. Instead, there was a lot running about. There were the sounds of babies crying and running shower water. Little by little the house calmed. Mrs. Norfeld's voice echoed up the stairs, "Hey boys, the twins and the girls are in the car. You know we're going to church this morning. We're leaving in two minutes!" Her special occasion heeled shoes clicked about the house, pausing for a long second. Then all was quiet.

Robert climbed from his covers to the window and peeked through the blind. What? Pressing his nose to the window he saw his mother at the wheel. She backed the station wagon down the driveway and was gone. Whew! He had to be extra careful not to wake both his father and brother. He dressed quickly, pulling on fresh jeans and a tee shirt. He glanced over at Paul who was snoring away. Good. Now to make a quick pit-stop to the bathroom, and not knock anything over.

Heading towards the staircase he heard a bump. Paul was up, he could feel him watching his every move— probably with that same anxious look his father used. Ugh. A pang of guilt filled him. He felt bad he had overslept and disappointed his mother—he had promised to attend church and had really let her down. But he had no interest in going to church. Not now, not ever. Robert hurried to the kitchen and fixed a sloppy peanut butter sandwich; leaving signature knife spikes in the middle of the jar. Gulping down the simple breakfast, Robert climbed on his bike and flew down the street.

Paul was in quick pursuit.

* * *

As he rode along, Robert didn't even bother to look over his shoulder. He knew his brother was chasing him. He didn't like this one bit! To lose him, Robert lifted his body like the pros on tour, doubling his speed. He left the paved road to a short cut on a dirt rough path. Many of the overhanging briars pulled his hair and scratched his arms. Robert didn't care. He wanted to lose his brother; and get to the cabin before the guys arrived for this extra meeting. Yet he really didn't want to be here at all. For him, Sunday was for sleeping-in and gorging down huge breakfasts; not for going to this meeting. He believed there were a lot of secrets, that these guys were hiding a lot of stuff from him. He needed to explore. Maybe he would find something … like hidden information that could give him a grip and some power.

Again, Robert looked over his shoulder. No sign of his irritating brother. Great. He must have lost Paul on that narrow, weedy path. He reached the dilapidated cabin. Hiding his bike in the brush, he began walking. The cabin had once been used to accommodate the area fishermen who liked to make a good catch from the stocked pond. Years back, the Tuttle family had created this waterway and used it to water their crops and livestock. At least he knew that much. He studied the shabby cabin. It must have once been appealing in its own rustic way.

Interest had fallen off; it was now a shack housing the Tuttle gang which he had been anxious to join. He had to complete all the initiation rites or be shamed and thrown out. The small stuff had been annoying but now things were getting out of control. Slashing the tires of the farm machinery and letting out the cows had not set well with him; it was an awful thing to do to the Sander farm. He hated how they bullied him into doing their dirty work. He really didn't want to hurt anyone, did he? And now he was working for the Tuttle County Store. He was hidden in plain sight. There was more for him to do, and he hated it. Yet he still wanted to be in with these guys. What was his problem? He liked wearing the black clothes, which enticed a sinister side, like a film villain. This part of him was thrilling and oddly satisfying. It was also very creepy. He was volleying back and forth. He was changing into someone he didn't know.

Lost in thought, Robert tousled his long black hair. He didn't want to admit it but he missed his friends and was irritated they had not called. He had to call them first. And what about Jessica? He had figured she was his girlfriend, after all, they shared that great kiss. At first, he talked with her on his cell but lately there was no answer. Now when he called her home, there was often the answering machine or nothing at all. All this was his fault. He couldn't believe Jessica had visited his home with her parents and he had missed her! He had been out messing around with the gang. "Idiot! I'm really dense in the love department," he said aloud.

There were other worries like the new high school where he would start as a sophomore. Just thinking about this made him nervous. He could cut classes like some of the guys, but his family would go ballistic. He was already sneaking around and not listening to them. To top it off, his brother and sisters looked at him like he was an evil character out of a comic book, which he probably was.

Once Robert stepped into the musty cabin, he went right to work. He opened long narrow drawers that were custom designed and positioned on the side wall. He wanted to trash every one and leave the place looking like a hurricane had hit. But his mind buzzed a strong warning. This could make matters worse and perhaps even be blamed for it, which would be quite true. There would be accusations and members would shun him; a situation he would like to avoid. He searched and searched dozens of drawers, but he was coming up with whole lot of nothing. Oh yes, he found a bunch of smelly notebooks that served to log fishermen names, hours, purchasing items. There were piles of outdated magazines, pipe fixings and dusty bottles of whisky supposing that some took a time out from throwing their fishing rods or celebrated a great catch.

"Hmm. This is very interesting," he said as he thumbed through yellowed papers showing the construction of the pond. Many families had contributed so as to gain access. But, stapled sloppily was a recent memo forbidding certain families use of the water. Including the Sanders and other families he didn't know. The letter noted numerous details and conditions, most of which he did not understand but sounded like contrived reasons to push them out. He folded the paperwork and shoved it his jean pocket. Funny how he was trying so hard to be bullied in.

He checked his watch. Time was getting short. There was one more drawer. Should he, or shouldn't he? He was tired and thirsty, and it was almost time for the meeting, but you never know. He bent over and yanked out the last wooden drawer, swollen with stuff. Quickly sifting through, he found the contents were disordered and unexciting. Then his thumb hit something—a small manila envelope with a hard object inside. His hand encircled the envelope as the fold popped open. Robert squinted into the packet; a key lay at the bottom. He poured the silver key into his hand and held it up to the light wondering why it looked so familiar. Ah! It looked like grandpa's key to the shed except his was a rusty mess. But if it was what would it be doing here, hidden away? He shoved it back into the envelope. Who knows? This could be what he was looking for.

There was a crash.

He stood very still, slowly tucking the envelope in his pants pocket.

A shadow went by the window. Eerie and very annoying. Swift and silent, Robert left the cabin and moved towards the back window. He halted and folded his arms on his chest like his angry dad would do. Robert stared hard at the tangled body in the bushes. Paul.

"Hey that hurts!" yelled Paul as Robert pulled him to his feet.

"You think that hurt! Well, how about this?" Robert waved his fist hard at Paul's head.

Paul ducked.

With increased strength another punch was launched.

With speed not seen before, Paul flew behind his brother and pushed him with the power of a superhero.

Losing his balance, Robert fell backwards into the prickly shrub.

Stunned, neither spoke.

Paul stooped over his brother, attempting to pull him up.

"Don't touch me! I can get up myself!" Robert twisted his body this way and that, as fresh scrapes bled on his clothes.

"Now you look like me with all those scratches. I also bruised my arm when I bumped into the window and then into the bush. Anyhow, I followed you out here because I had a dream about this place."

"Dream? I don't care about your silly stories that come right out of your ridiculous books. Don't ever bother me again or the next time you'll really get it!" Robert's distain pierced through liquid dark eyes. He turned and headed toward the front of the cabin.

"But Robert, it was just as I had imagined!" Paul licked his dry lips, his eyes bright. As he headed for his bike, a piece of paper caught his eye. Scooping it up, he realized it was a yellowish envelope that contained something small. Paul ripped the packet in half. Out came a remarkably clean padlock key as well as a folded note on stained paper. Scribbled in messy script it said, "key from the old man's place, the backyard shed."

As he reread the note Paul's head fogged, then flipped to clarity. He grabbed his bike and pedaled hard, his face to the wind.

* * *

"Paul, where have you been," asked Danielle, as she rushed out the back door. "After church mom picked up a chicken dinner for us and sent me to find you and Robert. She probably didn't think you took off on your bike." Danielle stared hard at her brother. "I wondered where you went. I had to go to church and you got out of it and it seems like you even had fun. Mom was angry with you but this time dad was on your side. He said to leave you alone because you were tired from all the house painting. I can't figure why you're on his good side and I'm not. It seems like I always am the one who gets ignored."

"Danielle, will you stop talking? Please. You're giving me a headache." Paul rubbed his scalp and made a face.

"It's only that …"

"Shut up, why don't you!" Paul tucked his hand in his jeans pocket and pulled out the ripped envelope. Taking his sister's hand, he opened the envelope and spilled the note and the key into her palm.

Puzzled, she read the note and stared at the key. Then a flicker of recognition lit her face. "I know what this is. I misplaced a key like this one, although the key I used was under the shed mat and was grimy and full of rust."

"Danielle, stop talking in riddles! Tell me what you see!"

She fingered the shiny key in her hand. "This is not grandpa's messy key, but it could be a copy." Danielle held the key up, taking in every detail. "It will probably open the lock to the door of what grandpa called, the great shed."

"So, you haven't used this key, and you lost the old one, how do you get into the shed?" Paul's impatience was increasing.

"I usually follow Natalie into the shed. I'm not sure how she gets in and I forget to ask her. Natalie says the shed is home of the "dream machine." I don't have a name for it, but I've experienced something in that far corner where the refrigerator box was dumped. There's …"

"Great, I found both of you! Come in now. Sunday dinner is on the table," yelled Mrs. Norfeld from the kitchen window.

Paul put his finger over his lips in a quiet sign. "Let's keep this between us. Later, once everyone is not paying attention, let's meet at the shed. I've seen some very strange things in there, I want to show you. And we'll try this new one and see if it works." Paul pointed to the key on Danielle's hand.

"Yes, but much later on, when mom, dad and the twins are asleep."

"As well as Natalie. You'll need to make sure she's snoring first."

"No, Natalie will come with us," said Danielle as she twirled the key in her hand.

Paul yanked the key and note and returned it to his pocket. He gave Danielle a long stare. "Including Natalie is a not a good idea, she is growing up, but she worries me."

"Wait and see. You'll be surprised to find out how much your sister can handle," Danielle said as she hustled into the house leaving Paul walking rather slowly, talking to himself.

10

Revelations

*T*he mantel clock played its English tune, beating out eleven chimes as Natalie stood beside Paul's bed, trying to control a huge case of giggles. Realizing she had to be church mouse quiet, she covered her mouth. It was because her brother slept so funny. He hadn't bothered with the bedding. Instead, he burrowed his head into fluffy pillows with his feet sticking over the edge of the bed. There were books piled in the middle of the bedspread and an assortment of his favorite snacks tossed everywhere. He glowed a yellowish color which was really a reading light. This would have been the perfect picture to take and show to her friends except she was on a mission—to wake Paul and silently bring him to the shed.

She would do just that.

"Hey, you alligator monster, get off of me," yelled Paul

as he thrashed about, trying to push away the nightmarish creature.

"Shush. It's me, Natalie. I'm no alligator, but if you don't shut up, I may call Captain Hook to come and get you."

Startled, Paul slid from the bed, all the books tumbling to the floor.

"Sometimes brothers are plain stupid," Natalie thought aloud.

"You know I heard you. I'm way past Peter Pan. In my dream I was exploring with George Irwin and his work with gators. I bet you never heard of him!"

"Well, if you don't keep you voice down all of Tuttlebury will hear as well as mom and dad."

"Yeah, we're supposed to go visit the shed tonight," said Paul boasting his signature know-it-all look.

"That's the plan if you don't wreck it. Hurry up and get ready. Robert will probably be home soon and we don't want to bump into him."

"I'm way ahead of things. I went to bed already dressed. I only have to throw on my sneakers. You know, I'm smart. I aspire to becoming a guru of Mensa.

"A blue tube of pasta? What did you say?"

"Now who's brainless … it isn't me. For your information it means membership in an extremely intelligent group."

There was a push at the bedroom door. Danielle stood at the foot of the bed wearing her annoying frown. Methodically using hand signs, she ushered down the staircase, through the dimly lit house and out the back door. Natalie and Paul followed.

* * *

"Did you hear that creak and thump? There were voices too, rattling on about something," said Ted Norfeld as he nudged his wife's shoulder.

"No hon, I heard nothing. I was in a middle of a dream."

"Are you sure you didn't? Listen. Did you hear that?"

"I don't hear anything strange, only the sound of the summer crickets … which we wouldn't notice if you would break the piggy bank and buy an air conditioner. Let me listen again." Nancy Norfeld sat up and leaned into the large pillows. "No, dear, I hear nothing unusual. But I really would like the hum of air conditioner."

"Yeah, but you wouldn't hear the twins screaming." He stood and reached under the bed.

"Don't bother. I moved it. You know we don't live in the city anymore."

"You didn't do that. You took my best wooden bat." Ted slumped back on the bed.

"But I didn't throw it away. It's on the porch for when you practice with the kids. Anyway, it's probably Robert making all the noise you heard. Not me. Maybe he decided to come home and not stay with the Tuttle's."

"I doubt that." Ted leaned over to get his robe and slippers. On cue, his wife gently stroked his arm. "Look hon, we're having a lovely sleep. If you get up and stomp around, you'll wake the babies and then we'll spend the rest of the night feeding them, burping them and changing them."

The furrows deepened in his forehead as he realized the truth of his wife's words. He gently tucked her in as he threw the covers over himself truly believing he had heard something.

* * *

The beginnings of a new moon lent an evening glow, as the three hurried to the shed. Danielle reached the shed a minute before Paul. Winded, they both stopped and waited for their sister. Natalie brushed by them and pulled open the door. "You know the shed's always open when I come."

Flicking on her flashlight, Natalie skipped in, followed by brother and sister. Three beams pierced the darkness.

Paul sensed hairs twitching on the back of his neck. Danielle breathed tensely as she deliberated taking a step.

But Natalie giggled and easily approached the refrigerator box. She lifted the velvet curtain and went into the flickering greenish glow.

"C'mon, you guys," Paul shouted, even though his sisters were not listening. "You could trip on a rake or hose, or walk right into a huge spider web. Maybe you'll go to a peculiar place, like the last time I was here."

Danielle halted and turned her flashlight on Paul. "You mean you were here before and didn't tell me?"

"Well, there wasn't time to talk with you. You're so busy. I came to get a lawn chair so I could read under a tree. So, what of it, you were here with Natalie. Right?"

You're changing the subject. You said you came for a chair but really something else happened, didn't it?"

"Um. I'm not really sure. It was like I was lost in another world. It could be I was dreaming again. I seem to be doing that a lot these days."

"Okay, now you're making me crazy!" Impatient, Danielle waved the flashlight around like a strobe.

"Alright it was like this. I was in a huge room with stacks of books from the floor to ceiling. I saw a gentleman seated at an expensive desk with papers all around as he ate lots of snacks and ham combo sandwiches. He was wearing black eyeglasses, dark slacks and a collared shirt. He seemed familiar, like I already knew him. This was all very curious, until I realized this person was like me and all of a sudden; he became me. The other me; or rather the me to come. Maybe. Well, he was working on some kind of writing project and never lifted his head." Paul stood very still; his face lost in thought.

"What a story! I could say you're making all this up except ... Paul did you see that?"

"Yes, and I hear something too!"

A pinkish glow surrounded the refrigerator carton, as soft music played. Danielle and Paul rushed towards the delightful strains, pushing aside the velvet curtain. As they stepped into the tiny enclosure the walls fell away. They were standing in a grand ballroom, listening to a live recital. Before them sat a solo presenter—Natalie. With mouths wide open, they watched their sister expertly play a prized Stradivarius violin.

A breeze swept by. The enchanting moment vanished. Abruptly appeared a rowboat surrounded by miles of ocean. The clouds began pouring waterfalls. Brimming with water, the small raft tilted to one side. Well-muscled arms appeared, hurling pails of water into the sea. In a blink, the pails began to fill with odd objects. Clothing. Shoes. Personal belongings including a wallet, comb, bicycle light. There was a gasp of surprise followed by heart clenching fear as the owner was recognized.

Robert.

All this stuff belonged to Robert. He was standing up in the middle of the boat. His form was clearly defined like thick pen strokes. Robert's eyes were focused, his body steady like a character from an action movie. He moved forward; glaring at an evil creature. Suddenly a loose floorboard tripped him. His arms thrashed about attempting to recover his balance. He grabbed an oar and held it over his head shouting warrior style, ready to attack this monstrous foe. Giant waves slapped the boat and he was gone!

Abruptly all three were standing in front of the open shed. Puzzled they shrugged and shook their heads in wonderment. They eyed each other with disbelief and confusion. What had happened? If anything. Perhaps nothing at all.

Silence.

Then Danielle coughed nervously and threw up her arms. "Where did Robert go? Why are you both looking at me so weird? You did you see Robert fight that ugly creature and fall into the sea. Didn't you?"

Danielle kicked a dirt patch hard, sending tiny pebbles into the air.

"I'm asking again—what happened to Robert?" She paused and looked around. "And why are we all standing in front of the shed?"

Paul and Natalie were still; their faces masked a frozen white.

"Come on guys, get with the picture, Robert is in danger and we have to do something about it!"

"You saw Robert?" said Paul.

Natalie cupped her hands around her waist like her mother when there was something important to say. "I didn't see Robert; we were in a boat on a beautiful day having a picnic. Before that I had a fantastic violin tucked under my chin. It played so smooth; almost like it was playing itself and I was pretending to pluck the notes. It was fairy tale music."

Paul rubbed his cheeks in frustration. "I didn't see any boat. I was standing in that creepy shed, at that fancy desk again, thinking odd thoughts that sounded like me but much more advanced. I was an older version of myself, figuring an upload of complicated data."

"I have to get back in there and play my violin again!"

"Danie," said Paul softly, "you really saw things we didn't see. I'm worried about Robert. From what you said he's headed for big trouble."

"Yes," replied Danielle. "Except he already has been in trouble and it's getting even worse."

Natalie pushed her brother and sister. "What are you both talking about? Robert was probably being his nasty self, like always. Like the night he went out and didn't come home. Did he have something to with that farm with the broken tires?"

Danielle cleared her throat and looked sadly at her sister. "Robert probably was involved but I'm not sure of the details. I'm very worried."

"It's always about Robert! I don't want to talk about him." Paul picked leaves off the nearby bush and pointed to the large shed. "Looking at this run-down building, we know it's real. We know that grandpa spent a lot of time in there with all this stuff. We also know the box that is in the corner with the velvet curtain really brought us a new refrigerator. But what happened to us in there … well, that's all very unknown." Paul took a deep breath.

"Yeah, you're right." chirped up Natalie. "The unknown is a dream machine! What you hope for happens. My next wish will be to play the harp."

"Are you kidding!" shouted Danielle, rubbing her hand together. "After what it did to me and what it showed us about Robert; it's some kind of forecaster, I think. I really don't know. This is so puzzling, and very exciting!"

"Yes, scary is right. Danie, I'm nervous. What did this weird box show you? You can tell me; I can keep a secret."

Paul's gentle eyes met the fear in his sister's large green eyes, his hand tapping her shoulder.

Natalie stepped between the two and gave her brother a little shove. "Hey, I can keep a secret too!" Natalie took a deep breath and continued. Didn't you hear what Danielle believes that box is? She thinks it can tell the future. Maybe it has shown her things to come, like it has done for me. I've been doing a lot of wishing and hoping."

"Okay, okay," said Danielle as she moved away from Paul. "Natalie's right. That box has shown me interesting possibilities that are amazing. I can hardly take it in. That's why I'm not ready to talk with you. I need time to think."

Paul then stepped closer to the shed door. "I understand. Sometimes I want more visits with that box, other times I'm so perplexed I want to smash it to pieces. But then I think …"

Danielle and Natalie studied Paul. He had that distant look he wore when he was trying to figure a problem, a kind of other worldly sense. No one uttered a word, the long pause dripping in anticipation.

"It's like this. The box could be telling future events, portraying hopes and wishes as outcomes. Maybe. Or the box could by projecting certain actions which are purely those wanted by the individual and not real events at all. Like playing a clip of a filmstrip. It could be that future events are only possibilities of what could happen not necessarily what will happen. There could be numerous options presented and other choices considered. Then there is the issue about the refrigerator box and how it generates these events. Maybe it is not the box at all. The box could be a temporary vessel exploring these assorted outcomes … a gateway of sorts."

Danielle's mouth, hung wide open. Natalie gasped and took safety in her sister's embrace. "Wow! Paul, what was all that? I think I got some of it. Actually, I'm not sure I really understand at all."

Suddenly the yard lit bright with the porch light.

Danielle pointed towards the porch. "Do you see that? The kitchen light is light is on which means that ..."

"Dad is up and getting ready for work. It's five in the morning!"

"You're right Paul," said Natalie as she broke away from her sister and ran towards the house.

Silent as mime presenters, Paul and Danielle hurried behind her.

* * *

Robert pulled the strange blankets over his shoulder as he tried to get comfortable in the unfamiliar Tuttle house bedroom. But he couldn't sleep. Hmm. Was it guilt? But he had called home to prove his whereabouts; also fending off the interrogation he would have encountered the next day. Across the room his friend was yowling and snorting in a deep sleep, which was very annoying. Robert was awake and unsettled like when he forgot to turn off the stove or study for a test. A kind of foreboding. What was it? It could be all the hostility experienced at the last meeting. The guys were demanding, wanting him do awful things. One older guy threw nasty questions at him about everything—especially things about his grandfather's house, where he now lived. He had been waiting for the punches to start, but then the gang stepped back. And stopped.

Now he was taking shelter in the lion's den with the two Tuttle sons. He should have run. But he was scared of being beaten up. He knew that the Tuttle family owned the entire county and wanted to own him and his family as well. If you didn't fit in there could be big trouble.

Robert's head began to sink into the pillow as sleep hovered over him. Suddenly he sat straight up. He remembered what he had forgot; the small manila envelope sitting in his hand. So plainly he envisioned the key but had no recollection of what happened to it. Except the last time he saw it was at the fishing cabin. He had quickly tucked the envelope in his pocket when he had heard noise. Paul. His brother had been spying and fell into the bushes. Then they argued. Umm. The key must have fallen out of his pocket. He had to go back to the cabin and look around.

Robert's eyes were acclimating to the early morning light. Gingerly he picked up all his stuff he had dumped last night. Then one sneaker lightly stepped, then the other as he left the Tuttle house.

11

Mounding Storm Clouds

*Y*esterday's humidity that had hung in the air like a wet army blanket finally lifted. Now a welcoming breeze cut through the summer rays and awesome blue sky. The plant and animal life loved it. The golden cornstalks reached for the sun as their stalks swayed and danced in unison. Grazing cows and sheep munched peacefully. Horses pranced about, elegant in their shiny coats. Screeching flocks and chirping birds filled the air. With open arms the fertile countryside called one and all.

Camera ready, well-kept farms sat proud amidst the surrounding crops. Sighted were moving tractors, irrigation sprays, and fences being mended by farmers with children by their side. All hard at work. Most likely they had risen to an early breakfast so as to milk the cows and perform an endless list of farming duties. Sweating through their work clothes, the long day's dimming light was most appreciated. It was time for a well-deserved meal at table with family followed by a good evening rest. Tranquility and harmony experienced at its finest.

Then tomorrow it began all over again.

Until finally the gentle rains yielded to the fiery sun, flowing into a colorful harvest with hopefully a bounty to smile about. This lovely postcard perfection had once highlighted the small town called Tuttlebury. However, this peaceful and simple life had fled the fields; times were changing.

Certain country roads have merged into highways. Tracker-trailer trucks and a parade of other vehicles fiercely rumble by; with not a turn of a driver's head. Remaining dirt roads have been cloaked with black top attracting two wheels of motor bikes as well as those humanly driven. Colors and riders blur as speed increases. Even more distressing are the grouping of some into a gang mentality. Witnessed are the trampling of feet through fields of crops, taking fresh produce at will, and decorating the countryside with the sparkle of cans and empty bags of chips.

Some riders are passing through. Others are homegrown like the cornstalks, but unlike the eager plants, have no aspirations to reach for the sun. They are a new breed of youth. Self-absorbed. Rambunctious. Unruly. And they have a testy attitude to match.

Discouragement is in the air. Farmers who had nurtured large families hoping children would help in the fields are sorely mistaken. The desire to pass along the farm and its rich experience to them had met with disinterest; such that parental expectations lessened as well as the birthrate. Slowly farms closed barn doors and sold off property. It was time to move on. However, some stayed and adopted novel ways to cultivate and harvest the land, although expensive and contrived.

These remaining hard-working farmers, looked with forlorn on the motor bikes and busy traffic, bewildered with today's young people. There was a collective disgust with the pollution of land and disregard for the pastoral life, trading it off for life filled with flash, dance and danger.

But it was not only the youth.

Facing troubling winds were the adults as well. The ways and means of the town's namesake, the Tuttle families, owned up to the root meaning of the name—gods of thunder. Heavy handed methods ruled the town with corruption found in every corner. There were bullying tactics in farming subsistence noted in the expensive pricing of fertilizer and seed and unfair usage of the town water supply. A choice to step more independently would eventually be a farm's demise. There were those who fought back. The Smiths. The Johnsons. The Millers. They fought hard but eventually threw away their farmer hat.

Then came John and Mary Norfeld, a young couple full of vigor and expectation. They farmed the land their own way fending off the harassment from the Tuttle family. Not an easy task since the Tuttle's managed huge necessities like the ownership of the area water for irrigation and banned access to certain families, including John and Mary. But the Norfeld's were tough and would not be pushed away. They planted a chief crop of corn and supplemental summer crops and were very resourceful to make ends meet. Farm animals were maintained not so much for market but for their own table. It was hard work but they both loved the freedom to earn a living off their own land. Even if the yield came up short and Mary Norfeld sold her famous pies and handcrafted items. The farm was well worth their effort.

Becoming proud parents to an elder daughter and younger son, they prompted a strong farming mentality in their household. Passing down this tradition was their hope.

Yet while the children obediently helped with the crops, milked the cows and fed the chickens, their hearts were elsewhere. Their daughter loved the city and helping people so she went to nursing school, later finding a position in a city hospital. Their son had a head for numbers, favoring math class even over lunch. He would spend hours over his books, caught in all kinds of calculations. Both studied diligently to pursue life outside the farm. Although the Norfled's were saddened by their children's departure, they both agreed to let them go.

As years past they were known as Grandpa and Grandma Norfeld. Now retired, Mr. Norfeld was as stubborn and cantankerous as ever. He was especially disliked by the Tuttle community for his honesty and fair play. Yet this was the way it had always been. Others were jealous of grandma's fine baking especially her berry pastries and moist zucchini breads from the crops she grew herself. In some ways the Norfeld's were relieved the children left for city careers, away from the Tuttle influence.

Sadness came one spring. One rainy afternoon, Grandma passed away in the kitchen. She had finished tying on her strawberry patterned apron when she felt dizzy and sat down. And didn't get up. The doctor said it was probably a heart attack but grandpa didn't bother with finding out for sure. It was grandma's time, and that was that. A year later grandpa died as well.

With the passing of both John and Mary Norfeld, the Tuttle family hoped to see the end of their problem. But not so.

That was because the Norfeld son returned, bringing his

very growing family. They were not farming people, which was a dilemma for the Tuttlebury farming community. How could the Norfeld's be rallied into the Tuttle domain? Should this new family be discreetly pushed away? Or bullied into acceptable behavior? Perhaps wooing them with an illusion of benevolence like the means to catch a fly ... with honey. Maybe this would catch them.

Dark clouds were mounding.

12

A Step into the Unknown

As usual, Mr. Norfeld took his place at the head of the table. Today he sat rigid in his large oak chair, his eyes large and stern—which was not usual. The playful table conversation cut off like the sink faucet. Four sets of questioning eyes gazed upon their father. Mrs. Norfeld abruptly placed a platter of golden fried chicken on the table, sat and nodded to her husband.

Mr. Norfeld huskily cleared his throat, and rubbed his cheeks. More silence. Not good signs. Danielle itched behind her ears. Natalie kicked her sandaled feet nervously. Paul played with his fork and napkin.

Robert's head looked down, fingers texting on his phone. Sensing the attention on him, Robert looked up. Mr. Norfeld's eyes stared hard, his face a stone gray. "Hey, I know this is about me, so why don't you leave everyone else out of

96

it. Okay, I go out a lot but I'm old enough to do some things alone. Besides it's summer and I have to have some fun and anyhow we're all …"

"Silence! I have had enough of all of you—especially seeing cell phones at dinner! I've had enough of your interests outside the house, doing exactly what you please. I'm at work and your mother is here with the twins all day. She's holding up the fort, doing everything. Where are all of you? You're not telling us where you're going or coming back or even asking permission. Some of you are going to who knows where; like you Robert." Robert opened his mouth to respond but Mr. Norfeld held his hand up in a stop motion. "I have the floor and I am not finished." He turned his head and nodded to the other three children. "You, Danielle are way over your head in softball. Natalie, you're spending hours and hours outside, especially in that old smelly shed, which I don't understand at all. And Paul, you're in own world with a stack of books. That's not all, there's the issue …"

Mrs. Norfeld sniffed and broke out into loud sobs. "Please stop. You're being too harsh on the kids. When you saw me other day, I was angry. Yes, I was tired and still am, but I can't blame this entirely on the them. There are some things only a mother can do and with twins it seems never ending. But the kids do help. Perhaps they did more when we first moved in, but Natalie often plays with the twins, Danielle has styled the nursery and Paul did a great job painting the porch."

Paul squirmed in his seat and eyed his mother curiously.

"Yes, Paul, I've noticed. I have seen the good things all of you have done." Mrs. Norfeld wiped her eyes and gently smiled. "But we all could do better. Sometimes I'm overwhelmed and Dad is working and you're involved in something else. I know you're willing to help. We need better communication. Perhaps we could plan a way to track our activities—like a special calendar on the refrigerator. For starters, I could note the upcoming church welcoming coming up in late August.

Dad nodded to his wife, his anger subsiding. "Yes, your mother is right. I like the idea of a calendar. After supper, I will tape one on the side of refrigerator and you can all write your activities and suggestions." He glanced around the table, at the large anxious eyes, on the juicy chicken and tasty macaroni and cheese that was beginning to congeal. "Well let's say grace so we can eat, while this meal is still warm."

Plates were filled and the usual around table banter returned. The days' accounts were shared as stomachs became full and satisfied.

Offering to clear the table before dessert, Robert removed the soiled plates and placed the iced chocolate cake and paper plates in the middle of the table.

Delighted with the surprise baked desert, everyone clamored for a piece. Except for Robert. Declining the rich confection, he sat quietly, staring at the back door as he tore his napkin into tiny pieces.

* * *

That evening rain fell with heavy gusts blowing this way and that. It was a night to stay put. Mrs. Norfeld happily tucked in the twins and then took her usual living room seat to watch a television drama. Dad was in his study figuring work problems on his computer. The rest of the Norfeld children had scattered throughout the rambling farmhouse.

Deciding against TV, Paul piled a stack of books on his bed, placing a juice pack on top. Grabbing a handful of popcorn, he tucked himself into the pillows. Dinnertime had hit a sore spot. He would lighten things up and enjoy himself. And for some reason, Robert was not in the bedroom, so he had the place to himself, the way he liked it. Placing a thick novel on his lap, he opened to the colorful bookmark. Ah, he had come to a good part. Throwing a handful of popcorn into his mouth, his head bent down, fully engrossed.

Then came a knock.

Paul curled on his side and flipped the page.

The knock became a resounding drum roll on the old oak door. Still absorbed, Paul did not move an inch.

Then came a huge rap like the sound of a horse whip.

"What was that?" said Paul as he sat upright.

"It's me," said Natalie as she quietly let herself in, leaving the door slightly ajar. "I want to talk to you."

"Come on, Natalie, can't you see that I'm reading!"

"It's about dinner tonight. Do you think mom and dad know about the shed and why I go? Do they know what really happens there? Will they nail it up so that I can't get in or even worse take the refrigerator box and throw it away?"

"What are you saying?" Paul threw his book down. "You think that they're watching us that closely? Usually, dad is at work and mom is tied up with the twins."

"Yes, but maybe they know things they're not telling us. Paul, I'm confused. What do you think?"

"What do I think? You're the one who spends a lot of

time in that shed and they know this. But I think they would have said more if they had experienced the box the way we have. Um. Maybe to stay on the safe side, think about taking a break from going there."

"But going places in the Box is great fun. Even though I'm not sure how it all works, you explained it very well so that I'm not afraid."

Paul hastened to the edge of the mattress; his eyes bright. Such a compliment didn't happen every day and usually ended up a kind of insult. But coming from Natalie was different. She might be young, but she was honest with her comments.

"Paul, are you alright? You have a funny look in your eyes."

Paul looked away from his sister's gaze to the far wall. There was that night he said a lot of things to both of his sisters but right now he remembered hardly anything. Except that the refrigerator carton was some kind of gateway to another time. "Well, that Box is very unusual, a place to step into the future and see how it feels."

"Yes, Paul it's a place where dreams come true! I get to be a concert pianist and play my violin in special places. I hope that I can become that person. Or am I that person already? I have to grow up and do the right things. But I'm not sure that I will do them right. All this could be a dream and not come true. Or everything will."

"Wow! Natalie, you can sure talk up a storm. The way I see it is …"

"Paul, being in the Box is like seeing life from the beginning to the end. Like God sees us. He sees all of us from start to finish, everything we do—what happened before, what is happening now and what will can happen in the future. It's because God is the Alpha and the Omega."

Natalie paused and took in a deep breath. "Although the Box sees all of time ... for us the past is over, the future is still coming, and right now is the only place I can be."

Paul nodded in agreement. "I couldn't have said it better. How do you know about these things?"

"Mom has been taking me to special meetings at church so we can join. These are meetings we're all supposed to go to. But dad has been working and somehow you guys are off doing other things. Anyhow the man in charge, I think they call him, oh, I forget, was talking about how God sees all things and knows all things that we don't know until later. Maybe."

Overhearing, Danielle burst into the room. "What do you mean Natalie, I went to some of these meetings, unlike our brothers. I met the man in charge, who is the pastor by the way. He talked a lot about the Bible."

"Tell us what you think he said."

"I'm not really sure. But when Pastor Jim talks about this stuff, the hairs on the back of my neck get prickly. And when I visit the Box the same thing happens."

Paul stood a few feet from his bed and gawked at his sisters. "Danielle, you've visited that Box, you've seen things. I know we asked before; how come you don't tell us about your experience?"

Danielle's full cheeks were ablaze in crimson. Looking down she took a moment to think. "Well, it's like this ... what happens to me is so wonderful, so out there, that sharing seems wrong or even boastful. Even worst would be that these happenings would vanish because I spoke too soon, although I hoped so badly for them to be."

"I can see you, even though you're trying to hide," said Natalie as she directed her words towards the door. "Don't pretend you haven't heard everything we've said."

All eyes bored through the weathered oak door as a dark form awkwardly stepped into the room. Robert.

"I can hardly believe it, you're finally home," said Danielle.

Paul rushed over to his brother. "Yeah, and I'm curious what you think about the Box, you know that tattered refrigerator carton in the shed; the one Natalie decorated with a messed-up curtain."

Natalie pouted, darting an angry look at Paul. "Hey, I think I did a really good job with mom's old stuff. Turning to face her brother, she said, "Has that beautiful Box taken you anywhere Robert?"

"What are you talking about? I haven't been in the shed since grandpa died. It's locked anyway with a rusty padlock; the supposed key under the mat is always missing. You guys are being so ridiculous!"

Robert stood militant in his radical black attire his face shadowed dark arrogance. He wasn't sure what they were talking about. Only that whenever he walked by the shed, even as a young kid, he experienced the start of a migraine headache. There was something weird in there—that's for sure. And the key found at the club house looked like grandpa's shed key ... someone in the club was interested as well. But he wasn't about to tell his family anything.

He spoke in a deliberate tone. "What I think is that you have become delusional, sucked into vain thinking and imaginations. Hard to believe you have succumbed to this irrational thinking to help adjust to our new environment. Your behavior is unwarranted and absurd."

Astonishment and confusion etched their faces.

Robert abruptly turned and left the room.

* * *

It was two in the morning and the steady rain continued.

Robert pulled his hoodie over his muscled shoulders, fully covering his head. He placed the tiny manilla envelope in his jacket pocket and carefully pulled the zipper. He had gone back to the cabin the other morning looking for this packet, only to find it on Paul's desk. Who would think? It must have fallen out of his jacket when they had that little fight. Now to prove his hunch— that this was the key to grandpa's old shed. Whatever is in there must be pretty interesting; it was making everyone crazy.

The house was quiet as he stepped from the back porch and ran through the heavy rain drops to the drenched shed. What was wrong with him— acting terribly self-righteous when in fact he didn't have a clue? He was so out there like the professor in Literature class. Patting the outline of the packet, he would soon know.

Approaching the shed door, he slid the key from the envelope and jammed it into the rusty padlock. He tried to turn it but his wet grip kept slipping. Suddenly the key eased out and fell into the mud. No way! Crouching with flashlight in hand, he aimed this way and that he attempting to rescue the silver key. This effort was going nowhere. He was usually not a quitter but already his clothes were soaked through and he considered heading back.

Suddenly the padlock fell over his arm into the same place the key had vanished. The weathered door now hung open, beckoning him. Losing no time, Robert bounded into the shed. A heavy earthy musk filled his head, the cold damp chilled his already wet body. Moving his flashlight, he surveyed each wall, corner and crevice. No surprises here. Not even a field mouse seeking shelter. Only the usual stuff; earthen caked garden tools, winter shovels and grandma's stash of canning pans and jars plus lids.

And a rundown, smelly refrigerator carton.

With a swing of his arm, Robert washed the entire box in light. It was the same as he remembered it in the kitchen—sturdy double cardboard, with thick lettering of the store brand and appliance serial number. The only difference was an impromptu piece of worn velvet that was fashioned like a curtain over the opening of the carton, landing in layered folds on the packed dirt floor. Natalie's design.

"What a waste of time!" Robert shouted and turned to go out the shed door. He was thoroughly annoyed.

A flash of emerald glow streamed from behind the curtain, swirling about into a strobe of starlight. Robert twisted around. The refrigerator box was spinning waves of dancing green and purple hues, the air alive and radiant. Swiftly he approached the it and swung aside the makeshift drape.

Then stepped inside.

Robert swallowed hard. The space was palatial like a grand room in a medieval castle, with a golden arched ceiling that stretched to the heavens and long ornate windows that did the same. A long table was festively arranged with a wonderful banquet displaying his favorite eats. Chords of familiar choir music echoed to the ceiling, blending several vocal harmonies. The air was electric as the guest of honor was ushered in. Robert strained his eyes to see who this special visitor might be.

In a flash the wonderous sight vanished. He felt a painful pounding on his shoulder blades and back. He gasped. His eyes widened in disbelief. This couldn't be happening. But it was. He was in the meeting cabin surrounded by all the guys—the victim of their fist fight. And their punches were brutal! Yet it all seemed unreal like he was watching a video of himself. The gang was hurling insults and demands; he had better follow through or worse things would happen. Why had they picked him to do all their dirty work?

"Now listen very carefully Mr. hotshot Robert!" shouted the gang member with the wavy blond hair.

"All the stuff you've done so far is like playing in the sand. Now comes the real deal to prove your loyalty," laughed the older fellow with the army haircut.

A snarly looking man they called Chief grabbed Robert by the shoulders, his eyes bulging as he yelled into Robert's ear. The angry mob surrounded closer and closer, cheering them on. Robert felt the room begin to swirl. Sweat broke out as panic seized him, making it difficult to breathe. Robert wanted to punch these guys, or run far, far away. "By the way you sleazeball, where did you hide that key? We know you took it. It unlocks future things. It supposedly connects to a kind of gateway to the future right in your shed. Butch knew about this but he is gone from us. But you know about …"

"Know about what?" Robert was so shaken with fear he couldn't think.

The next instant, the room folded into itself, went sideways and vanished into a mist.

Disorientated, Robert took in his surroundings. He was standing in a mucky puddle outside the shed. There was no key in his hand. The door of the shed was securely locked. He rattled the aged door, shouting, "I hate you guys. I hate this awful mess! And I hate that box!" Realizing he might have awakened his entire family, he sprinted back to the old farm house. He landed quietly on the porch steps, then scooted up the rickety fire escape into the hall window. Inching his way slowly down the hallway, he eased the creaky door to his room, sighing in relief. He was glad not to have been caught, especially after dad's dinner outburst. His head was electric with confusion, he hadn't a clue what to do.

Believing his life was in danger, he needed a plan. Now.

13

Making Choices

*D*ad had left early for work while most of the family slept in. The chilly rainy night found them burrowed in their covers. Even the twins were still tucked in. But not Danielle. She hadn't slept at all. Not after last night when she watched her brother bang on the shed door and then run away. That was really crazy. He was yelling, shouting something very strange. She glanced around the room, at her snoring sister and then to the chair where she had tossed her wet clothes. Boy, she had gotten drenched but she still didn't know what was up with Robert. Dad was right; she had been spending too much time at softball games.

And too much time in the weird shed— in that odd refrigerator box.

As the older sister, she needed to tune in more, especially to her brother. At first, she had watched him mess around with those weird guys. It was so unsettling; her eyes would twitch. There was that odd dream—or was it a vision—in the Box where Robert was in trouble on the boat. But Paul and Natalie didn't see this. Only her. She had no idea why. But things had to change. They had been friends once, riding their bikes, getting ice-cream in town. But all that was a lifetime ago when they lived in their old house. Funny it was only about two months since they moved here yet it seemed like forever. Today she was determined to track her brother's every move. There were a lot of questions she had ready for him. Maybe over an ice-cream cone they could discuss summer experiences, hers being softball and shed time. And his? This could be very interesting.

Finding a comfortable summer shirt and tattered jeans in the dirty wash pile, Danielle dressed and hurried downstairs. Before going out, she had to finish chores she had promised mom she would do. She had been too eager to please, so the list was quite long. Besides helping clean the upstairs rooms, she would rake outside, start the laundry and get breakfast going. What had she been thinking? First things first. She was hungry, breakfast was where she would start. Like mom, she did a kind of whirling dance in the efficient kitchen and soon coffee was brewing, French toast and sausages sizzling. Her stomach was gurgling in hunger, she didn't know if she could wait for everyone to get up. As she set the table, she snacked on a piece of cold coffee cake defrosting from the freezer.

Suddenly the front doorbell rang.

"Who can that be?" Danielle thought aloud.

"I was wondering the same thing," said Mrs. Norfeld as she pushed open the kitchen door, then abruptly turned towards the living room.

"I'll get it mom. You can help yourself to breakfast."

"But I'm all dressed and your clothes are wrinkled."

Danielle rushed to the picture window and lifted the edge of the lacy curtain. There was a man on the steps. A stranger.

Mrs. Norfeld peered through the tiny magnifying hole in the door. Then she abruptly threw open the door, her tall form so menacing the stranger startled. "Who are you? Why are you calling on me unannounced? Are you another salesman?"

There was a long pause as the short gentleman in the pristine gray suit smoothed his salt and pepper moustache. He righted his stance, his highly polished shoes planted on the cement step. "I am Mr. Mussmen, an administrative assistant from the Tuttlebury High School. I would like to speak to the young lady in this house."

"Well, that would be me, I am Mrs. Norfeld. I run this household."

"Yes, I believe this is true, that you're the woman of the house." Glancing down at his clipboard he continued, "However, I am looking for a young lady, undoubtedly your daughter, a Danielle Norfeld."

"You are correct, Danielle is my daughter. I wonder what business would you have with her," said Mrs. Norfeld, her voice tense.

"Mrs. Norfeld, May I please come in and give you the details?"

"No, you may not. Mr. Mussmen, I was not expecting you. You have not shown me any credentials showing who you are. Besides I have children to tend to." Mrs. Norfeld began to close the door.

"Wait! I have my badge here somewhere ... hmm, I'm not sure where it went!" Mr. Mussmen scrambled through his briefcase; his face flushed. "Please don't go! Take this envelope and have your daughter complete it fully, especially the required essay. We were impressed by your daughter's records from her previous school and want to discuss a special opportunity." He shoved the envelope threw the partly open door, side stepping Mrs. Norfeld and instead, handing it to Danielle.

"Just you wait a minute!" Mrs. Norfeld glared at the strange gentleman before her. "My daughter has no business with the high school and last week I sent on the required forms for Danielle to enter the eighth grade at the Tuttlebury Middle School. You are very mistaken. It is my older son, Robert, who is scheduled for the tenth grade in your high school."

"Mrs. Norfeld, you don't understand. It is very important that your daughter send in the essay, it will be the deciding factor in ..."

I certainly do. Good-bye Mr. Mussmen!" Slamming the door, Mrs. Norfeld glared at her daughter. Then at the large white envelope. "What nerve of that man! Giving you the packet and not me, your mother!" She muttered to herself as she watched the high school administrator rush to his shiny blue car and speed off.

Danielle was already sitting at the kitchen table, the contents of the envelope spilled in front of her. She began reading aloud. "This is an urgent matter requiring your attention and immediate reply."

"Well, why did you stop? Please tell me what is going on," exclaimed her mother, bypassing her favorite coffee cake to hover over her daughter's shoulder.

Danielle's head leaned into the paperwork, as she quickly read through the extensive letter. "Mom, it says here that they want me to attend the high school this coming Fall."

"What? What are they talking about? You're already

enrolled as an eighth grader at the middle school. Orientation starts in a few weeks."

"I know. But this letter states that the information sent from my old middle school system, has me functioning at the ninth-grade level. You see, they want me to skip a grade."

Mrs. Norfeld snatched the page from Danielle's hand and read it to herself. Her sneaker tapped nervously. "This can't possibly be. They think you're intelligent enough to skip a grade! Such strange news. Now you'll think you're as smart as Paul. Danielle, I really don't know. Middle school would be fine, wouldn't it? We need to talk to your father. Right now, we better have us some breakfast." She grabbed a plate and went over to the stove.

Danielle's appetite had vanished. Bewildered, she felt like the floor had swallowed her. Obediently she filled her plate, wondering if she could get away from mom and eat on the porch. From the upstairs baby monitor, husky cries of hungry little ones shook the room. Mrs. Norfeld took her plate and went to calm the babies. "Danielle, I'll take care of the twins and after you eat, please tend to those chores you promised. After that you can go out, but be back this afternoon to review this paperwork. This will give me time to read every word and go over things with your father."

Danielle rolled her eyes. She left her portion untouched on the table and headed out of the kitchen, bumping into her brothers as they pushed each other into the room. Paul was looking rested but Robert was in need of lots of coffee and a hot shower. Time to get moving. Even though she felt like soaking her pillow with angry tears, she had promises to keep. Then she could spend time with Robert. Heavy hearted, she didn't know why everyone always thought less of her.

* * *

Mrs. Norfeld watched Danielle rush past her to the laundry room. "That girl is so difficult all the time and now this. I need to catch my breath." Sitting on the edge of the couch, she slid the high school forms unto her lap and thumbed through, speed reading as she went, for she was every bit as intelligent as her kids, even more so. A flick of pink slipped to the floor. Due to the lingering post baby weight—it was time to diet—she had a tough time bending. She rose, her eyes roaming the room. "Ah, here it is." The note had perched itself under the side coffee table. Grabbing the fireplace poker, she snatched it up and glanced over the scribbled longhand. "What!" Taking in every word, she reread the sticky note ... *the Tuttle committee has decided to schedule Danielle for the ninth grade. This decision is final. Mandatory that this student be matriculated and included in the fall orientation. Any altercations will result in due consequences.*

"No! How dare they push us around!" This directive written on a sticky piece of paper was probably not meant for her eyes or Danielle's either. Mrs. Norfeld's hands began to shake, her head airy as sweat rolled down her back. Beyond irritated, her heart pounded in rebellion. She understood, although she wished she didn't, what it could all mean. But now she knew. Lies. Deceit. Grand trickery. She had been deceived by the showing of generosity with the picnics, the friendly phone calls, the access of a refrigerator. What to do? She wanted to rip up this note; pretend she never saw it and go on as usual. Because this promotion would mean accepting another pretentious gift from these awful people.

Mrs. Norfeld waved the paper over her head. She could reject this opportunity, perhaps losing her relationship with Danielle or pursue the promotion and give her daughter a chance.

Wait a minute … she should probably call a family meeting and tell everyone. As family, they were all settling into this town. But what about Robert and those strange guys; high likelihood these friendships were not any good. Natalie was so tight with the Tuttle girl, she practically lived there. Paul was trying but he lagged socially, finding happiness with books. Then there was her husband; who followed after the Tuttle men with that silly grin, he hardly ever wore. She hated to think it, but these men were becoming his close comrades. And what about the twins? She wanted the best for this growing family, which is why they even moved out this way. They had traveled to the middle of nowhere to grandpa's old homestead, her in-laws. A place that had once been safe and nurturing.

Mrs. Norfeld turned her head. Once again William and Joseph were wailing and Danielle was calling for help. It wasn't easy caring for two at once, although she was managing. "Okay, I'm coming!" She looked hard at the note, wondering how to handle this messy situation.

Suddenly her head was full of creative thoughts. Tucking the memo in her apron pocket, she went upstairs.

* * *

Danielle ran through the house, nearly knocking over her mother's treasured hurricane lamp. Although having refreshed with a shower, sweat was dripping down her back. She swiped her forehead discouraged by how long the chores had taken and how uncomfortable the thought was of skipping a grade. The offer was so flattering and also very scary. Yet, she believed she could do it. On the other hand, her mother thought she was not capable. Danielle was hurt and confused and now she was late. Rushing down the back steps she muttered aloud, "Oh no! I've missed Robert. I knew this would happen."

"No, you haven't. I'm right here," said Robert as he waved her to a patio chair next to him.

"Robert, you're still here. I thought you would be off somewhere by now with the guys, or at your new job. You're out here all by yourself." Danielle's heart leaped with delight, but she was careful to not show it. Right now, she didn't want giddy, she wanted self-control.

"Yeah, I kind of like this weird patio mom put together. It's only a dirt patch, mismatched lawn chairs and a blackened grill, but it's comfortable. Danie, have a seat and we can talk like the old times," teasingly said Robert.

For a minute, Danielle halted. Was this person really her brother? "Hmm, I was wondering about doing the same thing. How about we bike to the pond and talk there?"

Robert nodded in agreement. Jumping on their bikes, they rode at an even pace, pedaling into a simple park. Securing their bikes, they found a grassy mound to sit on.

"Tell me what's going on," said Robert as he leaned closer to his sister.

"You go first."

"No, Danie, you go first."

"Okay. I've been wondering how you've been these past weeks. You're always leaving the house so that I haven't seen you much and I don't know what you're doing especially with that strange gang …"

"Hey, let's not get into a parental lecture." Abruptly Robert stood up and sat on a rock across from her.

"I didn't mean it like that. It's that I miss you—my older brother and good friend. I'm trying to get used to this strange town, different house and brand-new friends. Now we also have two young brothers as well. I help mom a lot and play baseball but I still feel like I somehow don't fit in. How about you, Robert, don't you miss playing basketball with your team?"

"Yeah. I miss the way things were," said Robert soberly. "Especially practicing on the court. I'm not sure this place is for me either. I hang with these guys who can be tough. And you know I work at that Tuttle store doing everything." Robert's cheeks tensed and his eyes looked dull.

"You're finding it hard to fit in too. You know, I watched you with these guys and in many ways, they're rude and demanding. It seems like the same thing is happening in your job. I'm concerned. It would be a good thing if you called your friends from home, like George, Jamal or got back to your rocket and robotics projects. Both Paul and I are interested in helping ..."

"Really? You're always trying to fix us as family and now me! This time you don't know the full story. You should stay away. But you're already being dragged into things."

"Dragged in? What do you mean Robert?"

"I already know about the grade skipping. The plan to start you in the high school this year."

"What, I found out today! Mom and I read the paperwork this morning and she still needs to talk to dad. Nothing has been decided. How do you know—were you eavesdropping?"

There was a long pause, then a laugh of contempt. "Danielle, you think you're made special friends here. But the fact is you're being played by the Tuttle family."

"What!" All the rosy color faded from Danielle's face.

"That family arranged it all. They altered the

115

requirements of the high school application, with the intent to promote you to Tuttlebury High. They want to own you; they already have me. They watch your … our every move."

"They did what?" Danielle sat very still, her eyes wide and staring.

"Yeah, they want to take over our entire family. They had failed with grandpa and grandma. Now is their chance. And they're succeeding."

"What are you saying? Can you explain things a little more?"

"Well, take some control by making sure you send an exceptional essay to the high school. Let them know how smart you really are."

"I'm supposed to do what? I don't understand."

Robert lowered his head, then raised it. A flash of anger filled his face, his eyes dark and foreboding. "Danielle, they got me. I do things. I've changed. Better for you to leave me alone. I have things to finish." Robert stood again, his form casting an ominous shadow.

"But wait!" Danielle's head hung sadly as her brother grabbed his bike and was gone.

A few minutes later, she was peddling hard on her worn bike. She was heading home to their backyard, to visit the Box.

14

Danielle

*D*anielle felt like she had been slapped on the face. Twice. Emotions were toppling like bricks—rejection and humiliation. She felt plain stupid. Her entire body ached for comfort, for understanding. Perhaps a visit to the shed would help. However, the Box had gone completely silent. Inside its corrugated walls, she had sat a long time on the hard dirt floor. Wishing and hoping. The Box had shown her many things about herself. But not today. There were more questions with no answers. Like why did her talk with Robert go bad? One moment, Robert was a decent brother, the next he was an evil villain. It was probably all her fault. She had talked too much; she should have kept her mouth shut. Danielle took a deep breath and twirling a stray hair, tucked it into her messy ponytail. Listening would have been better. But she had lot to say. She was very concerned with his evil friends—what were they pushing him into? Was this gang responsible for the upset at the neighbor's farm, making her brother the fall guy?

There was a lot to be worried about. Scared too.

And what was all that talk about being tricked by the Tuttle's? They thought she really wasn't smart enough on her own to skip a grade. Instead, the Tuttle family was using their power. How dare they do such things! Maybe she should walk away. Her heart was thumping like quick percussion movement. Just great. Paul was the brain in the family. He had already skipped a couple of years ago; who knows when he might move ahead again. Natalie also did well in school; also showing her talent in everyday tasks and playing violin beyond her years. Robert had great grades even though his street smarts were falling off a cliff. Danielle sighed. She had to admit, most of the time she felt kind of average even though her report card was mostly A's. This was probably because too much time was spent with sports and not books. Deep inside she believed she could be an exceptional student; although needing to alter her priorities and improve the schoolwork. Probably the twins would grow up and outdo her as well, becoming state senators or brain surgeons.

Danielle figured she had become invisible. Heavy hearted, she felt like a complete failure. But c'mon, she knew she was capable. It was easier to do less to fit in with certain friends and have time to play softball. "Hmm, I'm smart too! I need to apply myself more," she said aloud. Why, with all the hours spent in the Box, she had viewed a wonderful future. At times she considered it all a fairy tale that was totally absurd. Yet she hoped for these possibilities, that she could become a successful happy woman.

Leaving the shed, Danielle walked over to her scratched

bike. She wheeled it slowly up the yard, leaning it by the porch. She needed to make a decision now, before her parents decided for her. So … yes! She would bypass her mother's low opinion and would accept the high school opportunity. She would do so well that she might even be promoted again. She would show them.

* * *

Still lost in thought, Danielle threw open the back door to the kitchen. She found herself in the middle of pandemonium—although it seemed to be a happy one. Something was up. Everyone was running from room to room, munching on sandwiches as they yelled to one another.

"Great, you're home Danielle. Grab a snack and get ready," said Mrs. Norfeld as she filled the diaper bags.

"Where are we going? It's a little after four and almost time to get supper ready. I came in now because we were supposed to go over that contract and essay for the school."

"Well, Danielle, your dad brought home free tickets, a gift from the Tuttle family, for a trip to the Fantasy Fun World amusement park." Mrs. Norfeld wiped her sweaty forehead. "You know the one that has that famous roller coaster. It's an hour drive so we need to leave soon. Your father and Paul will probably watch the younger Tuttle boys and you will be with Natalie and the Tuttle girls. Robert plans to meet us there with his group. We're borrowing the Tuttle van. Dad should be back any minute with it. Everyone let's get going," she bellowed like an army sergeant.

Standing close to Danielle, she spoke in a gentle tone. "I know I said we would go over those papers … your father changed our entire day. He's so excited, I wasn't able to talk him out of it. Personally, I'd rather stay home. Get yourself ready, we're leaving."

"But … but mom, we were going to have a serious talk about school. Besides you know how I can't stand amusement parks! Ever since I was little and was pushed off a ride. I had bruises for weeks."

"Well, Danielle, you recovered from that fall. Stop making such a big deal. As for school, I would prefer you finish at the middle school. I spoke briefly to your father as he was going out and couldn't answer. The eighth grade should be fun, you can find new friends and maybe join the Fall softball team. The high school would be a huge challenge that would push the envelope. This promotion seems like …"

"Seems like what? Too much for me? I want to go to the high school. This is a great opportunity and I don't want to miss it."

Mrs. Norfeld smirked, tightly zippering the diaper bag. "Danielle, let's talk later, okay? C'mon, everyone! Dad is here with the van. Let's go!"

"But mom, I don't want to go to the park. I'll stay home and watch the house."

"That will not work. You are needed to help the kids with the rides. I will be with the twins. You're going, so pack up."

Danielle stood very still, realizing their discussion was over. Throwing her backpack over her shoulder she tucked in a couple of bologna sandwiches, a mystery novel and the school envelope that was laying on the coffee table. On the way there, she wanted to check out every detail and who knows— she might send it herself.

* * *

"Everybody out," Mr. Norfeld shouted as he pulled open the van door. Thick, humid air poured in, which quickly emptied the van of its occupants. Happy chatter was mounting rivaling the twins' babbling noises. The pleasant ride, bathed in lovely air-conditioning had refreshed them. Pointing to attractions on their maps they were ready. Danielle had already circled hers with a red pen.

Anticipation soared as they hustled to each attraction. Mrs. Norfeld elected to sit in the shade with the twins, preferring to watch from a bench, licking a double-dipped pistachio cone. They didn't argue with her because someone had to watch the babies. Standing in line with Natalie and her friends, Danielle waved to her mother. But Mrs. Norfeld was busy finding a place with ample space to tuck a tandem stroller. Danielle sighed. She was on her own with Natalie and her girlfriends. This arrangement would have to be okay. Already the line snaked and twisted for this swirling teacup ride. It would be a long wait. The sun poured on the heat, her perspiring armpits were causing a dismal gray stain, her hands sweaty. This ride had better give a good breeze.

Danielle glanced about the area. It was an older park with updated renovations. An element of the historic remained. Like the railroad train and circus horse carousel that kept their old-fashioned appeal with a touch of paint showcasing a glistening finish. Danielle looked over her shoulder and watched her dad break out running to catch up with Robert and two of his gang friends. They were headed to the featured ride in the park, maybe in the world.

Paul and Stan also had their eye on this ride.

That would be the Roller Coaster—the Terrifying Boomer Rang—the TBR. It was a mean, well-honed thriller machine. This ride scared the heck out of her. From where Danielle stood, she could hear the tracking click uphill, the screeching of brakes, the screaming as it flew downhill. On the next climb, the higher one, the roller coaster demonstrated its special feature—the change-up. The coaster would charge up the rail and instead of flying down with face to the wind; it would pause, switch gears, and fly down backwards, the wind pushing hard on everyone's backside. Just great. Danielle shivered. This was one ride she could do without.

Suddenly the girls tugged at her arm, jumping up and down. "Danielle, we're tired waiting for the teacup ride. We want to see the zoo animals instead. Mom and the twins could come too. Can we go?"

There was a tugging on her other arm. "Danielle, Stan and I want to go on that exciting coaster. It looks fantastic! Can you go with us?"

"Dad and the guys can take you."

"Please, they voiced in unison.

Two pairs of eyes stared at her. Pleading. Wanting. Long ago, she had promised herself that she would never set foot on scary rides again. But these faces looked so hopeful. "Okay," she heard herself say. Really? What was she thinking! Out of her mouth came, "Sure. I'll take the girls over to mom so they can see the animals. Go wait in the coaster line and I'll be there in a few minutes."

* * *

Danielle was not happy. She would rather ride her bike cross country. Instead, here she was, waiting for this dreadful ride. And trembling. She had to pretend to be brave and be the responsible one. The boys were so excited, they were ready to launch into orbit. Then in a swift swoop they were all seated in a single cart, the attendant checking the locking gear.

"Get with the picture," she said aloud realizing the ride was about to begin, like it or not. The boys became church quiet. Expectations ready.

The engine of the Terrifying Boomer Rang throttled as the coaster began its uphill climb, click …click … calculated and sure … then faster and faster. Heartbeat's racing, sensing what is coming next. In in a flash the cart peaked and held for a sliver of a second then—woosh! Down it went. Swirling and plunging around curves. Awesome. Slowly it began its second most colossal ascent … click … click … click. This time with dramatic determination. And stopped. Teetering on the summit for a split second. Then it rocketed down at blinding speed—backward. Danielle felt the air being knocked out of her as the wind pushed at her back … a sensation of feeling light and being swept right out of her seat. Her stomach twisted, fearing for her life. Just great! She wanted this ride to end. The happy squealing of her two young companions turned to terror; as they screamed and screamed. With her arm stretched across their backs she held tight. "It's okay, I got you!"

Danielle caught her breath. A pause in the middle of the storm. Suspended in an otherworldly dimension. Floating… drifting. In the mist was the shape of a robust man whose kindly eyes met hers. His huge moustache fashioned over full lips, forming powerful words with earnest but with no sound. She leaned closer. His strong presence washed over her. Danielle had met this man; he was special to her. Then she knew; this was Grandpa, whom she had loved with all her heart. Reaching out to her. Calming her.

The moment was over.

Slowly the cart edged to the side and stopped. As she stepped out the earlier dread of the ride was gone; as well as worries about this strange town, the high school, Robert.

Understanding and assurance cleared the cobwebs in her head. In fact, she wanted to ride again.

Fear and anxiety had left her. In its place were strength and confidence. As expected, she took charge of her siblings, planning a fun and safe day. Everything was different, she actually was enjoying herself.

This must be what empowerment felt like.

* * *

Sliding to one side of her bed, Danielle attached the Tuttlebury information sheet and essay form to a clipboard. Working from notes she had scribbled in the car ride; she now wrote with exacting penmanship. Reviewing the composition, she smiled. She had written an essay to be proud of. Compiling the papers together there was still the last page, the one requiring signatures. She shivered as she held this paper. What? There in plain sight was written Mrs. Nancy Norfeld. Her mother had already signed it! Excited, Danielle signed her name and sealed all the paperwork in the pre-stamped envelope. She turned off the book light. Now to get some sleep because early tomorrow she was hitting the mailbox.

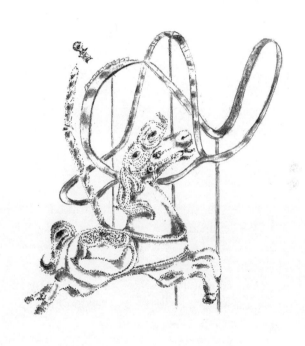

15

Discussions

"**M**other," yelled Sarah, the eldest Tuttle daughter. "We've finished setting up the meeting room. All the plates, silverware and cups are out. The finger sandwiches and side salads are placed where you told me. I'm getting out two large pots—one for coffee and the other hot water for tea. The juice as well. Sue is getting all the condiments ready. All we need are the cookies."

"They're almost baked," said Elsa, as she called herself, Elsanor Clementine Chester Tuttle to the general public, Mrs. Tuttle to the town folks. But to her children, mother was just fine.

"Yum! They smell so good. Can we sample one, please?" The two Tuttle sisters edged close to their mother and even closer to the giant chocolate chip confections, oozing semi-sweet goodness.

"Girls, don't get too close! These are for the board members, who should be coming soon for the advisory meeting. Here you can have the ones that are broken," said Mrs. Tuttle as she lifted the cookie pieces with a spatula right into their hands. "Don't let on to your brothers, especially Stan who will gobble them up! The meeting will start soon and when it is 7:05 the door will be locked. Your supper is on the stove; last night's stew. Any questions, ask your father." Mrs. Tuttle removed her apron and waved it about, "Now off with you."

* * *

It was seven o'clock. Exactly.

The Westminster chimes boomed from the ornate grandfather clock. Heavy and determined. Time to begin. Five minutes grace and the door would be secured. The late comers quickly took rear metallic chairs, the choice, cushioned ones already taken by the proud and the prompt.

The jangle of keys echoed harshly as the bolt clicked in place. The really latecomers hung their heads in dismay and went home.

Mrs. Tuttle took to the podium. Dressed in a polished slate blue suit, she stood regal and domineering. She wore no make-up and her short gray hair was combed severely back, staying in place with massive hairspray. From head to toe, the flash and dance from any accessory was not to be seen. Clearing her throat, she clicked the thick heels of heavy black shoes. Mrs. Tuttle became very still. Her angular cheeks were raised high, her stony blue eyes testy and distrustful.

The room went morgue silent.

Like a royal dignitary, Mrs. Tuttle waved her hand, "Now stand and declare our motto."

Uniformly springing to their feet, the twenty members recited, "We the women of Tuttlebury; do of one mind swear to honor our allegiance to each another, our families and to our town namesake, the Tuttle Founders. We will strive to perform to our upmost for the continual growth of our community, to protect, enrich and validate this county. So be it."

The air fluttered as the ladies resettled into their seats. As usual one woman remained standing. She held a thickly filled clipboard and began to speak. "Last month's minutes. First on the docket is the …"

"Silence! Sit down," barked Mrs. Tuttle. "Mrs. Duncan, today we will not review the minutes. Mail them to me at your convenience. In this session there are more urgent matters to deliberate." Mrs. Tuttle thumbed through her notes, positioning her dark rimmed glasses just so.

"As you are aware, to maintain a robust township, cooperation is required from every resident; especially those who have relocated to our county in recent months. Unacceptably there are those in our town and some present here, who have not taken this cooperation seriously." Looking up, Mrs. Tuttle looked upon every face, frowning at a certain few. She swiped a hair off her forehead and straightened her suit jacket.

Some ladies sat motionless; others stirred nervously in their seats.

A latecomer in the back, jumped up from her seat. Dressed in bold blues and violet, she stood tall; her words deliberate and strong. "Mrs. Tuttle, I'm quite certain I know who you are speaking about, since I am attending this meeting of my own accord. In the last seven months my family has tried to comply with this town's rigid formalities. We have heard your demands and have attempted to satisfy you. But our efforts are not working. My husband, three children and I are not accepted here. We are looked down upon. Nothing we do is acceptable. No one speaks to us at the county stores and we no longer are invited to any special functions. This is not the place I want to bring up my children!" With grace she gathered her purse to leave. Her confident steps were a drum roll on the glossy hard wood floor.

"Mrs. Steward, return to your seat now! How dare you come to my meeting uninvited and leave so abruptly! There are consequences for such behavior. Stop! The entrance is locked and you cannot leave."

Heads turned towards the back of the room, waiting for the dam to burst. Instead, Mrs. Steward headed to the left side of the spacious study and turned into the kitchen, to the alternate way out.

The room erupted like the roar heard from engines of heavy farm machinery. Voices cackled and screeched with no thought given to meeting formality and correctness. All opinions were fully unleashed.

"Order! I call this meeting to order!" bellowed Mrs. Tuttle, her face twisted in anger.

"Good riddance to you Mrs. Steward! You don't know what is good."

"We don't need you," screamed the hefty lady in the front row.

"We should teach her a lesson … you don't act like that in Tuttlebury and get away with it!"

"We will get rid of all these people who are hurting this town!"

"Yes, especially that terrible Norfeld family. It was a relief to finally see that old man and his wife be dead and gone," said a lady in a fancy pink pant suit, as she gestured with a strong fist.

"But we had a long wait until they died. Now we have another Norfeld family; the son and their six children, eight in all! The wife thinks she's better than us. The older son is utterly revolting! He can't even follow orders and light a match. Instead, he lets out the cows and slashes tires. Enough of this lack of respect … his family will be next!"

Like a lion's roar, the clapping launched to the ceiling.

Feet were stomping.

The hysteria ebbed. A hush filled the room.

Only a few feet from the podium, a slender middle-aged lady stood, dressed in a fashionable emerald suit, set off by expensive jewelry. She boasted an immense reputation as a state activist and dramatic speaker. All heads focused on her. With a touch of elegance, she placed her scarf around her shoulders. Then she nodded graciously to each woman, her eyes affirming, her affect gentle. Slowly she turned to meet the fuming face and twitching form of Mrs. Tuttle, gracefully took her hand and spoke in calming tones. Mrs. Tuttle nodded dutifully and left the podium, finding a seat behind it. The fury in her eyes fading.

"I am Mrs. Dudley," said the woman in the emerald suit as she commandeered the stage. "This afternoon I will resourcefully view all your grievances and work with you to create efficient strategy."

Expectancy hung in the air, as all eyes fixated on the lady before them. Even Mrs. Tuttle looked up at the speaker with expectation.

* * *

Natalie awoke to morning light, the air already heavy with humid air. Her hair was damp and the summer nightie was soaked through. Her first thought was about her sister Danielle... how strange she had been yesterday. But it wasn't a bad strange. Danielle didn't seem to mind helping her and Paul and their friends. Danielle always had to do stuff, but there was something different in the way she helped out; she took over like a teacher, who knows lots of things. Hmm. Danielle even walked straighter, more grown-up like.

Natalie's thoughts flowed through possibilities for the day. She figured her mother would want a hand with the babies, and she also promised Dad and Paul she would help clean out the garage. Not so much fun. But hopefully she would finish up quick so that she could visit the Box, she had now named Aurora. Things had been so busy the last few days; she really had lots of questions. She still worried everyday about Robert. Maybe Aurora would have answers.

Looking over to her sister's bed she saw that it was already made and the outfit hung over the closet door was gone. Natalie smiled. She had a few minutes to write in her special book. She slid from the covers and eagerly retrieved it from its floorboard hiding place. And this time she smelled the scent of cherry pipe smoke in the air.

* * *

"Hey, Nancy, these waffles are fantastic," said Ted as he broke a piece off and dipped it in syrup.

"Stop! No more sampling until we have enough for everyone. Please tend to the sausages, they're burning! Also, did you put on the coffee? If you didn't, please add a couple extra cups. I really need a full mug today."

"Coming right up! You see, I can do more than one thing

131

at a time," said Ted as he turned the sausages and measured coffee. "Well Nancy, once we have eaten breakfast and I finish sweeping the garage with Paul, I need to head out and meet with George."

Absorbed in stacking hot waffles, Nancy didn't speak. Wiping her hands on her apron, she gave her husband a puzzled look. "George who?"

"Why would you ask that, there's only one I know and that's George Amadeus Tuttle."

"Only wondering, that's all. You did see him last night at that men's meeting."

"Yeah, we all had a really great time talking about fish lures and booking a special fishing trip. There was so much to discuss, like renting a larger boat and having a special lunch. After the meeting I hoped to talk to George about a few things. I couldn't catch him because he left in a hurry. He said the wife was very upset about the women's meeting."

"Women's meeting … what kind of meeting was that?"

"Ah, you know all the wives get together to talk about ladies' stuff. I guess. I'm really not sure."

"Well Ted, I didn't know about such a meeting … although it probably wasn't about fishing. But it's strange that you were invited to the men's meeting and I never heard about the women's group."

Ted looked up from the stove, his wife's eyebrows arched upward. "Um … everything is still new, but I think the ladies meet about once a month. I'm not sure how regular the men gather, last night was a special fishing meeting."

"Somehow this doesn't make sense. The Tuttle's have invited us to other functions. Like the barbecue, the picnic and the amusement park. I have wondered about their intentions. Do they have all the control and we willingly follow?"

Puzzled, Ted looked away from his wife, to the pan of burning breakfast sausage. "Control? Not sure. I think last night happened kind of quick to decide things. Don't really know what the men usually talk about or the women either. Maybe last night was a special one for the ladies." Sweat was beading on his forehead.

"What's was so special that I never even heard a hint about it? Not even from you. It was like they left me out on purpose."

Ted fumbled with the spatula, blackened sausages falling to the floor. "I don't think they left you out. It could be they think you have a lot going with six kids, especially two being such little ones. They are giving us some space. You know, they were all very nice to you at the picnic and they wanted to give us a party for our church welcoming and they bring over food a lot, and they helped us get the refrigerator when you were in the hospital with the twins ..."

"Enough! You said it. They this. They that. They—the Tuttle family—have been sweetening us up; dumping the honey thick on us. They have absolutely left me out and have gone after you instead! Ted, this is all about control. To take us over as they have other families." Nancy's fair complexion darkened a deep crimson, her lips squeezed tight.

"Nancy, no more of this talk! Sometimes I can't figure you out, you're such an emotional woman. You don't know a good thing when you see it!" His hands were clammy, an ache was creeping up the side of his head. Ted stomped out, shaking the house with the hard slam of the back door.

* * *

Paul shook his head curiously. Something was off today. Dad had left suddenly. Mom wasn't speaking to anyone as she noisily cleared the kitchen. Danielle had left for a softball practice, and Robert was probably at the store working. It was him and Natalie. Moments before the frying food had kicked up their appetite. But the commotion and yelling from the kitchen had killed it. Figuring what to do, they both sat at the top of the staircase. The house phone began to ring and ring. Would mom answer it? Should they? Then it stopped. And rang again. Over and over. Finally, Paul ran to the upstairs phone and picked up the receiver. The exact same time someone else grabbed it.

There was a brief pause, as the receiver began to click in.

"Hello, hello. Mrs. Norfeld please don't hang up. My name is Mrs. Elaine Steward and I know why you were not invited to the women's meeting last night."

There was another pause, but longer.

Paul gently eased the phone down and nodded to Natalie, motioning silence.

"Yes, I'm listening," said Mrs. Norfeld, "and I have a lot to ask you."

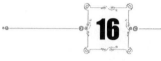

16

For or Against

$\mathcal{A}$ waiting them in the kitchen were the luscious waffles and burned sausage. That breakfast was out of the question. Mrs. Norfeld was still in the kitchen speaking on the phone in very serious tones. Instead, Paul and Natalie quietly raided the storage pantry loading up on peanut butter health bars, oatmeal cookies and single serving boxes of cocoa puffs, as well as several juice packs. Probably not the most-healthy, but it would fill their stomachs. Quietly, Paul headed out the front door to the patio table and threw all his goodies down. Natalie brushed past him. With hands full of lovely treats, she headed into the backyard. Paul called to her but she walking so fast, she didn't hear him. Or didn't want to. But he knew where she was heading.

To the shed.

Paul's first impulse was to run after her and get to there

135

first. Yet breakfast was calling and he was starving. Tearing off the plastic packaging he began munching on the grocery store delights. Tossing a straw in the juice pack, he slurped noisily, as the simple meal began to fill him. Ah. One more cookie and that would be enough. Then another form raced by heading to the same destination as Natalie. It was Robert and he was carrying something. Paul dropped the cookie and ran after his brother. Robert was carrying a shovel!

"Robert, please stop! What are you doing with that shovel?" shouted Paul, but his brother paid no attention. Robert was heading to the shed where he was sure Natalie had gone. His brother was armed and dangerous. Paul ran as never before, usually he would trip over his own feet.

But not today.

Paul reached the shed just as his brother drew up the shovel to smash the weathered door. "Open, or I'll chop you to pieces," yelled Robert.

The door inched open, a child's hand holding unto the frame. Robert lifted the heavy shovel over his head.

"No, Robert. You're going to hurt Natalie!" Paul threw himself at his brother. The shovel was tossed aside as they both hit the packed ground. Swinging the shed entrance open, Natalie stood very still her eyes round and questioning.

"Paul. Robert. What is going on! Why are you both fighting?"

Dizzy and disorientated, both boys sat up and stared at their sister. Their faces were a mixture of anger and confusion.

"Please talk to me." Natalie's positioned her hands on each side of her waist, glaring at her brothers.

"Natalie, I had to save you. Robert was going to smash you with a shovel," said Paul as he stood close his sister's side.

"Robert, why did you want to hurt me? I don't understand. What did I do to you?" Natalie's voice trembled.

"It's not you Natalie, it's that awful refrigerator carton. That thing is evil. It needs to be destroyed!"

"No, you can't ruin Aurora. This Box is my friend. I love coming here to visit."

Robert shook his head back and forth. "That's great, Natalie. You go and make friends with this awful carton and even give it a name."

"But Robert, she's not the only one," said Paul. "I like coming out here as well. It shows me wonderful things."

"I don't think so, this cardboard carton is full of lies and does crazy things! It's been bringing me terrible places. You're both falling for this. You had better watch out!"

"Robert, what has the Box shown you?"

Natalie and Paul turned around.

Danielle stood quiet and composed, holding the shovel in a tight grip. "Well, tell me Robert."

Robert shrugged and looked down at the floor.

Natalie cried with delight and hugged her sister. "I'm so glad you're here Danielle. Our brothers are really bad today."

"I'm wondering how long have you been standing there, Danielle," said Robert.

"Long enough to have seen and heard everything. You know, Robert, we discussed our views about the Box often, but without you. I believe you have had your own encounter with it. I suggest we all talk. Let's go in the shed."

No one spoke.

"You know, I think you're right; let's go in and straighten this out. Besides the longer we stay out here, mom and dad will wonder what's going on," said Robert.

They all nodded and followed their brother into the musty shed.

* * *

Elaine Steward felt encouraged after her chat with Mrs. Norfeld. She would have talked longer but the twins needed attention. She understood that routine perfectly well. However, now that her three children were in the town elementary school, there was more time to work on personal writing and magazine publications. Elaine refilled her coffee and looked out the open bay window … reflecting on her phone conversation. She thought on all that was said even considering things she had forgotten. The delightful scent of farmland and flower filled the kitchen; one of the advantages of moving here as family. It had really been her husband's idea since he had been raised on a farm. But she, Elaine, was a city girl! They had met while attending an urban college and he promised to stay in the city, although sometimes hinted about going back. The kids began dreaming about having a farm with chickens, cows and perhaps a horse. It took several years, but eventually it was her dream as well.

They had relocated to Tuttlebury.

It was charming place; with its winding roads through rolling hills and planted fields of grain and corn. Of course, there were many grazing cows and horses. Cradling her cup, she took a long sip. Those earlier days were the best … a lovely farm house to decorate, children happily involved with farm chores, a husband reliving childhood memories. Neighbors came by to greet them and chat. The town sent a welcoming basket of edible goodies and even helped them buy a larger vehicle for their growing family. Then there were the invitations to special town functions. Picnics. Dinners. The most fun ever county fair.

Less than a year later it all ended.

The generous outreach was over, followed by bullying and harassment. Now they were enduring a terrible shunning; no one spoke to them at all. It was all very disturbing; she couldn't put the children through this anymore. As a family they needed a change. Her husband agreed and soon they would leave this place. Yet there was some unfinished business. Elaine Steward smiled to herself. Mrs. Norfeld, her new friend and ally, would hopefully bring that about.

* * *

In a variety of lawn chairs the four siblings sat, staring at the cardboard refrigerator carton. The air was heavy with moisture and disappointment. One by one, they each parted the curtain and sat in the tight space waiting for something to happen. The Box was eerily still. There were no magical lights ushering them to another realm. There was no sense of any future reality.

Instead, the refrigerator box was one very dilapidated, smelly carton that should be heaved into the dump.

'So where do we go from here? We've been sitting for a long time being very patient," said Paul.

"Yeah, you think? I'm still as confused as ever," said Robert. "Let's see if I have this right. When this box used to work, Danielle saw me fall off a boat and probably drown which maybe means that I'm in big trouble and I could probably get badly hurt. Um. I'm not saying anymore because it might put you all in danger."

Danielle stood and walked over to her brother. "But we're already involved. You had us sneak you into the house after what happened at the Sander farm with the cows and tires. We've seen you hang around with that awful gang and how you've become like them. Even know how badly they treated you at their meetings."

"Meetings? You were all spying on me?" He stared hard at Danielle, Paul and Natalie.

Their voices went silent. Only bees buzzing on the windowpane could be heard.

Paul began speaking. "Okay, Robert, you already know I saw you at the cabin. We had that fight into the bushes. Danielle knows because I told her, but I didn't say anything to Natalie; didn't want to scare her."

"Scare me?" Natalie stood up and shouted. "Hey, I can handle myself just fine, thank-you! But I'm worried about Robert, always hanging out with that evil gang. I'm sad that Aurora has only shown him bad things. Now Aurora is not showing anything. And Paul I think …"

"Hey, don't look at me! You seem to have all the answers."

"C'mon let me finish," said Natalie.

"Yeah, Mr. Einstein, go ahead and tell us," said Robert mockingly.

Danielle elbowed her brother with such force he winced and rubbed his arm.

"It's goes like this. I think Aurora really is talking to us but in a special message. This quiet is the message. This means that for now, we have seen enough. It would be good to think about what we did see and what to do. It's up to us."

"Hmm. I think you're on to something, said Danielle. All these situations we've seen are possibilities. They are not actual realities. Not until we choose a suggested way will this possibility become real."

"Awesome! That could be it," said Paul, his face beaming. Even Robert nodded favorably at his sisters.

Suddenly the room went midnight dark. Brilliant rainbow colors washed over the four. There was a sound of a rushing train as a huge wind slapped against the shed. In a twinkling the shack like structure disappeared. As well as the entire farm.

Robert, Danielle, Paul and Natalie stood alone in a large field of overgrown grass. They stared at each another, mouths agape. Why were they outfitted in adult clothes, ready to do very grown-up tasks? Natalie was elegantly dressed in a floor length gown, violin in hand. Paul had on a collegiate sweater and pristine pants. Danielle wore a professional sports jacket oddly accessorized with a major league baseball cap. Robert stood proud in an expensive suit with a bright necktie and was carrying a strange silver briefcase. What was happening?

Time blinked and was gone.

Danielle, Robert and Natalie snuggled into cozy sheets fast asleep.

Except Paul. He sat straight up in his bed and looked at his familiar room and snoring brother. He was trying hard to stay awake. The yawns started. His head ached and his eyes were itchy and bleary. He swung his legs off the side of the bed and rubbed his head. He had to fight sleep, so he could figure out this strange experience and not forget it. "I have to", he muttered aloud, as his eyelids fell like a heavy stage curtain and he flopped onto the bed.

17

Tangles and Knots

$\mathcal{M}$r. Norfeld tapped on the steering wheel to a favorite song. His smile was so big, his teeth showed. Today he had been able to leave the office early. The major contract that buried him for several weeks was settled. It was one that could bring a huge profit to the company and he expected a sizeable amount would be in his paycheck. As a business man, he really liked this position but hoped one day he could take the plunge and start a private company. He could make something useful and simple, like the fellow who produces special pillows. He had the ability to do this; having graduated top of his class with a Master in Business Administration.

Yet on the other hand, his current office was relocating several workers to their headquarters on the west coast. Recently enlarged and renovated, employees were being moved around. They were even offered complementary housing for a limited time. In fact, already the district manager had mentioned possible options for him to climb the corporate ladder. But he would have to move his family. Again. Yet he had to admit, it was a tempting offer. Mr. Norfeld lowered his car window and took a deep breath from the planted fields. He loved the smell of the country ... corn growing, wildflowers by the side of the road and even the cow droppings. After all, as a kid, he had enjoyed an eyeful of brilliant green pastures. Mr. Norfeld rubbed his forehead. He had to be honest. Yes, the country was great but he hadn't stayed to make a life. It was his father, who from the heavenlies, had called him back. Now Nancy and the kids were getting a good dose.

They all seemed to like the farmhouse, as least he thought they did since he hadn't asked them. He already knew that Robert was having a hard time. He had lot of issues— high school, moving, his attitude towards family. Robert and he used to have a good father and son relationship; he could count on him. Nowadays he hardly got a respectful nod. Mr. Norfeld scratched his forehead. It could be everyone was having problems. Maybe he had made the wrong choice transplanting them. But he had not made plans for moving again.

At least not yet.

He was looking forward to surprising his family so he stopped for their favorite snacks and assorted fresh donuts. It was a huge bag full. But he couldn't wait until he got home; the sugary goodness was calling to him. He reached for a warm cinnamon bun and began munching. Finally, the last stop. He remembered that Nancy wanted to get back in shape and requested parts for her stationary bike, and Paul asked for paint supplies. He needed some fertilizer for the grass in front of the house, his attempt to maintain street appeal for the old farmhouse.

Destination, the Tuttle's country store even if they didn't have everything. He knew Serious Edy's Hardware really had more to offer but he wanted to give the Tuttle's his business. After all, the family had gone all out for them these past weeks. Maybe he would see Robert still at work, and offer him a ride home. That is, if he was even scheduled today. If he found George Tuttle there, they could discuss the upcoming fishing trip. Even though his wife found the Tuttle's to be too pushy, he liked them just fine. He really didn't get what Nancy was saying about all their controlling behavior. In fact, he had been honored by their generosity.

The parking lot was loaded and many drivers were trying to get in or out. It was the late afternoon rush. Mr. Norfeld decided to park way in the back where the trucks unloaded. He found the best spot, right under a silver maple tree. The car would be nice and cool when he came back.

Once in the store, it was shoulder to shoulder with customers as they loaded up on yard supplies, food goods, and barbeque stuff. Hurriedly he found the hardware and paint items and headed over to the farming supply area to look over the kinds of fertilizer. Then he peeked around the corner to see if George was in the office.

"Hey, where the heck is that Norfeld boy, said Mr. Tuttle as he searched the long aisles. "Never there when I need him … that good for nothing kid!"

"Now George, shush! You're too loud. Everyone will hear you!" cautioned Mrs. Tuttle.

"Don't get all goodie-goodie on me. I know you can't stand him either! This even came out at last night's meeting."

Mrs. Tuttle faced her husband, her nose flared like

a horse, her eyes unblinking. "Tuttle, shut up," she said, waving him away.

Mr. Tuttle ran into the stock room where Robert was heaving bags into a pile.

Mr. Norfeld lowered his body, pretending to read labels as he crept slowly towards the stock room. He heard voices and slapping sounds.

"Kid, you're too slow! Wait a minute. I told you to stack those boxes on the other side," admonished Mr. Tuttle as his large calloused hand swiped Robert's cheek.

"Sorry, I didn't mean to. Yes, sir. I will do it over, sir."

Anger rose like a tornado inside Mr. Norfeld. "How dare he speak to his son like that! And what was that slapping noise? George is supposed to be a decent man, a loyal friend," he muttered aloud, turning some customers' heads. He quickly eased himself up and walked alongside other shoppers. Finding an empty carriage, he dumped in his selected items and hustled to the nearest exit. He tried to act normal, but found himself almost running.

Behind the wheel of the car, Mr. Norfled rooted for the old-fashioned handkerchiefs tucked into the seat. There were once his father's and brought him good memories. He wiped his damp face then steadied his trembling hands so he could start the car. His brain was misfiring like crazy. He no longer was excited to go home. In fact, he should turn the car around and go back to work.

Mr. Norfeld really wished he had a passenger, so he could let some anger out. A good friend would be great right now. Who would that be; George Tuttle and his so-called fishing pals? Ugh. They really were of no use to him. His head swirled in confusion and his gut felt tight. How could that man slap his son around? How dare he! Nancy had been right all along; the Tuttle family was controlling and taking advantage of them. Mr. Norfeld took a deep breath. He had to calm down. He stared out the windshield at the giant silver maple. Lovely to look at, it was strong and weathered, having learned life lessons over the years—which he was still trying to do.

A sturdy hand now turned the ignition and the car roared, ready to depart. He turned out of the parking lot and steered the familiar course home.

To home sweet home.

* * *

Hearing the commotion, Mrs. Tuttle came flying into the stock room. Her husband was behaving bad; tossing heavy fertilizer bags, kicking cans around.

"What happened? Did you hit that kid?"

"What's it to you," said Mr. Tuttle, as grabbed a broom.

"Well, the entire store heard you. They watched as that idiot Norfeld guy ran out."

"Can't help that. I had to get Robert's attention. If he doesn't do his usual work, how will he pull off the big job we have for him?"

"Shush, you're talking too much," said Mrs. Tuttle, closing the large wooden doors. Such things are not spoken here; not with this place crawling with customers. Where is Robert now? Did he run off crying?"

"No. He apologized a lot. Because he was so ornery, I sent him up to the cow barn to haul some hay."

"Hope that boy straightens out. George, you need to control yourself. The town trusts us, we have to put on a decent face."

"You should talk, woman. That last ladies' group was

a disaster. Who was the one to lose control—you! Now we have to go crawling back to that awful city lady."

"Quiet! This is my business," said Mrs. Tuttle as she threw off her soiled apron and stomped out. "Leave me alone, I have a lot of phone calls and supper to make."

* * *

The house appeared quiet as Mr. Norfeld pulled into the driveway. The twins' traveling carriage was not outside nor were any of their toys. Many of the windows were only halfway open on such a hot day. He grabbed the pastry bags and his briefcase and hurried into the kitchen. "Nancy, I'm home! Can you believe that I got out early today? Got some donuts here! You think tonight we can order in a couple of pizzas?"

Mr. Norfeld dropped the bags as he his eyes bulged. "And who are you and what are you doing in my house?"

"Hello, Mr. Norfeld. We haven't met yet, but I'm Amy."

"You're who? What are you doing feeding bottles to my twins? Usually my wife feeds them, she hardly ever lets me give them a bottle. I don't understand. Why are you here, and where's Mrs. Norfeld?"

Amy slowly put aside the bottle, and placed little William over her shoulder, gently stroking his back to burp him. "My name is Amy Benton. I'm your neighbor from a couple of miles down the road. Mrs. Norfeld asked me to babysit two weeks ago. I have been coming over early afternoons to watch the twins when she goes out."

"Goes out? My wife rarely leaves the house and doesn't even have a car during the day. She's always so tired that I can't imagine her having the energy. Do you know where she is?"

"Yes, a lady picked her up a little while ago," said Amy as she placed the baby in the day bed and checked on his snoring brother.

"And they went where?" Mr. Norfeld's lips pressed, the muscles in his face tight. He edged closer to Amy.

Amy turned, grabbed her knapsack and rushed to the back door. "They both went to a meeting together and Mrs. Norfeld will be home soon," she said as the door slammed behind her.

* * *

Paul slowly edged up the hill, well, it was more like a mountain to him. His legs were throbbing and heart was beating in his ears. Getting out of the house had been his plan. Besides a new girl was coming over to watch the twins. Suddenly, the summit was before him. He had made it! Grabbing hard on the handle bars, his feet held the pedals for a single second. Then a change-up as his arms reached out. The wind soared as he flew down the hill, the gusts fingering his hair. "Awesome," he yelled. Now Paul was ready to head home, which would take some time since he had chosen this long route. But he didn't feel like it. Instead, he wanted to sit under a tree and think about things. Like what would happen once he started school in a few weeks and what classes he would get. Oh … and how come mom had hired a babysitter he wasn't supposed to tell dad about.

Flowing into the curved road he saw something. His brakes squealed and halted as he watched across the street. "What's going on at the Tuttle barn? Why is Robert hauling hay when he's supposed to be at their store?" Jumping off his bike he walked it over to the field.

"Robert what are you doing here? Don't you usually work in the stockroom?" said Paul, as he caught his breath.

Robert turned his back and piled hay into large piles, swinging the scythe in powerful heaving motions.

"Hey, talk to me!"

"Leave me alone! If you don't, they will make me bale this stuff," he said angrily.

"Get it done, why don't you! I'll wait so we can bike home together." Paul eased his shiny blue ten speed to the ground and sat.

Robert stepped to the side of the pile and stared. "So, you're going to sit there and watch me!"

"Um …"

"Here take this and help," said Robert throwing a large rake at him. "The sooner we finish, I can leave this place."

"Okay, I'll help." They worked in silence for several minutes. "Robert, you didn't tell me why you had to do this awful job."

"Mind your own business," Robert scowled.

Paul's eyes were wide and curious as walked over to his brother's side, sadly shaking his head. "Something happened at the hardware store. Something bad." Paul pointed to the discolorations on Robert's cheek.

"Alright, alright!" Robert flung the harvest tool to the side. "My boss, punched me!"

"You mean, Mr. Tuttle? Why?"

"They want me to do things for them to show my loyalty. It's like what they do in some colleges … a hazing; doing strange things to prove yourself worthy."

"Hazing? I'm not sure what that is. But I know these

Tuttle people are scary, always pushing you to do bad things. I don't know why you hang out with them."

"Yeah, they're tough, except for my buddy Alex, who seems decent. Anyhow, I already know the next assignment. Overheard a couple of the guys talking about it."

"What will they make you do?"

Robert shook his head. "This is very dangerous stuff. Better that you don't know."

"But I'm your brother and I'm already involved! You do remember I helped sneak you into the house after you cut tires. I know this much; you don't have to anything you don't want to. You can say no."

Robert turned his back and began to rake like a machine pushed on high.

"Hey bro, we need to be a team, including our sisters. Remember the Box has shown possibilities not definite outcomes. We can work together to do some good."

"Yeah, right," Robert nodded.

As they both rode their bikes home, Paul was lost in deep thought. He was thinking about that smelly carton Natalie had named Aurora. He knew it had shown each of them something remarkable; a special vision they had witnessed together. What was it? His brain fought off his effort at retrieval. One thing for sure, what he had seen had been truly awesome.

18

Scrubbing Kitchen Tiles

*W*aiting. Mr. Norfeld paced the black and white tile floor, alternating between the fussy twins, returning William to his daybed, then scooping up his brother, Joseph. Ah, babies are so hard to handle! He felt edgy, there was a lot to discuss with Nancy. He was trying to understand. Oh no! William began to shriek again as Mr. Norfeld lifted him up into his other arm. Now he was walking and rocking two babies. Ugh. How does his wife cope with this? What was he thinking? So many questions; like why his wife had hired a sitter and how come she hadn't talked to him. What was going on? William began to wave his arms and tear at his shirt. He was hungry. Quickly Mr. Norfeld set Joseph back in the daybed. Now to calm William. Looking about he grabbed a bottle of formula on the counter, and teased it into the child's cherubic lips. Mr. Norfeld tucked him unto his shoulder and soothed his back, coaxing a burp. "This isn't so hard," he said aloud. A sense of pride filled him and he wondered why his wife found all this so difficult.

Mr. Norfeld jumped and fell into the counter. What a startle! That phone was awfully loud; setting off one twin, then the other. Both were wailing and swinging their pudgy arms and legs. The oven timer was buzzing and wouldn't stop; definitely something burning. Probably the sitter had started supper and abruptly she left it. There was banging at the back door. A visitor now? Mr. Norfeld stood frozen in the middle of the kitchen. He had no clue what to do first.

Mrs. Norfeld pushed open the door, packages falling to the floor. "Hello, Amy, is everything alright? Please, can you help pick up these groceries?"

"Nancy, you're finally home! Where have you been?"

"What in the world are you doing home—at this time of day?" Nancy glared at her husband as she knelt and gathered up the packaged goods.

"I'm wondering as well … like why you went out and who is this Amy girl?"

"Oh my, my dinner must be all burned!" Nancy grabbed a kitchen mitt and ran over to the oven. Smoke filled the room as she removed the overdone potatoes and porkchops. "Now, look what you've done! The oven was turned up too high. You've ruined our supper."

"Well, that was Amy. She left and didn't mention the oven was on. But why was she here in the first place?"

"Nancy ignored Ted as she opened all the windows and doors, fanning the smoky air with the kitchen towel. She lifted Joseph from the daybed and abruptly turned to face her husband. In a quick swoop she eased William from her husband's arms into her own.

In a moment, she was gone, her feet pounding the stairs to the nursey.

* * *

It was Saturday and the air was so heavy that the smoke from last night's supper hung to every molecule. Natalie had the pile of old rags ready for her next chore. Dusting. This time every inch and cranny. She really wanted to play her violin, while visiting with Aurora. Or work on pencil drawings using her new colored pencils. But not today, since her mom had assigned extra household tasks to everyone. Even Robert. It was his day off and he was outside trimming overgrown bushes. Finished with painting the porch, Paul was busy scraping the house. Danielle had her list as well and if not completed the softball game was out. At first, Mr. Norfled declined the housework and locked himself in his office. However, a little while later, he changed his mind, and decided to mow the lawn.

Not wanting to annoy her mom, Natalie quickly picked up her dusting cloths and got busy. She knew her mother was really in a bad mood because there was no hint of the usual cheerfulness, instead her mother's bright eyes looked dull and sad. "I guess she has a right to be," Natalie said aloud, then looked around, hoping she hadn't been heard. Last night, everything had gone terribly wrong. There was too much yelling and hardly any listening followed by silence. It was all very upsetting.

Natalie moved the side table from the wall, loaded the rag with lemon oil and rubbed it in. In seconds the drab piece was glossy and smooth. If only people could be become shiny so easily. Last night mom had argued with dad about Amy. Mom only said that a sitter was necessary to give her a break from the twins. Dad pressed on; he wanted to know every detail. Mom didn't answer. Instead, she went to the table and readied the dishes for supper. That's when the shouting started. Dad was upset when he came home early with treats to share, and found his home taken over. He wanted answers. Her mom's voice was jittery, as she spoke about the meetings with the other mothers' having difficulty living in Tuttlebury. From this group, she heard that Robert had been abused by the Tuttle father. Also, that the Tuttle's were pushy about church attendance, a way of controlling the families in town. The angry discussion went on.

Natalie groaned, as she rubbed the pounding on the side of her head. It was all too much information and she hadn't been snooping. As family their lives were getting messy. Anxiety was like a noisy radio, lots of buzzing but no clear voice.

Finished with the living room, Natalie moved to the dining area and continued her polishing. There was something to be said of this mundane, repetitive task; it was comforting. As she bent to reach under the giant China-cabinet, she saw Danielle scrubbing and scrubbing the worn black and white tiles in the kitchen. The floor looked bright and bold, like new. Hmm. She hoped her housecleaning looked as good. As Natalie continued to polish the fancy cabinet legs, her hand hit something hard. Getting down on hands and knees, she touched what felt like grooved notches. She pulled at it, but it wouldn't budge. Putting her face to the hard wood floor, the object was cloaked in darkness and most likely stuck in the molding. Excited, Natalie dropped her oily rags and ran upstairs to find a long ruler.

* * *

"Hey, Natalie, where are you going? You still have the den and upstairs to finish," yelled Danielle. Very annoyed, she grabbed the electric polisher from the hall closet, plugged it in, her eyes following after Natalie. She wanted to walk away as well. After all, why do all this special cleaning when there was a chance there would be no church welcoming at all?

Daniele was hearing her parents' conversations loud and clear; even behind closed doors their voices traveled. She wished she could shut her ears. She heard they would no longer be joining the Tuttle church. Instead, they would connect with Trinity Church—the parish grandpa and grandma had attended. They hoped, or at least mom did, that an arrangement could be made to join the new church in a few weeks' time. It was already August, summer was waning. School would be starting for everyone, with new classes to step into. Yet in all this talk, there was no mention of the possibility to skip a grade. And the Tuttlebury High School had not yet responded to the essay she had sent. She was frustrated and anxious.

"Enough!" Danielle shouted as she pushed on the polisher and glided around the kitchen floor feeling like the whirling lady in a television advertisement. She stood back and admired her work, hoping it would stay nice for a while. There was a kick at the door and in came Robert, muddy and dusty from the yard work. Robert jumped, his eyes went wild as Danielle hoisted a broom and attempted to sweep him out. "Can't you see that I've just washed and buffed the floor! Go outside and clean off with the hose." She followed her brother out the door sweeping behind him.

* * *

"What's up with Danielle," Robert muttered to himself, "she's getting more like mom every day!" Well, since he couldn't get into the house, what should he do? He had finished cutting bushes and cleaning the garage. He was so done. What now? He could sneak to shed and see if the box would wake up. He could really use some help right now. But he didn't want everyone following and giving him advice. No way. Changing his mind, he went to check for mail. He walked over to the street side mail box supported by to a wooden post. Both were weather worn, needing Paul's paintbrush. Grabbing the mail, he turned and gazed at the rustic farmhouse. He remembered how grand and happy a place it used to be. Always the gray clapboards and the black shutters seemed to smile as his grandparents flew out the front door to greet them. They had smelled great as well ... grandpa wore an earthy tobacco essence and grandma was as sweet as the cherry pie she was baking.

Those were the good times.

"Am I happy to be here now?" Robert took his hat off and swiped the sweat from his forehead. A mixture of emotions sizzled up and down his spine. The house was great, but as a family, they were having a terrible time. The towns-people had appeared fine; even the guys in the gang, especially Alex. At first. Now they constantly watching him, bullying him into situations he didn't want, doing very evil things. He was sinking deeper and deeper into their quicksand; he could hardly breathe. He wanted to walk away and be strong, a man who would stand for what was right. But he was flip-flopping like a rotten banana peel. He hated himself for it.

Suddenly there was a pat on Robert's shoulder and Paul was waving his hand towards the back of the house. "Look, I finished painting that section, doesn't it look great!"

Robert grinned in spite of himself. His brother was truly

a sight, vibrating excitement about his masterpiece paint job, his blue dungarees covered with yellow paint. "Yes, I see it. Paul, you have made this old place look great. You should be very proud."

"Thanks, Robert. Your opinion means a lot. Sometimes I think I can only read books; that I'm pathetic with my hands. But I did this!"

"I'm proud of both of you," said Mr. Norfeld as he stood between his sons, has hands on their backs. "Now let's quickly finish up, so can go in and call it a day."

"Hey, you all," yelled Mrs. Norfeld's shrill voice. I have good news. This week we will again see the pastor at grandpa's church and become members. Next Sunday, they will introduce us and as family we will receive a blessing. Then we can have a little celebration." She took in a deep breath. "Dinner in twenty minutes!" With that she ran back into the house as Danielle rushed out.

All hands helped finish the back-yard clean-up.

* * *

Except for Natalie. Instead, she was again standing before the China- cabinet. With resolve, her hand tightly around the yard stick, she bent down on the hard wood floor and jimmied the object from the tight molding. Her body ached from the odd position she had taken, but it was well worth it. In her palm sat a dainty golden key. She turned it over and over, fingering it gently. It was nothing like the shed key that was tarnished and rusty. What purpose did it have? What tiny lock would it let open? She stood, and looked with different eyes at the cabinet. Since the key was found under it, could it be that a secret hiding place lay inside?

"Natalie, where are you? It's almost time for dinner and it's your turn to set the table."

"Ok, Mom, be right there." Quietly Natalie opened each drawer and let her fingers search for a special nook or corner. Nothing. She decided to try the lower drawer once more, careful to gently move the tablecloths and napkins. Again, nothing.

"Natalie, need your help now!"

"I'm coming!" Natalie went to close an upper drawer and a card caught on something. Pushing aside the card and other notes, she realized something behind the clutter. It was a petite knob on a small compartment. She grabbed and pulled. Locked. She looked again, this time below the blue knob. She had found it! There it was, a tiny keyhole. She pulled the key from her pocket and gasped; it was the right size.

Supper was a simple meal of grinders, zucchini soup and salad. Everyone focused on the food before them, busy chewing, slurping and burping. The usual was banter absent. They were tired from all the physical activity of the day, tired from all the quarreling. Sitting quietly with one another was really quite enough.

Supper clean-up was a record-breaking event. Danielle was off to the den to watch a baseball game with dad. Paul took a long shower, rinsing off all the yellow paint he missed with the hose. He went to his room to read and found Robert already snoring. Totally not normal. Mrs. Norfeld was in the nursey rocking and singing to the twins.

Finally! The kitchen was quiet. Natalie stacked away the last soup dish, and turned the Tiffany lamp down to a dim golden glow. The dining room was still, she could hear the gentle ticking of the antique grandfather clock. She reached into her pocket and fingered the tiny key. Natalie's heart skipped, her hands a little wobbly. Facing the ornate mahogany China-cabinet, she saw her reflection in the glass door. What a pretty young lady she had become! Suddenly her head felt airy. The image in the glass faded into a wise matronly woman. Grandma Norfeld. Undeniably, where Natalie stood, her grandmother had often lingered. As Natalie reached into the large drawer to the hidden compartment, she sensed her grandmother urging her on. Natalie eased the tiny key into the lock. There was a light click and the long drawer feel open. Into her hand fell a bundle of papers secured with thin red and white twine bakeries used for used for tying. Grandma's signature. Spasms tingled her spine, the light hairs on her arms standing up; like the swirling teacups ride—only better.

Abruptly beams of bright light flooded the dining room. Footsteps and the whooshing sound of opening the refrigerator. Holding tight the secured papers, Natalie found her way to the winding stair case and up to her room.

19

Launch Pad Week

$\mathcal{I}$t was Monday. Danielle awoke with a sunbeam dancing on her cheek. Stretching her arms, she was up early, before her cellphone chimed and even before everyone else. Sweet. She had big plans for today and was eager to start. All her clothes were piled on the chair—a combination of a dressy outfit and her baseball uniform. Having showered last night, she only needed to freshen up, and get well dressed. Danielle had even fixed herself lunch, hidden behind the veggies in the refrigerator where no one looked. And just in case, several power bars were thrown into her backpack. Her mother already knew of her whereabouts, well, at least the official softball game.

Time to go.

Natalie snored heavily as Danielle tiptoed by, pausing for

a moment at the long closet mirror. Yes, she stood confident in her lovely dark violet pant suit, a leather briefcase in hand.

Heading towards the staircase, Danielle noticed the nursey door was partly open. Peeking in, mom was tucked into the spare bed with one of the twins' blankets, as the babies purred softly in their separate cribs. Emotion flooded her; how she loved her mother. She didn't want to anger her, she really didn't. After all, she was grateful her mom had signed the high school papers Mr. Mussman had delivered. Yet today, Danielle, had to figure some things for herself. She only hoped her mother would understand.

The early morning air rushed over Danielle as she peddled her bike at a moderate pace. She could go faster, but working up a sweat was not her intent. Not now. Her attention wandered from what she would say to mindfully watching the road for any potholes or rocks. After all, this was her first time coming this way on her bike. She turned off the main road into a large driveway, nurtured at both sides with a variety of flowers and accent trees as it flowed into ample parking lots. Finding a bicycle rack, she parked her bike and secured it with a lock. As she walked towards the oversized building, she noticed a sign embossed in gold leaf plate, defining its purpose. She was finally here.

** TUTTLEBURY HIGH SCHOOL**

Danielle opened the heavy entrance door and stepped in. The halls were quiet, the wooden flooring gleaming, almost as good as her polished kitchen floor. Wondering where to go, Danielle felt a tap on her shoulder. It was a gentleman about her father's age, who was dressed in a gray suit and blue tie with a plastic identification card clipped to his jacket pocket. He frowned at her. She smiled weakly, squinting at the card—Mr. Jon Clark, Assistant Principal. Hmm, she was glad she had not bumped into the same man who had visited her home. Hopefully this principal could help or she might need to make a fast getaway.

Hello, I'm Danielle Norfeld and I live in Tuttlebury. That is, I recently moved with my family in June. I came here to speak with someone about school this coming Fall and I think ..."

"So, you are Miss Danielle Norfeld. This is very interesting. On my desk this morning there was a memo to call your mother. Something about orientation for middle school this Fall, and that you have a brother who has skipped a grade. You come from an intelligent family to have such a brother. He will do well."

"Yes, my brother Paul is very smart." Danielle said in soft tones, wondering why he spoke about her brother and not her. This situation was confusing. She remembered Paul had moved up a grade back in their old school. Mom had been her usual efficient self and had worked it out with the school personnel.

"My aim today is to follow-up and call your mother, Mrs. Norfeld. She had contacted the office on Friday and seemed quite concerned. The secretary said the connection was bad, a lot of commotion with fussy babies and believed your mother declined signing the final papers until she had all the correct information." Mr. Clark's eyes met Danielle's. "Do you know anything about this?"

Danielle looked over the gentleman's shoulder to a case filled with sports trophies. She had to think quick. What information was her mother looking for? Danielle remembered her mom had sent out the initial paperwork for the middle school. That was before the envelope from Tuttlebury High had been delivered by a strange man with a large moustache, a Mr. Mussman. Danielle had read them thoroughly; it was a formal notice to skip a grade, from the 8th grade to the 9th. A wonderful opportunity. At first her mother had declined this promotion, but then signed on the bottom line. Danielle couldn't wait to drop it off at the post office and everyday hung by the mailbox for a reply. Maybe her mother called because she also was anxious to know the decision.

Danielle's neck prickled with irritation; her brain ached.

"Ah, Miss Tuttle, are you going to answer the question or daydream all day?"

"Mr. Clark, I believe my mother called to find out the results of the high school application including an essay, which could promote me to this high school. I am here to check on my enrollment status." Danielle coughed nervously, searching the principal's eyes.

Mr. Clark was still, his eyes blinking with a mixture of confusion and doubt. He nudged Danielle on the shoulder and pointed down the hall to the main office. As they began walking, he brushed his hand across his right cheek. "You see, I haven't had time to review all the material. There was another staff member who worked on it. He would know about all this but he's on vacation. Besides a parent should be here, since you're not legally an adult."

"But my mother had already signed the papers for the middle school and Tuttlebury High where promotion to the ninth grade was offered to me. The essay counted a lot so I work especially hard on it. I was hoping that someone had reviewed this essay and found …"

"Miss Norfeld, from what I read in your file, Mrs. Nancy Norfeld cooperated in finalizing forms for this coming middle school year." Mr. Clark gave her a stern look. "Formal consent was verbally given as well as written signatures. You will be starting soon. I'll have the secretary print out your course schedule.

Danielle felt her confidence deflate; her face flush a bold crimson. Now she was really confused; were there other papers her mother needed to sign? She thought she had asked the right questions. Danielle licked dry lips and spoke; her voice hoarse as she forced her thoughts. "Wait a minute, I thought I was about to begin the ninth grade as a high school freshman. I know I wrote a great essay!"

Mr. Clark avoided Natalie's questioning eyes, instead he quickly walked down the hall.

As they entered the main office, Mr. Clark pointed Danielle to the available seating. He went behind the plastic window and spoke to a professional looking woman rapidly fingering a computer keyboard. Abruptly began a search of the room, opening this cabinet, that drawer. There was a dramatic sense to it—their faces haggard, their movements hurried. Finally, the secretary thrust a paper into Mr. Clark's hands. As he scanned the document, his eyebrows arched like question marks.

Danielle approached the working area. "Is there something the matter?"

"Yes, young lady, there certainly is! Turned out the paperwork for the 8th grade admission was incomplete. This included failure to transfer academic records showing proficiency from your previous school. Also, some essay you sent was found to be unsatisfactory." Mr. Clark gave her a long stare. "It appears that in place of skipping a grade, you will be heading back to seventh grade. Sorry, Miss Norfeld. You had the picture all wrong. Please tell you mother, Mrs. Nancy Norfeld, that the office will inform her of this correction to grade seven. Mr. Clark waved her away, pointing at the door.

"But I was told I had a very good possibility of moving into the 9th grade."

"Miss Norfeld, I don't know who told you this," Mr. Clark remarked in a nasty tone.

"That guy … I mean a gentleman came to our house and spoke to us. His name was Mr. Mussman and he had very black hair and a gray moustache. He said he was the office manager."

"Who? I have never heard of him young lady; you need to be careful not to make up stories." Ushering her out the door, he secured the lock.

Danielle felt her heart pulsating, every nerve vibrating. Her hands clenched into tight fists. As she reached the exit, there was another tap on her shoulder. There was an urgency about it.

"Miss Norfeld, I am Mrs. Peterkin, the principal's assistant. "There has been a serious error in your placement. Finalizing your results, I was pleased to read your extremely strong essay, and found it very engaging." The older woman with stylish white hair, smiled kindly. Looking cautiously about, she slid a note into Danielle's hand. "Tomorrow is my day off, please call me."

Danielle stuck the paper in her pocket and climbed on her bike. Now to head to the softball game. She really wanted to go home and have a good cry and really talk to mom. This was what she wanted to do. But it was already into August. The team would be wrapping up the summer league and getting ready for Fall softball. Heading unto the main road she leaned right on her bike. Then abruptly turned left, to the softball game, an activity that made sense to her. She would play this game like no other.

As she rode out, she saw that strange man in with the big moustache speed by in a fancy blue car. Mr. Mussman.

* * *

Robert rolled his bike unto the field to meet up with one of the guys from the gang. Also, it was almost starting time for the softball game Danielle was playing in. Today he would cheer her on. He had wanted to tell her, but she was up and out very early. Robert laughed, his sister was getting like him, which was not so good. His thought was to watch the game from the sidelines and get some details about this next dirty job from a member called Chief. He didn't know this guy, and found him creepy, so that meeting in a public place seemed safer. He believed this job involved the mega-size store, Serious Edy's Hardware located a couple of towns away, near his father's job. But he wasn't sure what they wanted him to do. He found a thick tree to lean against where hopefully a wild ball would not hit him but where he could get a decent view of Danielle. He hadn't gone to many of her games and paid little attention if he did. He found softball tiring; he would rather shoot basketball hoops. Before moving, he had played great even for a rookie in ninth grade. But all that was long gone.

The softball game had begun. His eyes roamed the field, looking for a girl with a ponytail dressed in a black and yellow uniform. There she was playing second base. Nice. The pitcher was throwing balls, there was an out at first base and a pop fly was caught. The third out really caught his attention. A small player hit the ball hard. It soared over the pitcher, as the hitter ran like a race car. The ball went thump into the mitt of the short stop and sent over to second base— to Danielle who instantly tagged her out. Sweet. This game held promise to be very entertaining. The next few innings flew by as he watched Danielle do amazing things. She hit well and scored. Even had an exciting home run. She also pitched using that softball windmill form and struck batters out. Danielle was a mean machine. But she also was a team player and played fair. He had no idea she was this good. As he cheered, his sister turned briefly, smiled and waved. He was so proud.

The game was now in the eighth inning, and Danielle's team was in the lead. What time was it? Robert glanced at his watch. Where was this guy? Had Chief forgotten, or had Robert missed him? He had been so involved in this game; he hadn't been paying attention. It could be the gang had changed their mind and were going to leave him alone. He hoped. A flash of sunlight on metal caught his eye. A motorcycle pulled next to him; the engine revved high. A tattooed arm raised in greeting, as Chief smirked, raising the furrows of facial scars.

"C'mon Robert, let's ditch these silly girls. We have a lot to do. Leave your bike by tree, you can get it later."

"Yeah, I'm coming." Disgusted, Robert left his ten-speed by the tree and hustled over to the noisy motorcycle and hopped on the back. What had Paul said the other day; about the box telling them things? Something about choice. Robert had the ability to choose the right way. He took a deep breath … if only he had the guts to do so.

20

Complications

*N*atalie settled Joseph and William in for an early afternoon nap and turned on the baby monitor. All was quiet. She went to her room, to the special hiding place and pulled out the letters she had found in the China-cabinet, as well as her favorite pens. She tucked them inside the violin case and tiptoed down the long staircase. Now to have some fun. However, her mother's phone loud conversation was pounding in her ears, she hoped the twins would not wake. What was her mother so angry? It seemed to have to do with Danielle, and she heard the words grades and softball. Probably about school starting. She wasn't sure why her sister was having school trouble; Danielle always had a great report card with many high marks. But this was the last year of middle school, maybe there was a lot to do before graduation. Natalie felt differently; she couldn't wait to begin a new school! Her new friends would be there and she loved to learn. She wasn't as brilliant as Paul who had already skipped a grade or Robert who seemed all grown up. This year she would do her very best and surprise everyone.

Passing through the kitchen, Natalie nodded to her mother and pointed outside. To the shed. All weekend, she had wanted to spend time in the refrigerator Box, her friend Aurora. There had been so many interruptions. Silence had greeted her the last time she visited, she hoped today could be different. She stood by the shed door and smiled. The sight of peeling paint and decaying wood greeted her, definitely in need of Paul's paintbrush. As usual the rusty padlock hung crooked; the door slightly ajar. She believed Paul had the key or was it, Robert? They both had fights over it. She had no problem getting inside, for her, the shed was always open.

Natalie skipped through the familiar shed to Aurora. She lifted the velvet drape she had fashioned from mom's old curtain and went inside. She perched cross-legged and took out her violin as well as the packet of envelopes tied with red and white string. They released the fragrance of fresh picked strawberries. Sweet like her grandma. Carefully she untied them and stacked three piles. One was for letters she knew the person's name scribed on the designer envelope. Another pile was for letters that looked business like; perhaps bills. The third were a mixture of sizes and of unfamiliar names. She had a lot of questions and hoped today Aurora would visit. Hmm. But this special Box had only been forward looking, and did not lean back for them. Unless for some reason, something in the past is happening again. That's a lot to think about.

Natalie was certain that some of the letters were written by her grandfather. She recognized the awkward use of capital letters and oddly spelled words. Two envelopes were already open, filled with sweetheart poetry. She knew at once that grandpa had penned them to grandma long, long ago, before they had been married. Grandpa also had written to his two children, who now were her dad and aunt. Unopened and waiting. Curious, Natalie held them tight in her hand, then carefully put them aside, knowing her parents would want them. She reached for another pile and stretched her legs such that the confined space appeared to expand. Not noticing, she stared at this mound, the confusing ones. She selected a messily opened business letter. It was confusing with several pages of diagrams and graphs with numbers, and signatures from people who wrote very sloppy on a dark line. Probably very important stuff.

She replaced the letter and eagerly grabbed one from another pile; ones she recognized as family. There were eight in all. Natalie spread them on the box carton floor like petals of a flower. Then gently eased one from the middle. Cradling between both hands, she realized something was different. The envelope was much heavier and when she turned it over it was sealed tight with red goop and fancy letters. This could be the wax seal she often read about in favorite mysteries. Turning it back over she realized another oddity. The letter was penned with grandma's artistic flair with graceful sweeps and curls, and was simply addressed; For the Twins. Natalie leaned forward and quickly scanned the others— one for dad and mom, her sister and brothers and one for herself. And the one she held tight addressed to her two baby brothers. At the bottom left in tiny letters she read, William and Joseph. She gasped. This couldn't be right. She knew grandma had died a while ago, way before they had moved to the farm, and the twins were born. How did grandma know any of this, including their names? Natalie wasn't sure what to think, finding these letters all very strange.

Abruptly the Box began to shake. The four sides of the ribbed cardboard folded in on her, closer and closer. Rainbow sparks of emerald, ruby and blue burst into brilliance of color, as she floated to the roof of the shed and into the sky. She was dizzy with excitement; wanting more, wanting to know. Natalie's feet softly set down in a meadow, wild with pink and violet flowers. Trees laden with green leaves ushered breezes to direct her path. Storm clouds were gathering, rain began falling like football size teardrops. But she was not afraid. From her pocket she pulled out her glasses and watched the silver blue puddles, then snagged her foot on a branch. She was falling, falling.

* * *

"Natalie, where are you?" yelled Mrs. Norfeld out the back door. She really wanted her daughter home. Now. The sitter hadn't shown up and she needed to get to the school right away. One of the neighbors had offered her a ride and would arrive any second. She wished Danielle was here to straighten out this mess at school but her daughter was on a field somewhere. Oh, goodness, her mind was a rambling mess. But Natalie could help with the twins, as well as Paul who should be home from his bike run. Where was her younger daughter? Then she remembered. Natalie had pointed outside while she was on the phone, having words with the people at that school.

Natalie was in that shed.

Mrs. Norfeld ran out the kitchen, through the mowed grass to the rough, that was thick with weeds and branches. Why the kids liked coming way out here, she didn't know. Yet she was about to find out. The shed door was open enough for her to edge herself in; baby pounds were coming off! The damp, heavy air rushed her; she couldn't breathe, or hardly see. She blinked hard. She saw a blanket covering a childlike form on the dirty floor; with hands holding tight a bundle of papers; papers that resembled her mother in law's stationery and handwriting. She quickly stuck the envelopes in the deep pocket of her apron. What? She moved aside the tattered coverlet recognizing the velvet curtain that had been thrown away. There was Natalie. Her daughter was in deep sleep, her face flushed and sweaty. As if the weight of a feather, Mrs. Norfeld gathered Natalie in her arms and rushed out of the shed. But she turned to glimpse a greenish light dance across the lop-sided refrigerator carton, as it settled firmly in place. Mrs. Norfeld's eyes moved back and forth, remembering something. Yet she had no time to consider what she had seen. She only knew she had to help her daughter.

* * *

Expecting to be late for supper, Danielle rushed into the mud room near the kitchen hall, dumping her grubby softball equipment on the worn floor. A dust cloud rose to the ceiling, along with the pungent smell of sweaty dirt. "I'm home!" she yelled. "Sorry, I didn't come home earlier but we had a double header. It was really hot out there, but I played hard. Some of the teammates and parents said I was awesome! Robert came to the first game for a little while and gave me a thumbs up." She loosened her tight ponytail as she approached the middle of the kitchen. Paul sat alone at the table; ear plugs tuned in. His plate was packed full with offerings of simple food; variety sandwich platter, potato salad, coleslaw, corn chips and store-bought cookies. Certainly not the usual feast, but she was so hungry, she could eat dry toast.

Paul looked up, as he took an earphone from his ear. "Hi

Danielle. About time you came home," he said as he bit into a ham and cheese combo.

"So where is everyone? I thought you all would be having supper."

"Danielle." Paul stared hard at his sister. "Everyone is stressed out right now."

Washing her hands quickly, Danielle reached for the tuna salad on rye and a handful of chips. "Is something wrong with mom? This sandwich is tasty but not her style."

"That's because Dad ordered it all from the deli. Mom has been busy putting Natalie in the tub, and Dad is feeding the twins. And Robert is out there somewhere." Paul waved his hand wildly above his head.

"What," said Danielle, the tuna falling from her mouth. "What is wrong with Natalie? Is she sick? I have to go see!" She threw her paper plate on the table.

"I wouldn't if I were you, because you're part of the problem."

Danielle froze like a mime in a circus show. "What did you say?"

"I only have some of the pieces but from what I heard … you have big problems at the high school or middle school. Not sure. Mom was planning to talk to some principal but then she found Natalie in the shed with a fever and so she's trying to bring it down and …"

"Natalie got hurt in the shed? Mom found her … our mother was in there?"

"Yes. Please let me finish." Paul adjusted his seating, avoiding eye contact with his sister. "Dad doesn't know yet about the school problem. Mom wants to talk with you. Dad is lost in his own thoughts about a new job that he is considering … could be a transfer to another state. There's one more thing. I only know about this, but now you will. The softball commissioner called to say that you have been banned from the team. Something about the poor sportsmanship you showed today." Waiting for the eruption, Paul reached for a handful of chips and gobbled them.

Danielle's mouth opened wide and stayed that way for some time. She piled food on a plate and went outside. There was the sound of rushing water. Paul leaned into the kitchen window watching his sister take the hose and spray freezing water all over herself, uniform included.

What he didn't see was her quiet visit to the cellar laundry to change into a clean outfit, then head up to her room. Danielle fell into bed and within seconds was counting stars.

Mrs. Norfeld sat by the door of the bathroom as her now awake daughter splashed about cups of water on her head, using wash cloths to dripple cool water on herself. "Mom when do you think I can come out?"

"When you're not hot anymore. Let me come in and feel your forehead and take your temperature." Mrs. Norfeld noisily pushed aside her chair.

"Don't come in yet! Let me get ready!" Natalie yanked dry towels from the rack and fashioned them around herself. "Okay, now!"

"Wow, what's with all the suds on your head," chided mom. Natalie's soapy curls, resembling a cartoon character were gently washed away, then Mrs. Norfeld toweled dry and dressed her daughter.

"Hey, you know. I'm like that mermaid we saw at the movies recently." Natalie's arms wrapped around her mother's neck, giving her a sloppy kiss on the cheek. "I'm much better now. I'm a little tired. I only want warm milk and my violin. I will play for you before I go to sleep … it's a new song I wrote."

"Yes, we'll see but first stay still while I take your

temperature," said Mrs. Norfeld. Concerned the fever had not lowered enough, she settled her daughter into bed and went downstairs to get some medicine and a little something to eat, perhaps a piece of dry toast and tea. That was the nurse in her; as a mother she would have loaded a generous spoonful of fresh strawberry jam over lots of butter. Approaching the girls' room, a sweet harmony of gentle breathing greeted her. Natalie eyelids were already fluttering in a dreamy dance. Surprisingly her sister was in the room as well. Danielle had flopped into bed, not bothering to even pull down the sheets. Mrs. Norfeld put the food aside and sat on a corner of Natalie's bed. She would sit her awhile, making sure Natalie was comfortable. Her eyes swept around the room; her heart filled with thankfulness as she watched them slumber. Such wonderful daughters; she was very proud of them. She bent her head and folded her slender hands as words of gratitude flowed into simple prayer. Peace filled the room and wrapped around her. The concerns of the day eased, as her eyes grew heavy and sweet dreams embraced her.

Revolving Door

*T*he early reddish streaks of a summer sky awakened Mr. Norfeld. He reached over his pillow to nudge his wife but his hand fell on empty sheets. He sat up and realized that Nancy's side of the bed was perfectly tidy. Where was she? Throwing on a light housecoat, he quietly approached the nursey. Nancy had to be there, although he had spent a good deal of the night there himself, settling the twins. No Nancy. He walked by the boys' room which was usually slammed tight, but this morning was slightly open. Enough to stick his head in and peek. Both boys were still tucked in, rocking the house with their heaving snoring. He couldn't believe Robert was sleeping in his own bed; that they slept through the all the racket. Amazing. Now standing at the girls' room, he had to lean in to see anything, since the rays of the sun were slow in visiting.

Focusing his eyes in the darkness he noted his two daughters burrowed into their pillows. There was someone awkwardly positioned at the bottom of Natalie's bed—his dear wife. He took one step into the room and halted. Oh, how he wanted to wake Nancy and have morning coffee before he left for work. Maybe even share a plate of scrambled eggs with ham and cheese, his favorite. But he couldn't do it. Not after her rough day. There were always the needs of the twins. Natalie taken ill with fever; the comings and goings of the other children. Children who were fast becoming adults. Suddenly a sadness swept over his heart. He was losing track of them … in many ways they had become unfamiliar to him. Natalie, so gentle and kind, was asserting herself. Paul was attempting new things, like painting the house. As a dad, he was very proud, but also full of regret. He wished he had taught them more. Danielle was showing confidence in all her efforts around the house, probably in other things as well. Then there was Robert. Things had changed between them. Robert was becoming a difficult teenager; taking on a defiant attitude that could care less about family.

His stomach felt awfully queasy.

Mr. Norfeld took the blame. Leaving friends, school, favorite activities, his family had been transplanted to this farming community. A country life that was alien to them and even to himself who had been raised in it. These past weeks, he had done little to acclimate them, instead he had buried himself in work. With the little spare time there was, he had befriended the Tuttle family, especially George. Nancy had warned him about their bullying tactics; to watch becoming overly involved. He half heard his wife, since he was enjoying having a pal in George, a friendship he had wanted for a long time. So much so, that he even wanted to brush aside the incident at the store when George slapped his son, Robert—hard. A streak of guilt cut through him. For reasons dark even to himself, he had often chosen to defend the Tuttle family and blame his son.

What was wrong with him?

To top it off, another position had been offered several states away. He had been close to signing the papers without telling his wife or the kids. He had hesitated … knowing this move wouldn't go over well with any of them. On the outside, he wore the image of a happily married man, yet he knew his big thumb was stuck in other puddings. Enough thinking! Time to leave for work.

Mr. Norfeld grabbed his briefcase and headed out the back door nearly falling over Danielle. With a cell phone close to her ear, his daughter spoke in an adult tone. "This is Danielle Norfeld. Mrs. Peterkin, I am calling as you had instructed. I want to discuss the essay, and all that is involved with promotion to the ninth grade this Fall."

Danielle's earnest eyes, met the curiosity in her dad's. She jumped up and ran into the house, the aluminum door banging behind her.

Mr. Norfeld cleared his throat. Skipping to high school? Then he remembered. Nancy had mentioned this possibility and even showed him the paperwork. He hadn't given it much attention, instead he told his wife to work it out. Rubbing his chin briskly, wayward hairs pricked his hand. He needed to start paying attention.

* * *

Mrs. Norfeld dressed quickly and headed downstairs. This morning she was relieved that Natalie's fever was close to normal, yet wasn't sure if the doctor should be called. What was the matter with her daughter? She had found her in the shed; could that dank place cause this? And why did Natalie like it there anyway? It certainly wasn't where she cared to visit. Once Natalie was feeling better, they would have a talk.

Perhaps making breakfast for Natalie and anyone who was hungry would help her sort this out. Mrs. Norfeld put a large pot of coffee on and packed the frying pan full of thick bacon. Scrambled eggs were next. Finally, she pulled one last box of cheese coffeecake from the freezer and placed in on the table. A breeze flew by and there was a quick nudge on her shoulder; then a wet kiss on her cheek. It was Robert. Instantly her hand lightly touched the sloppy kiss. She couldn't remember the last time he had shown affection … she really missed it.

"Morning Mom. Breakfast smells great! But can't stay. Have to get over to the Tuttle store. I will be working most of the day," said Robert as he pulled apart a large piece of pastry and wrapped it in a napkin. He winked as he rushed out the door.

Danielle came in next. Robert kindly stepped aside, instead of his usual style of shoving and muttering mean things. He even smiled at her. His sister returned a puzzled look.

Mrs. Norfeld turned towards the door, the cooking spatula in hand. "Danielle, is that you? What were you doing outside? Never mind, breakfast is about ready. Grab a plate and fill up. I'll be right back after I bring Natalie a little toast and egg. Oh, can you make sure the top of the stove is turned off?"

* * *

Danielle filled her dish, admiring the good food. With the first bite, her appetite soared. She hadn't realized she was this hungry. With all the upset with the Tuttlebury high school, as well as the awful accusations from their softball commission, she had felt numb. But she was a little better now. Pouring a cup of coffee, she picked up the morning newspaper and thumbed through. She decided to flip from back to front, so she wouldn't get stuck on the first page. She read as she munched. The news was all the usual fare, nothing very exciting. Although there was an article from the state governor, citing issues of tax evasion and fraud with the town of Tuttlebury and the mayor. This was interesting, although the article was too short to fully understand. As she stuffed a piece of cheese pastry in her mouth, she turned to the front page; the juicy stuff. Her eyes open wide, crumbs fell from her lips into her mug of coffee, as she stared hard. At top of the page, she read—Tuttlebury High School Staff Missing.

Danielle held the paper close to her face, taking in the facts. The woman found missing from her home was widowed and had been living alone. Neighbors had called authorities upon seeing doors open, all the lights on in the house as well as hearing the howling of many neighborhood dogs. There was evidence of a household robbery and possible physical abuse. The owners' vehicle remained in the driveway. Danielle's vision blurred as she read and reread the name of the missing person. A woman named Mrs. Stella Peterkin. "Oh no!" This was the woman she had been calling all morning.

What to do? Danielle considered running upstairs to find her mother. Mom would doubtless be checking on Natalie and readying the twins for the day. Danielle could already hear the rattling pipes drawing water for baths. She really needed to talk to someone—but who? She would sneak upstairs and wake Paul. He wouldn't be happy but once he saw all the breakfast food … As Danielle jumped up, the table cloth stuck to her arm and her plate of luscious food fell on the floor. "Oh no!", she shouted for the second time.

"Glad I woke up in time to see your circus act," said Paul pointing a finger and laughing. "So much noise upstairs and in the kitchen too!"

"Yeah." On her knees, Danielle was hand shoveling her breakfast into a large napkin. As she rose to the table, Paul passed her a fresh paper plate. "Thanks, Paul." Maybe her brother would hear her out.

"Danie, haven't talked to you much lately. How are things going?" he said as he jammed eggs and coffeecake into his mouth.

"Well, now that you've asked. There's quite a bit. Got some time?"

Paul nodded, pouring himself a glass of orange juice.

Danielle took a good breath.

"I think I know what you're going to say. This is about the call you got from the softball committee. They left a message saying you were off the team. Poor sportsmanship? What's with that?"

Danielle coughed; a piece of coffeecake stuck to the roof of her mouth. The team wasn't what she wanted to talk about, not yet. She pointed to the newspaper article and her brother began reading. In moments he dropped his fork. "Huh. Not sure why you're showing me this."

Suddenly Mrs. Norfeld burst into the kitchen. "What's that I hear about softball?" She grabbed two bottles of formula that had been warming. "Here, Paul, it's your turn to feed your brothers."

"Thanks, Mom." With a look of relief, Paul grabbed the bottles and ran from the room.

Mrs. Norfeld laughed. "The first time he fed the twins,

I had to chase after him with the bottles. But he seems to be getting used to it. Anyhow this gives us time for a little chat."

Danielle nodded. "I guess so. First, I want to bring up something important … like school next year. I know you signed the papers for the high school and I really appreciate what you did. But as my mother where would you really want me to go?"

Mrs. Norfeld poured milk in her coffee and stirred. "Danielle, at first, I wanted you to finish the eighth grade. I didn't think you could handle the high school," she paused to sip her coffee.

"And now," asked Danielle.

Mrs. Norfeld smiled with tenderness in her eyes. "In the last weeks you have been maturing, not only in stature but in responsibility. You are becoming a delightful young lady."

"So, you think I am ready to skip a grade like Paul did?"

"Absolutely."

Danielle cheeks flushed, as she folded her hands. I'm a little confused. "From what I understand, you and I had filled papers for 8th grade and you sent them in. Then Mr. Mussman dropped off the application and essay to promote me to the ninth grade. They were completed and we both signed the on that dark line. I mailed it out right away. Is this correct?"

Mrs. Norfeld's head nodded in agreement. Yes, that's what happened. Danielle, you've been offered a special opportunity and I believe you will be an exceptional student."

"But the high school said you had questions before finalizing the paperwork and that you have tried to call them …"

"Stop right there, Danielle. Let's clear this up. There has been no such contact. I only recall contacting the middle school when we first moved here. I have not called the Tuttlebury High School." Her eyes darkened, trying to understand. "However, there was a call last week from some woman who wanted to discuss your promotion to the high school. She was very excited but we were cut off right away. I believe her name was um ... Mrs. Peterkin."

Danielle felt her neck hairs stand up and her mouth go dry. Mrs. Norfeld's eyes searched hers, wanting answers, but there were none to give. Instead, Danielle pointed to the newspaper and to the article, about the missing lady, Mrs. Stella Peterkin. Neither spoke, as her mother read the column, and read it again. Then like the burst of heavy clouds, questions and emotions poured like a steady rainfall.

22

Pieces in Play

Robert pedaled the two-mile trip to work, grateful to have found his bike in the yard after leaving it at the game. Today he was full of good feeling and even the awful thoughts about the Tuttle family and their henchmen had left him. At least for now. It wasn't only his intense workouts in the basement. He knew the reason; thinking positive thoughts. Last night proved this when he visited the shed. The box broke its silence, instead of angry waters and jail sentences, the ugly cardboard carton, had greeted him with a rainbow of light. Awesome. As well as an incredible view of things to come. Briefly he glimpsed his future … of becoming a man of science and research, on the cutting edge of new happenings. Yet as Paul and even Natalie had said, these were possibilities for the future. He had to do his part. Yes, he had the ability to make decisions for himself, the capacity to create a future by how he thought and what he did right now. For the only time "zone" to live in is the present. The past has already been lived and the future is yet to be. He had the power to step into great things.

Starting this very day.

Robert secured his bike into the rack and walked with a gait of confidence. His was completely determined; tonight, he would leave the gang. Enough of their terrible plans! When he met up with Mr. Tuttle, he would give him his notice, and walk away from this job. For he, Robert, was taking back his life.

He patted the hidden pocket inside his plaid shirt—where the key for the shed was. Last night he had been encouraged by the box, fondly named Aurora by Natalie. He figured the key would bring him good luck today. Although carrying the key was dangerous since the gang had once owned it, he believed it opened special connections. Connections that could empower; he already felt this strength.

As he headed to the stock room, he noticed that the aisles were unusually packed with customers. He wondered why. Then he remembered their rival store. Edy's Hardware. They were on vacation the rest of the week. How could he forget? He wished he could. Robert threw himself into his work; running crazy trying to help customers anxious to purchase and quickly attend to their projects. Then to the big job of unloading the trucks. The cartons were piling and his back aching since the other guy, Tim, had not shown up. But Robert kept a steady pace and was so occupied, he missed lunch. Instead, he decided to take a short water break. With his sleeve Robert swiped sweat from his forehead. Entering the makeshift employee lounge, to the corner table with metal chairs, he heard voices that were inaudible but very irritated. The Tuttle office door burst open and suddenly the voices were all around him.

Voices from select members of the Tuttle family and gang.

"Hey, Norfeld … you're done for the day. After all it is Friday!"

"Robert felt his tooth bite his lower lip. They couldn't wait to engage their evil plan. But wasn't this a little soon? He wanted to quit; should have already.

"Get out of here kid! Go with the Chief, and Jim to Edy's Store. It's time to arrange the place for this little job, which will happen tomorrow morning." Mr. Tuttle's eyes bulged and his breath reeked of garlicky salami.

Robert could sense a tidal wave rise in his belly. His hands began to shake. Their game plan wasn't making sense. Why were they changing things? He stared at his boss. "What? We're not doing this thing tomorrow night? I don't understand."

A look of disgust flashed through Mr. Tuttle's face. "Oh, you didn't know? Plans have changed. We have decided to carry out this mission Saturday, with the first light."

"But we were supposed to do this during the night," said Robert, his face becoming a ghostly white.

Mr. Tuttle turned his head, ignoring the comment.

"Hey kid, don't worry. Everything you'll need will be there," said Chief. We'll head there now to leave the materials in Edy's rear garage. You both will do fine, especially since you will be able to see."

"And be seen! These are evil plans! Even worse that Jim is coming—he punches me all the time." Moving closer to Chief, with his fist raised, Robert continued. "I will not do this! I have decided to leave you idiots and quit the Tuttle store. Find some other loser to push around." As Robert stepped towards the door, a large hand yanked his shirt, tearing the collar. Mr. Tuttle.

"Norfled, you're in too deep. There's no turning back. If you try, there will be consequences—bad ones. To you and your family." Mr. Tuttle turned to the muscular man with arms full of tattoos. "Chief, please escort this kid out to van. He can come with us to ready Edy's for some action. Convince him of his importance."

"No, no!" Robert tried to pull away from Chief's grip. He wanted to scream and fight his way out. Instead, he heard his own voice, small and scared, "What about my bike?"

Mr. Tuttle caught Chief's eye. "Take Jim and Robert and his ridiculous bike to Edy's. Leave the bike there so tomorrow Robert will have wheels to get home. Once you're done putting things together, take both boys to my place; they're not going home tonight. Make sure they both get tucked in after telling their mommies about their sleep over. These airheads have to be ready before dawn breaks." Standing close to Robert, Mr. Tuttle continued, "Chief will come by in his pick-up to get you and Jim. But afterwards you'll need to pedal the long way home yourself. Better get your beauty sleep." Mr. Tuttle laughed so hard he lost his balance.

* * *

Danielle had not felt this close to her mother. The last couple of days they banded like two detectives trying to solve a case, which in all practically, they were. They created a list of objectives, hoping the flashlight would shine brighter and brighter on the next step. They began with addressing the Tuttlebury sports committee that accused Danielle of poor sportsmanship at the last game and terminated her.

They needed facts. Mrs. Norfled already had neighbors to assist since they had formed a committee. No longer allowed in important town functions, they felt the oppression and had a keen desire to help. Mrs. Steward, her mother's key assistant, had known of the sports program corruption and was planning her own strategy.

Others in the committee were gathering information on Danielle's last softball game. They were interviewing onlookers and the coaches of both teams—visiting as well as home. Taking the information, commentary was presented in the opinion and sports page of the newspaper. So far results were a mixed review. Some painted Danielle as a sloppy player wanting to make her own rules. Others observed Danielle as possible all-star material, a team-player in a fair game.

But the town of Tuttlebury would not yield an inch. Danielle was off the team.

Danielle was crushed.

But her mother considered they were only momentarily detoured. They would regain their steam by trying new strategy. Somehow, they would find a way and win! So encouraged by her mother's confidence, Danielle smiled sheepishly. Yes, they had been seriously wronged. But they would both climb out of this sink hole.

The next issue was the skipping of a grade. Mrs. Norfeld called both the middle and the high schools, requesting an appointment. No one would speak to her. The next day there was paperwork siting in their mail box—details for Danielle to start the seventh grade. That's when her mom went explosive, pounding her feet on the floor and praying for help. Placing her hands on Danielle's shoulders, Mrs. Norfeld looked deep into her daughter's eyes, and said, "We have to find this Mrs. Peterkin."

"But how do we do find her? We have no idea where she went." Danielle's usually rosy cheeks looked gray, her eyes tired. "All the work we've done and all we know for sure is that I'm off the team and still going to middle school, horribly demoted to the seventh grade."

Mrs. Norfeld stood by her daughter, giving her a tight hug. "No worries. We will find a way. I need to think a bit and make more phone calls. Danielle, since the twins are napping, why don't you grab a sandwich, go outside and watch the birds. You can sit awhile or move around to feel better. Thank-you my wonderful daughter. Everything will work out!"

Danielle nodded. She really couldn't think anymore. But she was hungry and wanted a break from all this upset. Could be her mother's suggestion was what she needed.

* * *

"Oh, there you are," said Mrs. Norfeld chuckling at her berry-stained yellowed apron, her favorite. It had been misplaced the last few days, but now found! Too weary to start kitchen work, she tossed the apron on the arm of the den chair and sank into its soft cushions. But she couldn't relax, her mind would not shut off. What's next? She had spoken with confidence to Danielle, when she really wasn't sure about anything except feeling exhausted and nauseous. Mrs. Norfeld was executing a reasonable plan to help her daughter but it needed more tweaking and time; if she didn't run out of gas first. It was such a lonely place to be. All of it. The twins always needing her. Natalie's fever. Robert's ornery ways and his brother's aloofness. Now Danielle had a wheelbarrow full of issues. Then there was her husband, it seemed like he was helping but sometimes … oh, well.

189

Mrs. Norfeld's eyes grew heavy, then opened wide. Yes, Ted's ways of doing things could be annoying, but he was a really good father with a kind heart. He was trying and so wasn't she. Both of them could do better if they worked together and not go off on their own. Then as family they could become a strong engine roaring to great things. First, she needed to talk to Ted. She jumped up ready to pencil a list of creative ideas.

As she rose, there was a fluttering sound, like when a stack of newspaper falls over. By her feet, she stared at several envelopes strewn this way and that. A familiar scent hung in the air as she knelt and gathered them in her apron. It tickled her nose like ripe strawberries. Some of the card stock bore a special hand script like no other. Her mother-in-law! Excited, Mrs. Norfeld leaned over the dining room table and sorted through the curious treasures.

* * *

Ted Norfeld drove his rusting station wagon home with the efficiency of a race car driver. Already late in the afternoon, he wanted to get home. Then his foot let up on the gas pedal. It was Friday and he hadn't gone shopping for Nancy. Now if he could only remember the list. She must have told him several times, but he hadn't been listening. But he knew they were items for the Sunday's gathering. Ah ... party goods, that's what he needed! Edy's Super Hardware carried selections of almost everything.

Mr. Norfeld turned left to the quiet plaza of stores, up an incline to the large building tucked into a grove of trees. Hmm, his wife had visited the Tuttle church, but they decided to join the parish his father had once belonged. Planned was a simple welcoming ceremony at the end of the service. It was for all of them, but the twins would have center stage. Right after, there would be a little celebration at their home; not the Tuttle's elaborate hall. This was his wife's idea, again in his face about the Tuttle control of people in town. Yet he was seeing more things like Nancy. He also was concerned with the Tuttle family control and very disappointed with George Tuttle … he had thought they were friends. But that man had been a tyrant to his son Robert, yelling and slapping him around. He couldn't respect a man who acted this way, or even call him a friend.

Heading into the parking lot, he quickly jotted a mental list of things to purchase; plastic tablecloths and eating utensils, plenty of paper plates and napkins. He figured he would find everything since this store outdid the one George owned, with better quality stuff.

As he looked for a space, a store sign greeted him. Store Closed. It went on; stating the owners were on vacation and would return the following week. Not good. Now there was only the Tuttle store and he wasn't going back there.

As he turned the clunky station wagon to leave, his eye caught movement outside the store. Had the owners come back? Wishful thinking. Curiosity tugged at him. Parking in a wooded spot, he pulled his bird binoculars from under the seat and focused towards that area. "What?" His mouth became dry and his hands were sweaty. Fumbling, Mr. Norfeld adjusted the lens. What was he seeing? Yep, it was as he had thought. Guys from the gang. He recognized them from the social gatherings; about a half-dozen of them. They were led by a big guy with a head bandana. At the rear was a lanky man who was angrily waving his arms with some sort of stick. Oh, no! His son Robert was being prodded by this guy like a cattle ranger. He couldn't believe it. What was happening to Robert … had life really come to this? His son was in big trouble. Mr. Norfeld, wanted to grab Robert and get out of there. Yet he sat glued to his seat. Fearing the worse, his mind zipped about hunting for a solution.

He had a plan. Mr. Norfeld would call and tell Nancy the situation. He would become a kind of detective and find out what these nasty people were up to. Probably stay the night. Food? No problem, he thought as he sipped the vanilla coffee and dug into the donut bag for a sugary cruller. She had to say yes, he was doing this for Robert.

The phone kept ringing until there was a pause, then a connection. "Hello, Ted. You're late. You better have a decent excuse."

Mr. Norfeld swallowed the last bite of donut and took a deep breath.

23

Dark Skies Brewing

$\mathcal{M}$rs. Peterkin startled awake from a nap. Was it morning? She really didn't have a clue. At first being in this dark space was scary. Becoming familiar with every corner had helped her calm down. She figured she had been dumped in a rundown veggie stand that had long ago been deserted. She loved buying fresh fruits, but this place triggered none of those happy times. It was nasty here, smelly, with lots of creepy bugs. Although still summer, this place held a damp chill. Finding a musty blanket; she wore it around her shoulders like a cloak. But her wrists ached from the metal hand cuffs, twisting and turning to release them only bruised her muscles. She wanted out from this cloistered room with a its one door heavily padlocked and a tiny window only a mouse could push through. She flicked on the flashlight she had found hiding in the wall beams. It was still dark but morning was already here.

Soon they would be coming.

How long had she been here? Well, since she was taken on Sunday, it had to be a weekday... perhaps even close to the weekend. Being very disorientated, she wasn't sure. But she sure was angry. How stupid she had been to fall into the Tuttle's evil scheme! She knew better and should have called the police or walked away from her administrative position. The Tuttle family was corrupt; controlling everything, even the high school. Boy, was she glad she had told her boss off! Even though their gangsters took and dumped her in this awful place, she had no regrets.

Yesterday all this musing had left her depressed and teary but this morning she awoke alert. And strong. Somehow, she was getting out of this place! These hoodlums came by every day and this time she would play the cards in her favor. She had to help this town, starting with the Norfeld family. The Tuttle clan had offered the older girl, Danielle, a promotion to grade nine, contingent on an acceptable grade average, paperwork and an impressive essay. Danielle followed through with an exceptional essay that she, Mrs. Stella Peterkin, found so well written she read it through several times. The essay was definitely academically fit for high school. Danielle had her endorsement but the Tuttle family threw their nasty weight around and yanked this honor back. Mrs. Peterkin kicked the dirt floor. She would help that Norfeld girl, if it was the last thing she would do!

The heavy oak door burst open. They had come. Posturing herself confident and sure, Mrs. Peterkin stood up, barely five feet of her. Two masked men, walked in; one thick and muscular, the other rather skinny. One dropped off a bag of groceries while the other peered into the empty bucket and scowled. "You need to use the outhouse?" Mrs. Peterkin nodded as the gruff man grabbed her shoulder and pushed her out the door, to the nasty outhouse stringy with cobwebs.

"Let me go! You're hurting my arm. I have done everything you have asked. Take off these handcuffs!"

"Woman, will you close your mouth! You know you messed up big time helping that Norfeld girl. This is what you get! You should be grateful that the Tuttle family has such mercy," he said as he removed the cuffs. "Now hurry up," he said, pacing in in the damp grass. As she came out, the handcuffs were slapped back on her tender wrists. Roughly he walked her back to the decaying building and ushered her in. "Soon this will be all over," he said and took off.

The wood beams of the roof shook as the door slammed. Mrs. Peterkin felt her insides seize with anger. "No, you will not win!" she shouted at the door. Dumping the contents of the bag on the floor, she laughed. Enough food for someone on death row. Usually, they brought meager offerings. Today there was a large sandwich, two bags of chips, a container of coleslaw, one box of fig cookies and two large bottles of water. Hmm. They probably went to a deli somewhere. She hoped they had been seen and someone followed them. Now she would eat, and be able to think with a clear mind. As she grabbed the sandwich, the metal cuffs fell on the floor. Amazed, Mrs. Peterkin rubbed her sore wrists. Had this been an oversight or intentional? Her eyes roamed the enclosure with renewed vision. She was getting out of this place.

* * *

Paul threw his books aside. His focus was gone. It was mostly due to the tension in the house that was like a harbor fog. Dense and disturbing. What was going on with everyone? He felt like he was the last one to know about anything. Paul was becoming like Dad; who often stared across the dinner, lost in thought. He needed to get with the picture. Let's see … he knew that something was up with Danielle and the sports committee since he had taken the phone call. But there were other issues discussed in angry tones between his mother and Danielle. It all hurt his ears. And being behind closed doors, he was only catching fragments of their conversation. Yet he knew they we both changing. His sister spoke up for herself and his mother was speaking like a teacher to callers over the phone. A confident, no-nonsense approach.

There was Robert. Paul shook his head. He didn't know his brother anymore. They used to call each other bros. Like the tough characters in the movies, they promised they had "each other's back." They had really meant it. This all changed with the move to their grandparents' old house. He had tried to get his brother's attention. Instead, their fists were up and ready. There was that nasty fight over that shed key, for reasons he couldn't figure. This was not what he wanted, but knew he had become lazy. He just didn't understand Robert and had chosen to ignore him. He had to do better.

Natalie was left. He probably spent the most time with her; doing different things side by side; she would play violin and he would speed read through book chapters. Even when they visited Aurora, they didn't talk much. Somehow, they had to find a way to get along.

Beginning right now. Leaving his stacks of books, Paul walked over to Natalie's room. She had been quiet this week, probably because of the sudden fever. The cause was uncertain; mom thought the musty shed was the reason, the doctor thought it was a summer cold of sorts although not fully certain. But Paul hadn't talked to his sister. Only once had he spent a few minutes, dropping off breakfast at her room. Standing near the door; Paul heard his sister singing to herself. Amazing. She sang pretty good for a girl. He tapped the door and walked in.

Natalie lifted her head and groaned. "Paul, just like you to come right in," she said, irritation in her voice.

"Sorry, Natalie. I wanted to see how you're feeling."

"I'm fine. Well, don't stand there, shut the door and sit down," she said, waving her hand towards the pink wicker chair.

Paul grinned and sat like his sister had ordered. In the corner, Natalie was sitting cross legged on the oak floor, surrounded by papers, sketch pads, and a colorful bound book that appeared to be a dairy. In his chair, Paul leaned over, watching his sister. "What are you doing?"

"Lots of things. I'm drawing the woods around here. And I'm writing little poems and thoughts in my notebook."

Paul walked over to the corner. Looks like a dairy. Must have all your personal stuff."

"Paul, it's a journal, not a diary. Being as intelligent as you are, you should know the difference."

"Hmm, does that mean you write in only when you feel like it, not every day?" asked Paul as he stood behind Natalie's back. Then his eyes opened with surprise. "Hey, why are the floor boards moved and what's that hole in the floor?"

Natalie startled, slamming the journal. "I told you to sit in the pink chair!" With a swift arm, she swept everything into the floor, secured the floor boards and shut the closet door. Her secret hiding space, a secret no more.

"What are you doing? This is so exciting; having a hiding place. Did you create it yourself? Can I have another peek?"

"Paul, I would be happy if you go away and forget you ever saw any of this."

"Another secret to cover up."

"Yes, in this family, mysteries jump out at you," said Natalie as she winked at her brother.

"What do you mean?"

"Well, there's the secret about the new shed key that you and Robert fight about. And the rusty one that used to be in grandpa's jacket pocket always is missing."

"That's because you have it."

Natalie laughed. "The shed door is open for me. I don't need it. Although it's often under the mat. Also, there's the letters I found."

"Okay. I get it. The letters in your special girly place. I think it's pretty cool and makes me curious. I promise not to say anything." Paul playfully tousled Natalie's curly hair.

Natalie looked up with a sheepish grin, deciding not tell him about the special letters she found in the China cabinet.

"How about you play me a little tune on your violin?"

"Paul. I've been wanting to play all week. But my violin is in the shed. It was left behind when I got that fever. Mom thinks the musty shed got me sick, she wants me to stay in the house today."

"Oh. It would seem to me that you have been in your room for a long while. How about we go out and get the violin?"

"No."

"Why not?"

"Because mom said to wait until the weekend to go to the shed. Besides, I'm not ready to see Aurora yet."

"Can I go and find your violin?"

"Let's wait until tomorrow morning. Early. I want to go then. I'll bring Danielle."

Paul looked out the window lost in thought. Natalie, I don't understand the reason for going in the morning."

"It's because I think that it will be time to see things differently, as they really are."

Paul shook his head. "Not sure what you mean, but I will knock on your door early. Be ready."

Natalie nodded, as she closed the bedroom door tight.

* * *

Mr. Norfeld dialed his home number and closed his eyes as he counted the number of rings. Darn. He might need to leave a message.

"Hello, hello, Ted is that you? You're late."

"I know. That's why I called. I'm caught in a strange situation. Right now, I'm on a stakeout."

"A stakeout? Ted you're talking like the police."

"Yeah. Nancy, I saw something here at Edy's. I had come out here to buy the paper plates you wanted and the place was closed so I went to leave but riding up the hill I saw guys walking about. Kind of strange."

"Strange to see men at the store? Maybe they're the owners."

"Could be. But I think I recognized them. I want to be sure so I'm watching from the car."

"Do you have an idea who they were?"

Ted gulped down coffee and cleared his throat. What

should he say? That he saw Robert and the Tuttle people? Ugh. Maybe he saw them, maybe not.

"Ted are you there? Who did you see?"

"I have my binoculars out. Can't be sure ... could all be nothing. Um. I'll stay for a while longer."

"What about supper? You could leave for a minute and pick up burgers and fries."

No, I'm good. Bought myself donuts and a large coffee. My sweet tooth will keep me going for a long time."

"Okay. Promise you'll call me, or even text, so I won't worry.

"Okay. I'll be fine. Maybe after you tuck the twins to bed, you could have a cup of special tea and watch that series you like."

"That's a good idea. That show always relaxes me. As for you, please be careful and don't get into any trouble."

Mr. Norfeld nodded into the cell phone, setting it on the car seat. "Well, that went pretty well," Mr. Norfeld said aloud. Yes, there was a twinge of guilt ... he should have mentioned he saw Robert. Yet he wasn't sure, these people were a good distance away. He held the binoculars up. The evening outdoor lights were on but he thought he saw thin light beams waving from a flashlight. He couldn't be sure. He leaned back in the car seat and balanced the binoculars as he ate donuts, drank coffee, called home and ate some more. Mr. Norfeld's eye lids grew heavy and the hillside became a blur. His graying head dipped into his chest, as wheezing snores quaked the station wagon.

Until the inky evening sky yielded to creamy yellow rays.

Bursting Sky

$\mathcal{I}$t was morning. Chief tightened the black and red bandana around his head. Menacing dark hairs poked out and upward, matching his pitch-black eyes. Turning, he watched Robert and Jim dawdle like they were window shopping at the mall. He waved his arm, and shouted. "Get in the truck—now! Making a tight fist he shoved it upward. "Or I'll show you who's boss!"

Both boys ran toward the beat-up truck and tugged on the rear door handle. "Stop," shouted Chief. "Jim, sit in the back but you, Robert, stay next to me." Robert stood very still; his defiant eyes met Chief's. "Oh, you had better wipe that smirk off before I do," said the muscular man, his cheeks arched in warlike fury.

Robert froze like a pantomime in a circus act. But his insides were a spinning tornado, his mind flicking through possible options. He could walk towards the truck and last minute run off like a deer. Or make it seem like he was going along with things and then jump from the truck. Maybe he could wait until they were at Edy's; then grab his bike and fly home. Such plans were possible. However, it would be best to stand up to these Tuttle gang and be a man. As they neared the Edy's parking lot, Robert took a huge breath and boldly voiced his intentions.

"Chief. I'm out. I've decided not to join you. I'm going home," said Robert with strong conviction. Since the truck was slowing up, he opened the door and stepped out hitting the ground hard. As he stood up, he felt a lightning crack to his cheek. Chief's fist. Shaken, he fell again. A strong arm lifted him up. Jim.

"Where do you think you're going, you stupid kid?"

Robert fought away from Jim's strong grasp. Chief and Jim towered over him, their lips clenched in disdain. He looked away, knowing he couldn't fight them both.

With urgency, Chief spoke "Time to get on with it! Jim hustle that Robert into the building so we can have a little review of the game plan. Then I'll take off and watch your huge bonfire from my rearview mirror. Oh yes, remember not to be seen by anyone. Jump those bikes and make some tracks!"

* * *

Everything was in place. It was time to burn the building. Robert glared at Jim. It was the two of them now.

"Robert, you have the honor, get this fire bomb going!" Jim said, throwing the box of long matches at him.

Robert missed the catch, matches falling everywhere, as he gripped a broom and swept Jim off his feet.

In a blink, Jim recovered like a boomerang, lit a match to the accelerants; then lifted a shovel swinging with exceptional aim.

But missed Robert. Incredible. But not for long. It had become a dangerous competition volleying between the hefty shovel and puny wicker broom.

The hurling shovel sliced through the air scraping Robert's ear as he fell into the pile of smoking hay. Around him, the flames erupted into a frenzied dance; billowing clouds of smoke filled the room.

"Sheer luck, Norfeld. Great place to land. You can go out with a blaze because this time I'll get you." Jim gripped harder on the garden tool weapon, spun around and with immense power, charged.

Suddenly Jim tripped and fell heavily on the wooden floor, now engulfed in flame. He lay motionless.

With the broom arched fiercely over his head, Robert froze. From the corner of his eye, he recognized a familiar gray tee shirt. "Alex, what are you doing here?"

"I'm here to help. Can't put this on you."

"Alex, you're just in time! We have to hurry—this place is going to blow!"

Reaching under Jim's shoulders, Alex lifted the unconscious body, his muscles oily from sweat. Robert held unto the feet as they hauled Jim through the crackling fire. To safety.

Outside a good way for the building, Alex removed his belt and bandana securing the wrists and feet of their captive.

"Hey, Robert you had better leave!"

"What? You want me to go. Now? But we still need to call the emergency people and …"

"Robert. Let me do this. I should have been the one to set the fire. By using you they knew it would hurt me. It did."

"But I can't let you take all blame. It's not right!"

"I'm already in a mess of trouble. There's a lot about me you don't know. I'm older than you think. I ditched high school a while ago. I've been arrested and have done some time. But you're still clean. Get out of here!" Alex shoved his friend landing a sharp elbow in his side.

Rubbing the sore muscles and even more sore feelings, Robert glared at Alex, his dark eyes questioning Alex's crystal blue.

* * *

Sadness in his heart, Alex watched his friend ride out to the main road. Having hurt Robert would probably lose him as a friend. He wouldn't take any of it back. Chasing Robert away was the right thing to do … he felt good about that.

With nimble fingers, he called 911. Time for all hell to break loose. He stood watch over his hostage; he couldn't wait to turn this loser over to the authorities. He didn't care that this decision would mean handcuffs, a ride to the police station and possibly a trip to jail. Because it was time to spill all the Tuttle secrets.

* * *

Arousing from a deep sleep, Mr. Norfeld thrashed about. A dusty cloud had covered his face choking him. His arms waved it away as he twisted his body in the car seat. Smoke! His eyes popped open as he fell out of the station wagon. Oh no! Edy's on fire! Trembling he slid the cell phone from the right pocket. He moaned. Without a recharge this phone was useless, like a prop in a school play. Worse. How to call for help? He leaned his head towards the distant throb of an emergency vehicle. The shrill of siren grew louder, help was on its way. And there would be plenty.

* * *

It was finally morning. Danielle slipped into Paul's room and nudged his shoulder. Then another. Paul grunted and turned over. "Get up you hibernating bear!" Danielle laughed at her snoring brother. Glancing to the other side, was Robert's bed. All made up and not slept in. Yep, her older brother wasn't home much. He had found a new family. The Tuttle's. He worked for them, hung with their awful gang and often spent the night. The last time she tried to talk to him, she was put off by all the insults he flung. Probably for the best; she had her own life game going on and she was very stuck. "C'mon Paul! You were supposed to wake me. Oh well. Natalie and I are heading to the shed."

A few minutes later, Danielle and Natalie eased into soft blankets on the packed dirt floor facing the velvet curtained Aurora. The room was still. Thin early sunbeams danced through the shed.

So still, they sat in the quiet.

"Natalie, you think something would happen if we went into the Box?"

"It's too tight for two of us in there. Aurora's not ready."

"What do you mean?"

"Shush. Today is very important. Things are happening."

"Natalie, I don't understand."

"We need Paul and Robert here. They're coming." Natalie placed the quiet sign index finger on her lips.

"You know, I'm getting hungry. Hope Paul brings snacks. Could you could play something while we wait?"

A bewildered expression crept over her face, changing into expectation. Natalie took out her violin and tenderly cradled it under her chin. Delicate notes swirled in the air. Soothing. Calming.

Abruptly the shed door burst open.

It was Robert.

Followed by Paul as he tightly closed the shed door.

Urgency in his voice, Robert spoke with authority. "Get out of here. This place isn't safe! The Tuttle's are aiming to get everyone. Right now, Edy's hardware is burning! The Tuttle family is behind it all! And I was a total screw-up."

Abruptly the entire structure of the shed violently shook, the sound of aggressive voices growing louder and louder. Then came a huge thud as the gang members banged on the wooden beams and kicked the padlock off. The defiant group piled in, hostile and fierce. Chief was first to speak. "Well, this suits us fine, no key so we get to trash this place. There's Power in here we've come to get." Chief glared at Robert. "Yeah, you worthless idiot, start talking or you'll get punched in the gut!"

"Hey, Chief, the port is probably in the that corner where the big cardboard carton is."

"Let's have a look."

Like cicadas in their outfitted black jackets, they swarmed the refrigerator box. As they shouted, feet and hands pounded, tearing the huge corrugated carton to shreds. In the commotion, the thick velvet curtain was thrown to the other side of the room. They turned and glared at the four Norfeld's. "So, where's this Power? Ha! That's because you're hiding it? Maybe even playing a trick." Chief held up his hand, giving the command. "Make them talk!"

Robert and Paul went forward, fists held high, their demeanor clad in war armor. Ready to fight. Danielle yanked

Natalie to the other side of the shed, arming themselves with garden tools.

Readiness on both sides.

The front lines went forward.

Not a sound to be heard.

Then came the flash of crackling lightning. The brilliance of a huge star erupted. Blinding. A swirling radiance of ethereal color, of greenish and blue tint. Bold. Commanding. Gathering the strength of a hurricane storm, it became a swelling rainbow … the speed of light in a blinding flash.

The gang members held their hands to their eyes and shrieked. Out they went, tumbling and pushing one another. The shed door flew open.

There was a pause—like from the arch of a dive to the splash into water. Robert, Danielle, Paul and Natalie stood motionless. The small room was without boundaries, as it ebbed and flowed around shooting stars and mysterious planets; a piece of the universe itself. Their hearts quickened with excitement. Although the refrigerator box lay in shreds, the decorative curtain torn, this visitation from Aurora was like no other. Barely minutes long, the visit stretched across the cosmos in utter timelessness. A tangible moment of sheer delight.

In a twinkle, the blissful whirl of energy calmed and retreated, leaving the faces of the four, shiny with tender emotion. Eyes shone bright full of wisdom, affirming hope and direction.

Paul was the first to talk. "What just happened?

"Hey bro, not sure. I know I was about to punch those guys. Then there was this dream. A peaceful place where doubt and confusion were changed into understanding." Robert playfully scratched his head and grinned.

Natalie's gaze fell on both of her brothers. "Now you

know that Aurora could bring you to great places, like a carpet ride, while staying right where you are."

"And even though the box was trashed— the Power— as the gang called it, still happened," said Paul as he waded through the heap of ripped cardboard. "This power is a sort of port to future things that exists without the refrigerator carton. It's still around us."

'Yes," interrupted Robert. I can feel that strength. I had witnessed many events that were scary. But now I see great opportunities before me, nudging me to change and step up."

"Robert, I'm so glad for you. For me, Aurora showed all the butterflies in the backyard. Many of them flew around me, but only one stayed in my hand. The beautiful orange and red one. Natalie closed her eyes to think. "This is the one I choose."

Danielle nodded. There is so much to learn. Yes, this Power has been a port to the future. For us. Yet it is a continuous timeline; of happenings from the past, to this very moment and things still to come. We can remember our past, be in the present but we were only given a glimpse of the future. Until now. During this experience with the Power, I saw a moment into the past of someone else, the secretary from the high school; a Mrs. Peterkin who was recently kidnapped. She is in awful danger."

"What are you talking about?" asked Paul.

"I think I know where this lady is hidden. We need find her!"

"But what about the fire at Edy's? I was there. The police will be swarming us any minute. We need to figure what to do and quick!" Robert's face was set firm with determination.

"Robert, then you take the lead," said Paul. Since you're

the oldest and you've been involved with the Tuttle's, tell us what to do," said Paul.

They sat in a kind of a team huddle, getting ready for the clouds to burst.

25

Tighten the Homefront

There was a thunderous rap on the shed door. "I know you're all in there! Maybe you think that I'm oblivious and don't know anything. Better think twice, because I'm still your father and responsible for you." Mr. Norfeld, lifted his hand to again knock, as the door gently eased open and four heads appeared. "Sorry," they voiced in a most · respectful tone.

In came Mr. Norfeld, his five-foot eight stature seeming more like seven feet. Although his business suit was rumpled from the stake-out, he wore a professional tone as he addressed his family. "Robert, Danielle, Paul and Natalie. We are involved is very disturbing situation. This is what I know. Edy's Hardware is on fire. The emergency people are securing the scene. I did see the police arrest two young men I believe are part of the Tuttle gang. Last night I thought I saw Robert among them, and I was terribly worried. But this morning he was not there." Mr. Norfeld glared at Robert, his eyebrows arched and questioning.

Robert's eyes held fast to his dad's, a mixture of youthful trust and teenage boldness. "Dad, I've been doing my own thing. I have made some very bad decisions, like getting tight with the Tuttle gang. I didn't care if I hurt you or mom ... I was angry with everything and everybody." Robert swiped tears from his cheek, and looked at his family with a face of humility. "I was wrong and I'm sorry. Yes, you saw me at Edy's last night. I was forced to set things up. But this morning, I walked away from the scene. Alex took my place."

There was a hush that filled every spider filled corner.

"Wow, Alex is a great guy, even covering for you ... then you're not going to be arrested," said Paul.

Robert shrugged. "Don't know. Like I said, the Tuttle family demanded my help. I was an accomplice of sorts, but a protesting one. But by leaving I put another person at risk, a lady unknown to me, and I will probably be blamed. This woman is somehow important to them. She is being held captive in ..."

"In a broken-down vegetable stand and her name is Mrs. Peterkin," said Danielle.

Like synchronized swimmers, they all turned and stared at their older sister.

"What," shouted Paul as he grabbed the sides of his head. "I don't get what's going on ... please tell me!"

Danielle took a huge breath. "It's a long story. To begin with, school is starting soon and the high school administration required an application and essay submission that could possibly promote me to the ninth grade. Mom and I completed the paperwork, and I wrote a great essay. If everything was accepted, I could start at Tuttlebury high instead of the middle school. Believe it or not, I thought I was promoted."

"What!" exclaimed Paul his eyes wide.

"Quiet! Please go on Danielle," said Mr. Norfeld, nodding to his daughter.

"I was excited to get this opportunity. But later I found the Tuttle's had arranged it all. When I visited the high school to straighten it out, the staff denied everything, telling me the opposite; that I would be repeating the 7th grade. The main secretary was very concerned, and kept giving me sad glances. As I was leaving, she looked worried and silently handed me her phone number."

"Oh, no! I bet this woman was Mrs. Peterkin," said Natalie.

"You're right. It was Mrs. Peterkin. When I called, she didn't answer. I hoped nothing was wrong. But the next day when I read in the newspaper that a woman was missing from her home, I figured she had been taken by the Tuttle gang. I believe Mrs. Peterkin was looking out for me. Just a few minutes ago, I realized where she might be hidden."

Mr. Norfeld cleared his throat. "Wow, that's some story Danielle! Your mother mentioned paperwork from the high school but I didn't really get it. I hadn't a clue about the baby sitter either. And come on, Robert, you're in a mess of trouble. Hey, now I'm listening—if you think this lady is in that shack, we need to call the police. Now!"

Danielle stood close to her father, speaking in a soft tone. "What if I'm wrong and Mrs. Peterkin isn't there? The police will be asking us a lot of questions. It might be better to go and see for ourselves."

"Danielle is right," said Robert. I've overheard the Tuttle's planning to bring someone food and water … in a town near here. East Elmsted, I think, but don't know for sure."

Lost in thought, Mr. Norfeld closed his eyes, itching his forehead. "Let's head over and find out. Get in the station wagon. Danielle sits in front with me and navigates. Paul, call your mother and tell her we'll be home soon, and Robert be ready to contact the police."

"Me?" Robert put his head down, his hands fidgety.

"Yes, you. It's time to take back Tuttlebury," said Mr. Norfeld the engine roaring as they headed out.

* * *

Hearing the upsetting message on the answering machine, Mrs. Norfeld rolled her eyes. "I guess that's that, no babysitter today," she said aloud. Placing the twins in their kitchen day seats, she yelled, "Hey, where is everyone?" Having not seen them upstairs, she did a quick walk through the living and dining rooms, the den and the home office. "Robert, Danielle, Paul and Natalie ... where are you?" No answer. And what happened to Ted? Her husband's side of the bed had been tidy and there was no evidence of night snacking anywhere. Maybe Ted hadn't come home from his stakeout. Or he could have slept in his favorite recliner and right now be reading the newspaper. She ran to the living room and peered into the dim space. No husband. It was barely seven o'clock and no one was home.

This was all very strange.

William and Joseph began shrieking, wailing a distinctive harmony. Leaving the porch screen open she stepped back into the kitchen. She hummed to them as her hands quickly readied their bottles. Her mind was elsewhere, wondering if the family was in danger; who should she call to get answers. Her head was spinning. She would have to feed the twins at the same time. Cradling Joseph in one arm, moving William's day chair close, she eased the bottles towards their lips, but the fussy babies refused to take their formula. Abruptly the jingle of the phone began ringing and ringing. The twins were howling their lungs inside out. Hastily placing Joseph back into his seat, she tripped over a loose rug, fell into the kitchen table, knocking her coffee mug to the floor. The oozing hot brew missed her feet by inches. Yanking the phone, she heard her younger son's voice. "Paul are you okay," she asked realizing the tense voice was a message. "Mom, all of us are fine. Taking a ride with Dad. A lot is going on … the fire at Edy's Hardware and …" The message cut out.

* * *

Mr. Norfeld pushed down on the gas pedal like a race car driver, but it still took twenty minutes to find the town and the country road. Sighting a dilapidated building ahead he slowed and stopped. "Danielle, is this the place?"

"I'm not sure. I have to get closer. I've never been here but one of the girls from softball told me about it. She said the family used to sell the best summer corn and tomatoes. But it lost business once the Tuttle's put veggies in their store."

"Then how do you really know? The place could fall in on us and there would be no Mrs. Peterkin. This could be a waste of time." Paul annoyingly thumped his feet.

"When we were in the shed, there was an intuitive flash, where pieces of a puzzle moved into place. It all made sense," said Danielle.

"Then we need to check this place out," said Mr. Norfeld. "Robert, you can stay in the car with Natalie. Better not to leave your fingerprints. Since your phone is still working,

214

we will use it to call for help. Paul can come with us but stays outside as a look-out. He waved Danielle from the car, turned and stuck his head in the open window. "Please keep quiet, and remember safety first … no heroics."

Although roadside, the wooden cabin was tucked into trees and creeping vines appearing abandoned. Its boards were broken, weathered with slimy green mold. The entire structure was leaning to one side and as the wind blew, it creaked like a great mansion in a scary movie.

"Paul, stay here and be our look-out," urged Mr. Norfeld as he and Danielle stepped towards the battered front door. Curiously it boasted a new lock.

"Now what Dad," whispered Danielle.

"Seems like there's something of interest inside. Try looking under that dingy doormat."

Danielle gingerly eased her hand under the wet mat. In her slimy grasp she held a muddy key. Laughing, she handed it to her father.

Mr. Norfeld winked. "Even crooks take the easy way and do dumb things."

The paint chipped door swung open. Then unnerving silence. Suddenly there was a whooshing sound as a piece of sharp lumber was hurled. Mr. Norfeld shoved Danielle away; the board grazing his gray hairs. Then another attacked him. Reacting quickly, he ducked and pushed the wood aside. There was a loud thud on the ground followed by angry words. Speedily, Mr. Norfeld leaned over and assisted the stunned woman to her feet. "So, you must be Mrs. Peterkin. We're here to help."

"Who are you people," asked Mrs. Peterkin, releasing herself from Mr. Norfeld's strong grip. Her gaze flit to his side. "Oh, I know you, you're that student the Tuttle's sent me. You're Danielle Norfeld. Looking back at Mr. Norfeld she smiled. "You must be Danielle's father. I'm so glad you're here!" The wild look in her face softened. I'm so sorry. I thought you were those hoodlums coming back to get me."

"Well, we're here to bring you to safety." Mr. Norfeld shook Mrs. Peterkin's hand and Danielle tapped her shoulder.

"So glad I listened to Danielle. She told us to come here." He turned and smiled at his daughter. "Let's get out of here."

Mrs. Peterkin waved her hands about. "Let me talk first. Last night I was disappointed that I didn't leave this place. But the usual guys brought me a great meal—a large sandwich with sides, cookies and bottled water. They told me to enjoy because tomorrow everything would be different. I wondered what they meant, if they were up to no good. Then there was a pardon of sorts. One guy told the other to make me behave and went out to the car. I expected the worse, but instead he put the handcuffs on loose. Leaving, he tipped his cap and tightly secured the door. I was so hungry I tore into the sandwich and wouldn't you know it, the cuffs fell off. With my hands free, I was strong. I found a rotting loose plank and broke it into sharp pieces. No one was coming back in … I would get them first."

The room was still. Eyes stared with disbelief at the woman standing before them.

"We have to get out of here," said Paul as he hurried into the dingy room. "This Tuttle gang could be here any minute!"

Suddenly the wooden door was beaten down, breaking the hinges.

"Hands up! Do not move!" The rustle of dark uniforms encircled the Norfeld family and one very scared lady.

Not a breath was taken.

"Are you Mrs. Peterkin?"

"Yes, I am. Officer."

"And the rest of you must be also the Norfeld family."

"Yes sir, we are. This means you have met Paul and Natalie," calmly replied Mr. Norfeld.

"Also, a young man named Robert, who called in the emergency. I am here to assist; my name is Officer Gregory." The patrolman's neck stretched here and there, scanning the room. "This structure is in bad shape, but it should stand while we finish our business here. Norfeld family … you appear not to need medical help. Is this accurate?" All heads nodded in unison. "Mrs. Peterkin, since you have been restrained here for over a week, you will be taken over to Mercy Hospital and evaluated. At the least you may be dehydrated."

"Officer, I feel fine. I don't need medical service," said Mrs. Peterkin as she raised a half full bottle of water. "They gave this to me this last night."

"Sorry, Mrs. Peterkin. Kidnapping is a serious crime. Your current health requires documentation that will be used to settle this kidnapping case. The paramedics will take you to the hospital. The ambulance will be here momentarily. After you finish the medical evaluation, you will be requested to give us a full statement."

"Can I go home to wash, change my clothes, and get my car, so when I leave the hospital, I can drive to the station?"

"No." Officer Gregory looked up from his writing pad. "This has been a difficult time for you. We will do our best to fully document your case after you are released from the hospital … unless you are kept for observation. A policeman will be assigned to assist you. Could be me. Officer Gregory's face softened as he nodded to Mrs. Peterkin.

"Will you arrest that criminal Tuttle family?"

"I don't know exactly what will happen; but I can tell

you this, whatever you tell us today will be essential in determining this case."

Mrs. Peterkin sighed. Her taunt face relaxed, the color returning to her cheeks. "Then I'm ready."

As they left the former vegetable stand, swirling red and white lights of two police cruisers and an ambulance met them. In the first cruiser, two rowdy men with nasty attitudes were cuffed and seated in the back seat. Members of the Tuttle gang. Seeing them, Mrs. Peterkin let out a loud gasp. In the second police car sat Robert. Exhausted and speechless. To his right perched Paul, his eyes yanked wide like he had met his favorite author.

Mr. Norfeld, and Danielle halted. What was going on? Natalie's warm hand gripped Danielle's. "They're taking Paul too. I overheard them say the Tuttle's have accused us of serious illegal activity; something about breaking into the Tuttle fishing cabin and stealing their property. I really don't understand any of it. I think they wanted Aurora so they're being mean."

"Wow, Natalie, that's quite a mouthful." Curious, Danielle looked at her sister, younger, yes, but very with it. Both looked over at their father who was walking between cars, voicing his own style on interrogation.

Confused, Mr. Norfeld nudged another policeman. "Officer, what is going on here? Why are both of my sons in that police car? How are they involved? What is the extent of Tuttle involvement in this matter?"

"You must be Mr. Norfeld. I'm obliged to not comment, but they're headed to the station for questioning," he said crisply, walking away.

Mr. Norfeld ushered his daughters into the station

wagon and leaned into the soiled napkins from last night's donut supper.

No one spoke a word.

* * *

Good new travels fast but bad news travels even faster. As the Norfeld car pressed towards home they were passed by more emergency vehicles, some going to the veggie stand and others headed to Tuttlebury. What they didn't see was the police attempt to stop a pristine black SUV. The huge vehicle picked up speed instigating a chase. The police car was faster than the limbering suburban and caught up. Side by side they commandeered the tight county road, like a scene in a movie. The runaway vehicle slammed into the cruiser pushing it off the road into the brush. Gearing up, the Suburban plunged ahead right into a police road block, bordered on each side by thick maple trees. The black vehicle came to a screeching stop. All the occupants piled out—the driver, a woman and three teenagers, pushing aside suitcases, pack backs, and a mound of bagged household items.

The Tuttle family.

26

Smoothing the Rough Places

*W*hile keeping an eye out the window and an ear for the telephone, Mrs. Norfeld played with the twins in the den. The day was going by fast, it was already almost lunch, and the televisions in both the kitchen and living room were up full blast. It was not her thing to watch shows during the day, but the unthinkable was happening. A fire at Edy's Hardware was being detailed by one channel as the reporter stood in front of the smoldering building. The total damage not yet known. Those hurt were taken to the nearest hospital, Mercy General. No information was given on how the fire started and who was responsible. Another channel profiled the kidnapping of a school employee in a nearby township but again details were limited. Flipping channels, brief interviews were in process, with mayors from involved towns, including Tuttlebury. Looking closely at the screen, she recognized a congresswoman who was involved with the town women's committee. This woman had ignored her family and others, using bullying tactics. Mrs. Norfeld yelled at the TV, her arms waving about in anger.

Following came a news update. There was live footage of Mr. and Mrs. Tuttle and their family being escorted into the police station. The crowd swelled around the reporter, coaxing for answers from the Tuttle family. Law enforcement personnel stared directly ahead, ignoring their demands for answers.

A surge of emotion tightened her gut. Anger. Fear. Yet she had known this rogue wave was coming. It was here. Hopefully her plea would be heard and fair justice put in place. Suddenly there was a newsflash, a disturbance was being covered—live. As she raced to the other room, she caught a glimpse of several gang members being taken into police headquarters. Getting closer to the screen she gasped. Robert and Paul were with them! How could this be so? She followed their every move, as they were ushered up the steps and into the station. Oh, she hoped she was mistaken.

Moments later the back door rattled. With heads down, piled in Mr. Norfeld, Natalie and Danielle. No Robert and Paul. Long stares broke as the kitchen filled with upsetting voices, confused and afraid. They were all speaking at once, even overriding the blaring television. All were wondering what would happen next. They agreed that Robert and Paul were innocent. The guilty pointer had directly hit the Tuttle family.

They talked and talked until throats were raspy. Mom put out several bowls of chips and filled glass after glass of ice tea. Drinking and nibbling, they watched out the window for police lights, even the TV had been muted. High pitched anxiety was calming.

Talking was done. Now to sit and be patient.

Abruptly came the eruption of howling, ear piercing wails of hunger. The twins. Somehow the babies slept through all the thunderous noise in the house. Very interesting. This would be something to remember once things get back to normal.

Waiting. This was hard to do. They decided to put their nervous energy to work. Again Mrs. Norfeld became the captain of her home team. First, she prompted Danielle to take charge of her baby brothers. There was no rebuttal as with a smile, Danielle dashed off to the den. Natalie was next. The long cord of the carpet cleaner was plugged in as the younger daughter vacuumed corners on the first floor and assisted with preparing special filling for the sandwiches.

Mr. Norfeld was left. At the kitchen table, he was seriously thumbing through this morning's newspaper. His disappointed eyes met up with his wife's. There was nothing yet about the Tuttle's. As Mrs. Norfled cleared her throat, he threw on his dirty shoes and flew outside; to the lawn mower and whatever else needed attention. He had to do something to calm his nerves. Besides yardwork took him back to when he was young; when he had gathered garden herbs and picked berries from bushes his mother had planted long ago.

Mrs. Norfeld was busy doing everything else. Tomorrow was the family welcoming at grandpa's lifelong church with a small gathering at their house. Since no invitations were sent, she wasn't sure who would come, but with all that was happening she didn't mind. The sheet cake was sitting in the refrigerator soon to be joined by finger sandwiches and a salad. Since Ted wasn't able to buy additional paper goods, she counted what she had and hoped it would be enough. She readied her dress for the next day, threw in the laundry and ironed the twins' outfits. She wiped the sweat from her forehead and retied her sneakers. "Just keep going," she said aloud.

But every eye kept a glance out the window.

Except for Dad. The grass catcher on the mower had gone kaput. The lush carpet-like lawn was full of lumpy mounds of chewed-up grass clippings. He needed a rake … which was in the shed way down the backyard. Great. His long stride got him there in no time. Grimy and needy of paint, the shed door was slightly ajar. With the swipe of his large hand, the door swung open. Into the gloomy space he stepped, his eyes attempting to focus. His entire body shook, a thin ray of light clearing his vision. Mr. Norfeld gulped. What had happened here? Had a tornado swirled through … or maybe a large animal was living there?

The shed looked like their old house when they were packing to leave; like a demolition ball had been dropped. The farm utensils, once hung evenly and neat, were thrown around, coated with topsoil, grass seed and leftover manure. Lawn chairs were broken; their weaved canvas tangled in the debris. There were shreds of velvet material, that remined him of his wife's favorite curtains. Flies were buzzing about the broken window, fragments of glass scattered about. Looking to the far corner, his saw something strange. Cardboard pieces. It seemed familiar … it could be the refrigerator box that had brought their new appliance.

Quickly he picked his way through the rubble. Yes, it was that carton, or what was left of it. It was a reminder of one of their happiest days. The twins had been born, they were making friends and they had acquired a new refrigerator. He shook his head: wondering how this carton had become such a terrible mess. They should have just stuffed it in the garage. But maybe the kids had used it for something. For what?

He didn't have a clue. If Grandpa could see this disaster, his eyeglasses would have fogged.

Grumbling, he yanked a broom from the clutter and gathered the decaying cardboard into a heap and threw it out the door. He then swept the broken glass and tossed away a wheelbarrow full of broken items. What was left he cleaned and straightened. Two hours later his body ached and he really needed a shower. But as he closed the shed door, he took a quick peek. Grandpa would have patted him on the shoulder.

* * *

The windows of the Norfeld farmhouse were thrown open, exchanging scents of Lysol and bleach for good fresh air. Every surface had been wiped, waxed and put in its place—prepared well enough to receive a famous personality. Better yet, it would greet any parishioner who cared to drop by after the church service.

It was already getting late. Tired but satisfied with all their work, the family took a break out on the patio. With the twins in their tandem stroller, Mrs. Norfeld, Natalie and Danielle were sipping ice tea, and snacking on tasty lemon cookies. Mr. Norfeld joined them a few minutes later, toweling his hair after a hot shower. The choppy waves of worry had receded … for now.

There was the sound of crunching stones in the driveway. The dark police cruiser halted.

Faces full of surprise, they hurried over to the police car. A different policeman stepped from the car, his manner stern, his words straightforward. "I am Officer Stelley. I understand this is the residence of the Mr. and Mrs. Theodore Norfeld. Are you present?" Both heads rigorously nodded. He moved to the back door of the cruiser and ushered the occupants out. Robert and Paul appeared. "I believe these young men are your sons. They have finished their questioning intake, for now. Since they could be summoned again, they are required to not leave the area." He turned and sat in the driver's seat.

"Officer Steely, before you leave, can you tell us what will happen next? Please tell me my sons didn't commit a crime and won't have to go to jail," said Mr. Norfeld.

The rest of the family, caught their breath, pleading eyes staring.

In a stoic manner, Officer Steeley waved them away. Then paused, his eyes softening as he looked upon the troubled family. "I cannot tell you anymore at this time. You can watch the latest news report. The Tuttle family is being interviewed as we speak."

No one watched the cruiser leave. Instead, they piled into the living room and yanked up the volume of the television. The Tuttle family had been detained as they attempted to leave the state. They were being questioned regarding arson, kidnapping and other criminal activity. The channel was tuned to varying reports; as they picked at every morsel, hoping for clarity. Many pieces on the board game were yet to be moved. But they did know this, the Tuttle family and their gang were in big trouble.

* * *

She had seen enough. Mrs. Norfeld tiptoed away from the blue screen to throw a supper together. She wasn't hungry but everyone probably was, at least a little. The refrigerator was full of goodies for the next day's gathering. The finger sandwiches were tempting her, tasty mouthfuls of tuna, egg salad, ham and cheese and a fresh crabmeat she had creatively mixed. Prepared for tomorrow, she was ready to serve them now. She pulled the tray out and placed it on the table. Then put in back into the refrigerator. What to do?

There was a loud rap on the front door. Wondering who was calling, she lifted the curtain. There stood a young man intently keeping his balance while holding an armful of large pizzas and a bunch of colorful balloons.

"Hello. I'm Jerry, from the Italia Pie Shoppe. You have seven pizzas here. And rainbow-colored balloons … they're a gift."

"Hi, I'm Mrs. Norfeld." Oh my! Where did all this come from? Please set the pizzas down on front step. I'll hold unto the balloons. Very kind of you. The pizza smells so good and these balloons are lovely. Hmm. I count eight in all and …"

"Yes, there's one each for your family and they're from everyone at the pizzeria. You guys have really helped our town. But the pizzas are from a mystery person who ordered the best pies we have. She really wanted that."

"She?"

"Enjoy!" Jerry adjusted his delivery cap and jogged back to his car.

As Mrs. Norfeld waved to the young man, another vehicle pulled into the driveway.

It was Mrs. Peterkin.

* * *

Everyone darted around the kitchen table like flies choosing landing sites on a butter pecan pie. Cartons were pulled open, as the pizzas were admired, and devoured. But not until everyone thanked Mrs. Peterkin for such a luscious present. The table was buzzing with one contented Norfeld family and one grateful woman—Mrs. Peterkin.

Easy pop music was put on by the boys, as the girls shut off the radio and TV. Questions were flying, voices were speaking over one another until Mrs. Peterkin commandeered the floor. With an engaging manner she fully detailed her story, even considering questions before they were asked. There was still much to find out; but they agreed her kidnapping was a serious crime that deserved full legal deliberation and justice.

Dominance of the Tuttle clan was close to the end.

* * *

Walking the upstairs hall to each bedroom, Mom had the last word. "Good night. Sleep well. Be up early and in the car by 8:15. Tomorrow is our special day at church. Be ready!"

One by one lights dimmed and faded out. The Norfeld house was quiet as it rested in the dim shadows, it occupants sinking deeply into pillows and sheets hopeful for tomorrow.

27

Stirrings

The twins had not awakened and Danielle, Robert, Natalie and Paul were in the station wagon. Ready to go.

"Everybody in the get in the front and back seat—right now," demanded Danielle.

Paul shrugged. "Why? I like the way-back."

"What's the deal? Danielle, you're acting like mom," said Robert with a shrug.

Danielle nodded. It's like this, we need to talk, about all that's happened … about the refrigerator Box."

"About Aurora you mean," said Natalie.

"Yes, you're right Natalie. There's been no time to visit the shed since the gang attacked us on Saturday. It's a wreck. We really need to go there."

"I agree," said Paul. It was like a hurricane hit, pushing

the Tuttle gang out. Like we were weird spectators in the eye of the storm."

Danielle spoke again in a determined tone. "For me that time with Aurora was awesome. I was perched on a cloud, seeing the world in different ways, seeing myself in that world."

Leaning into Danielle's shoulder, Natalie nodded in agreement. "There was no storm. What I saw was so wonderful … a wave of pastel color that wrapped around me like grandma's crocheted blanket."

"What are you talking about? I felt I was being slapped around a thousand times," shouted Robert.

"I believe you were," said Danielle. "It was the strangest visit from Aurora; bringing us all what we needed."

"You know Robert," started Paul, "one day Aurora showed you a boat being pounded by fierce waves and you were falling out."

"Yes, I know," said Robert. The boast was sinking and I was going under."

"Yet you didn't drown," said Danielle.

"'How did you know that?"

"Because you're still with us … not locked away in a jail cell."

Paul scratched his head in awe. "Danielle this is getting intense, more than my mystery novels."

"That's because …" Natalie took a breath and looked over the seat at brother. "Robert, that's because you decided to change and get away from those bad guys. It was like the faith that the disciples had. At times they did good and other times, they messed up. You were scared and almost messed up but you had enough faith to do the right thing. And you did."

Robert shook his head. "But do I even have faith? I don't go to church."

Paul began to speak but this time Danielle jumped in. "You may think you haven't any faith, but I've seen you read the family bible and hide it under your bed. You do have some."

No one spoke for several seconds.

Again, Danielle broke in. "Quick, out of the car. Mom and Dad are bringing the twins. Let's plan to meet tonight—at the shed."

They all scrambled about, taking their usual seats.

* * *

"Well, looks like the kids beat us," yelled Mr. Norfeld to his wife as they both hurried to the car. He was amazed that the older children were ready and waiting for them. He was late. It had taken a while to dress since he couldn't find his favorite shiny gray suit and striped tie; clothing he hadn't worn since the move. Lifting both baby seats holding the twins, he followed behind his wife who was balancing diaper bags equally on her shoulders, new church missals in her arms. Quickly they were seated as usual, except the boys were gracious and took the books off their mother's lap.

The Norfeld family was off.

As Mr. Norfeld's began to drive he felt his head clear, his hands were steady and sure. He had no idea why. Yesterday's upset had thrown their lives over the top, with no outcome in sight. Every nerve had been jumping; his chest heavy like an elephant was sitting on it. But this morning was different. He was refreshed from a sound sleep and a quick breakfast. But it was more than that. There was a sense of well-being; like everything was alright with the world and clearly it wasn't.

Could it be because they were all together, tucked into the station wagon? But they were going to church, a place he had avoided. Yet today he was looking forward to this service. Mr. Norfeld glanced about the car. His wife looked lovely in her emerald suit, with her hair in a fancy twist. Danielle and Natalie were so grown-up in their summer dresses; the twins handsome in their soft blue suits. He strained his neck to see the guys in the rear mirror. Seated in the way-back seat, they came into view; heads turned, both with a grin and a wave. Mr. Norfeld gestured back. Things felt almost normal.

* * *

With a gentle turn and a loop around the bend, they were in the church parking lot along with a handful of other cars. "Where is everyone," asked the kids in unison. "It's okay," said Mrs. Norfeld, we're a little early. Most folks show a few minutes before the service begins. We need to head in and pick our seats. The pastor recommended we sit close to the front."

Using a convenient, less obvious entrance, the Norfeld's found their way into the brick faced building, selecting the second row on the right side. In moments they all wedged in. Mr. Norfeld held fast the handle of William's baby carrier, entering the long pew from the side and inched his way towards the center aisle. He was followed by Mrs. Norfeld and baby Joseph. Without giving it a thought, the four siblings slid together in birth order— Robert, Danielle, Paul and Natalie. Wanting to do things right, they kept an eye on their mother since she knew what to do. Appearing calm as they sat, yet each sibling was experiencing a personal butterfly dance.

The organist swept his nimble fingers over the organ

keys as the lively melody reached to the arched ceiling. Pews were now full. All stood to sing and watch as the priest, deacon and altar servers processed up center aisle to the altar. The church rumbled as everyone sat.

A hush filled the majestic space.

The service had begun. The pastor, a robust man with a gentle manner presided. After presenting several prayers, he was seated. The deacon dressed in a white robe then rose to the podium. Everyone stood. With a strong voice, he read the gospel for the day, a story of a boat battered by huge waves, of disciples fearing for their lives, of strong winds becoming calm. They had been saved although having faltered in their faith. The deacon spoke about his life; that with faith he was able to work through some impossible situations. And find that his faith increased. "Faith is a gift," he said, "to open and use daily."

Paul took in every word, nodding in agreement. Danielle leaned forward. Natalie smiled. Robert's cheeks flushed and his hands trembled. He sat motionless; his eyes focused straight ahead.

Taking in the sermon, Mrs. Norfeld's head bobbed up and down in agreement. Mr. Norfeld's face was moist with tears.

It was a moment of conviction.

The service was over. Before the dismissal and last hymn, the priest had a final word. He walked over to the Norfeld's, and extending his arm exclaimed, "Today we welcome the Norfeld family to our church community. We are blessed to have them join us." With a giant grin he looked up at the congregation and said, "Our events committee has arranged a surprise pot-luck to celebrate this occasion. Everyone is invited!"

All clapped with enthusiasm and robustly sang the final song.

* * *

Robert walked slowing down the stairs to the church hall, allowing people to pass him. Be invisible, he said to himself. Or better yet, dash out and wait in the car. As his hunted for an exit, folks looked at him with friendly nods, and pleasant conversation. They knew who he was. Yet they were genuine in their kindness. This was unusual; a kind of no judgement zone.

Smelling the food, Robert's stomach craved a heaping plate. His eyes were overwhelmed; there were so many delicious dishes! He tried a little of everything creating a mushroom type mound. Light music was playing which could hardly be heard over the chatter. Facing the exit, Robert considered taking his food outside and finding a tree to lean on. Not! He would spend time with his family. After all they were celebrating their first time in this church. Today was special. Even though he was distracted—wanting to know the consequences of his behavior—he needed to be patient. Natalie seemed to think he would not sit in jail, but he wasn't so sure.

Robert felt a nudge on his shoulder. "Hey, how about we eat over at that table?"

Robert stared hard at his good friend Alex, who seemed different, older somehow. But Alex had taken his place at the arson. He really should be in jail. Why was he here?

"You look like you're seeing a scary movie!" Hey, I'm not Alex, he's, my cousin. I'm Andrew. People tell me we could be twins and by the face you're making, they're probably right."

"Oh, so you're not him. I hope Alex is okay," said Robert at they both sat at the card table in the corner.

"Well, that depends on what you call okay. Alex is in the hospital for smoke inhalation and a broken leg. Once he gets better, he will be given prison time for arson."

"But he didn't start the fire! He came in and kicked me out before I got hurt or arrested. I would like to have a chance to fix things; it wasn't his fault." Robert put down his fork, his mouth a tight grimace.

"Actually, Alex sent me. He figured you would think this. He knows it wasn't your fault. You were set up. Being in this gang is not for you or for him either. He had wanted out for a long time but felt trapped. That's why he showed up that day, to make things right. You see, Alex has been involved with the Tuttle family for several years ... he has a long list of criminal activity. By rescuing you, he was trying to redeem all the wrong he had done. He gave you a chance to have a decent life and leave this gang for good.

"Alex told you all this? Are you one of the gang as well?"

"Yes, Alex and I have had our talks. And for a while I was with the Tuttle gang. When things got ugly, I decided to leave. It wasn't easy; they threatened me. Then they found my cousin and recruited him."

"So, one moment you're the bad guy and now you're a good one?"

"It's not like that. I beat myself up for a long time. At one point I found this church and am now a leader in the youth outreach."

"Robert. Mom wants you to come to our table. Pastor John is about to visit us. C'mon. Hurry!" Natalie and Danielle gave their brother a wary look.

"Great talking. See you around," said Andrew as he picked up his plate and waved.

"Who was that? He looks like that gang member Alex," asked Danielle. "Is everything okay?"

Robert nudged his sister's shoulder kindly. "No worries. Everything is good. Let's go meet our new pastor." Robert felt a flush of happiness in his chest, yes, it was all good.

28

Going Forward

*T*he ride home was quiet. Even Mr. Norfeld's usual chatter was replaced by easy jazz music on the old car radio. The last few days had been a remarkable experience for all of them. Commotion and upset with the Tuttle family. Mrs. Peterkin. Celebration and festivity at the at the welcoming with a new church family. There were so many sentiments. Balancing these emotions from the mountain top to the valley had them excited one moment, then bone weary the next.

Once home the four collapsed into favorite chairs in the living room and turned on a live baseball game. Mr. Norfeld took charge of the twins urging his wife to put her feet up and take a nap.

The sunlight was dimming and evening shadows were

covering the farmhouse and yard. A cooling breeze gently flowed through open windows.

Ping! Ring! The sound of the antique dinner bell clanged through the rooms. "C'mon everyone! Time for a little snack in the kitchen. Let's go!" hollered Mrs. Norfeld.

"But we all ate too much. We don't want dinner," complained Paul.

"I said come to the kitchen, now!"

"Okay Mom we're coming!"

They all knew that voice; the no nonsense sergeant mom. And she meant business! Within seconds, everyone including Mr. Norfeld, took their usual seats, waiting for an explanation.

"Like I said, we're having a little snack," continued Mrs. Norfeld as she placed the tray of finger sandwiches on the table.

Danielle gasped. "Mom, we spent all that time making these for the welcoming. Instead, the party was in the church basement."

"Yeah! So sweet, we get to eat them,' said Paul.

Mom winked and smiled. "Sometimes along with an unexpected surprise, you get a bonus. I don't need to cook tonight. Let's say grace and start."

After leading the dinner prayer, Mr. Norfeld was the first to grab a stuffed sandwich; chewing and talking at the same time. "Well, I wasn't a bit hungry, but these are really good, I want to try each one, especially the tuna. You know I'm glad we're gathered here. I have personal news to share." He nodded at his wife who smiled urging him on. "I have to say how very proud I am of all of you. Natalie. Danielle. Paul. Robert. This has been an intense couple of days, and you have shown to be strong and responsible. Even with the police hovering around us, you had shown respect. And you … Robert, have amazed me with keeping your anger in check." He paused and took a sip of iced tea, connecting eye to eye with his eldest son. "I believe this Tuttle situation will be resolved and you will be cleared."

No one spoke as they waited for their father to continue.

"There is another issue I need to bring up. Mom and I have discussed this already. I have been offered a promotion in another company with a great salary with room to grow. As part of the package, they offer luxury condo housing and scholarship monies for college. The position is in another state and they want to know soon."

The munching and slurping stopped.

"Oh no! I will miss my new friends, the backyard and the shed." Natalie's voice was thin, as she slumped in her chair.

"What! We're moving?" Danielle stood up and shook her head.

"No way. And let the Tuttle's continue to take over this county! We can't do that. I left that family for good … and I will not be chased out!"

"But this is grandpa's house. I'm been working hard painting it. We can't leave!"

Mom walked over to her husband and placed her hands on his shoulders, loudly cleared her throat. "Dad and I have talked all of this over and wanted your input before we decide." She paused, as her bright eyes rested upon each one of her children. "We appreciate hearing your strong opinions. Now let your father continue."

."To make this a family decision, we will take a vote. Please nod your head if you want to leave Tuttlebury."

No one moved or even seemed to breathe.

Now, a raise of hands of those who wish to stay."

With a whoosh all hands went up—the four siblings and their mother and father.

With a great cheer that awakened the sleeping twins, the family clapped and stomped. "We will take over Tuttlebury!"

"Yes, and then we'll call it Greenfeld," said Natalie.

"Hmm," said Mrs. Norfeld, giving Natalie an odd look. "Well, I'm glad we're staying. Before we ready for bed, I have one more item to bring up." She reached into apron pocket and pulled out several envelopes, piling them on the table. Everyone leaned over except Natalie who nervously picked her nails.

"I found these lovely letters the other day. They were hand written by your grandma and sealed in berry scented decorated envelopes. There is one for each of you, with your name penned in delicate writing. Grandma left no instructions. I suppose you can read it now or put it away for safekeeping." Mrs. Norfeld looked over to the window, her face hinted of sadness, then delight.

"You might be wondering why I'm choosing today to do this. It's because we could use grandma's strength by embracing her memory and wise sayings. Grandma's words are very heartwarming; words that can help us all go forward. I read mine over and over again." She carefully lifted the lovely envelopes off the table. "I will leave them in the dining room for you to find after supper. Remember these are personal letters but if you want to discuss them, I'm here for you." Abruptly she collected the letters and left the kitchen.

Dad stroked his cheek and shook his head. "Wow. I didn't see that coming. Your mother didn't tell me. Looks like she's not coming back so let's clear this supper mess. Then go pick your letter."

All heads leaned towards the dining room. Thinking.

Why did grandma write each of them a letter? How strange. Yet how wonderful. Grandma had always been in their corner, with a giant grin and sincere word. She must have penned reassuring, important thoughts or why bother to write at all?

In record timing, the kitchen was cleared as the four siblings hurried to the dining table and found their letter.

Remaining at the kitchen table, Mr. Norfeld savored the last sips of coffee. This weekend, so much had happened with his family. The worse and the best of life had visited them. Hardship had been dumped into their laps as well as the optimism from church folks he hardly knew. He probably should feel depressed yet he felt a sense of hope. Somehow all this trouble was bringing them closer. As a father, he was proud of his family no matter what happened, they would work together. Leaving his coffee cup in the sink, he headed to the dining room. The sole letter left was his. In his mother's delicate cursive was written ... to my dearest son, Teddy, all my love. He edged his finger under the flap and eased it open. As he read, he held the paper gently in his large hands, his mind capturing times past as they streamed by.

* * *

All was quiet in the Norfeld house, a kind of anticipation in the air like Christmas morning. Up and ready, Danielle, Robert, Natalie and Robert tiptoed through the halls, flashlights in hand. Thin yellow beams lighted the way to the shed. The door was jammed shut, the metal lock in snugly in place.

"Natalie, I thought you said this door was always open," said Paul.

"It usually is because I'm alone ... or sometimes with Danielle."

Paul shrugged. "Dang, I can't help. I used to have a key, found it sometime ago, But I've lost it again."

Robert shook his head. "You had the key I found in the gang's fishing cabin. I couldn't find it, so figured I misplaced it, then ..."

"Yup. I found it in the grass after we had that fight outside the cabin." said Paul.

"You got that right. It was the day you were spying on me. Paul, you had the key for a while until I found it in our room. Somehow, it's missing again."

"That's okay," said Danielle. "Because I have grandpa's master key from the old house keychain, hidden it in my bureau." I don't use it much because I usually visit the shed with Natalie."

"So, there are two keys," supposed Robert.

"No, there are three." By her feet, Natalie lifted the heavy soiled mat, and pulled out a tarnished, rusty key. "This key is for just in case."

"Yeah, I remember that one, grandpa always used it." said Robert.

Paul stood closer to his sister. "So many keys. And the gang broke in without one! We want in. Natalie, open the door!"

Grabbing the key from under the mat, Natalie awkwardly approached the lock, the key slipping from her hand. Curiously, on its own, the padlock shifted to its side, then fell to the ground. The shed door creaked ajar, begging to be thrown wide open.

* * *

Little Joseph was stirring, whimpering in his sleep. Mrs. Norfeld gently swooped him up and sat in the rocking chair near the window overlooking the yard. Flashlight rays, weaved and intertwined at the shed. She leaned in closer, careful not to awaken William. She laughed softly to herself. Yesterday if she had seen this, she would have raced out of the house like a crazy woman. But after reading grandma's letter, she understood. The children had some business to finish of the most unusual kind.

Across the hall the she could hear feel the house shaking with the snores of her husband. He needed this sleep and so didn't she. She tucked a summer blanket around baby Joseph and set him in his bed. Many thoughts flowed through her mind; the day they moved, their connection with the Tuttle family, the helpful people she had met. She pondered the kidnapping and Robert's implication in all this; what this could mean for his life ... for all their lives.

Once more she gazed outside; the yard was dimly brightened from the fading moon. Somewhat visible were the outline of trees around the patio and the garage on the side. Mrs. Norfeld inched closer to the windowpane, squinting towards the shed. Did she see something or was it her imagination? But there it was again. Streaks of violet light zipped about the shed. There was something about that place. Ah, grandpa had spent a lot of time in there, working on projects. Grandma kept an orderly shelf of her best jams; waiting for the day to flavor a piece of toast. A simple place that held strong memories ... and something else. There was a kind of manifestation showing significant things. This was apparent when she found Natalie with fever. She had also discovered the unusual letters from grandma. Ah. There was a presence of sorts, this she knew. Her eyes blurred and her head felt light as she sat back in the rocking chair. Perhaps after a few minutes of rest, she would better understand. Her chin tucked to her chest, as she snored softly.

Lunar light dimmed as the early sky drifted in.

29

Growing Pains

*A*ll three Norfold children hovered around their younger sister. "No way! Natalie, you've dropped the key," Paul grumbled.

"Shush! But the door is open, isn't it? Watch where you're going. Don't worry about the key; it will be under the mat later," said Natalie.

Danielle shone her flashlight at their faces, "It's scary coming back here. Those Tuttle bullies charged in, really wanting to hurt us. Plus, they trashed the place badly."

"C'mon what's taking so long," said Robert, his huge foot pushing the door.

The four flashlights powered into the space, creating menacing shadows.

"Oh no! What happened here," shouted Paul.

Standing still, feet anchored to the floor, they all stared.

The shed was showcase perfect. The broken glass and wooden boards were restored and the place perfectly swept. All the farming and garden tools were hung and grandpa's workbench was tidy and spotless. Whiffs of fresh paint and cleaning solutions tickled their noses.

Their father had been in here. And he had cleared out everything.

There was a thud as Robert bumped into the worn worktable. "Hey, here's grandpa's sturdy lamp." There was a clicking sound as a blast of light filled the room.

No one spoke.

Paul rushed to the far corner and yelled "the refrigerator box isn't here. It's all gone!"

"Aurora is missing! Those awful men took it." Tears were streaming down Natalie's face. "My velvet curtain has disappeared too!"

"Robert shook his head. "Dad got rid of all of it, including that musty curtain. Like it never happened at all ..."

"What's going on here?" Danielle put her arm around her sister's shoulder. "Let's chill a minute. We saw that box carry in our new refrigerator, and it was hauled from the garage to this shed. Natalie cleaned up an old curtain for the entrance. We all had experiences with Aurora, even you Robert."

"Yes, Robert, you were in that boat that turned over and you almost drowned!" Natalie wiped the tears, her face fully animated.

Paul's eyes twitched as he remembered something. "Robert, a few weeks ago you told me that story, that you did go under. But you were saved by a great light."

All eyes settled on Robert.

"Okay, you're right. I did see that image of the boat and

some weird kind of light. I'm not sure what it all means … there definitely was a message that I'm still learning from."

"So, let's figure this out; what really was that Box?" asked Paul. "Was it some kind of fantasy that rooted in our minds, or a window to the future? Maybe it was a kind of magic? Or a special kind of helper since Natalie gave it a name?"

"Not!" said Natalie, I made Aurora my friend with this name. Aurora was not magic—but awesome power. It let me see things that made me happy."

The four siblings talked at once.

"The Box suggested possibilities of what could happen in our lives if we decide to choose that way."

"Yes, it is a kind of portal … which is part of a complete timeline of the past, present and future. With us it went to the future and glimpsed those possibilities. On our own, we can only recall past happenings as we stay in the present moment."

"This is what the pastor had mentioned on Sunday, that a higher power knows us and knows the very beginning, the now, and through the end of time. I cannot know all this. But there are many choices I can try. For starters, I want to stay right here with you all."

"Then …" Natalie looked very thoughtful. "It's like the highway dad drives to bring us somewhere. There are many exits to take. Dad will try the first, then another and finally picks the next one. He tells mom, that some roads are the wrong way, others are the long way, then there is the best way."

"What?" asked Robert.

Danielle jumped in. "It's like this; there are many highways or prospects around us, but we have the opportunity to choose the road that leads to the best way … to a meaningful and good life.

"The Box has given us each a gift; from showing the most dismal side of ourselves to seeing the absolute best." Paul went on. "We have the capability to pick which way to go."

Robert shook his head and looked down.

Paul stood tall by his brother, "Robert, believe it or not, you have taken another way and have changed. You risked your life by breaking off ties with the gang, choosing yourself and those people close to you."

Looking down at his feet, Robert shook his head. "I suppose you're right but I still don't know what's going to happen to me. I've made such a mess. It's not easy to climb out of this mucky trench. But I'm ready do the right thing." The deep hostility had lifted. Now there was a sparkle in his deep brown eyes like honey on a sunbeam.

* * *

Finding a worn bedspread, Danielle, Robert, Natalie and Paul sat for a long while in the shed. Often looking at the corner where the Power had once been and wondering why it had left. There was much speculation; they had come to believe that the Box had finished its work—the rest was up to them. One determined step after another.

Their shoes off, they kicked back and enjoyed the light melody of a violin arrangement. With eyes closed, Natalie played an inspired melody, full of rich tones. One by one each of them found a place on grandpa's worn blanket and fell asleep.

Soon the rays of early morning were shining through the window. Danielle was first to stir. Shaking the blanket, she then nudged her sister and brothers on the shoulder. "Do any of you think the Aurora will return?"

Robert tied on his sneakers. "That box will never return. I bet it's in the dumpster right now. Possibly the power will …"

"I agree. The power Aurora has is always there. Like an electric outlet. But the plug has to fit just right to reach the power. Time is always happening. Each minute can move us forward. Then that minute becomes the past as the next one comes. We were plugged in for a while and were shown wonderful things. The way I see it … we have to try out what we learned and make our future happen," said Natalie.

"Natalie, you're right; we have to take that step."

Paul nodded with excitement. "We're on to something. That power didn't just come and suddenly disappear. This time port never left."

"That's what I said, Aurora, is always there for everyone. It has another plug getting ready."

"I like this explanation. But for now, I want to be here in this town, starting high school in a couple of weeks," said Danielle.

"Me, too. I can't wait to begin the fifth grade and make new friends."

"Ugh. Leave it to our sisters to be so logical. I want to see my course schedule and go to the school library. Who knows, I might make a friend, maybe someone who likes to snack."

"Yeah, Paul. We're all in for big changes this year. But I think we'll be okay," said Robert with a kind smile.

Not looking back, one by one they headed towards the door. The pungent scent of pipe smoke followed them out.

The shed door flung wide open as they stepped forward. Huge smiles dimpled their cheeks as they ran swiftly to the farmhouse.

From behind the shed came a spark, a crackle; a rising celestial light.

30

The Return

*T*he planted fields of green had become a harvest of plenty to be roasted and feasted upon with decorative dinnerware and fancy napkins. The clouds swirled marble in a sky of pale blue, the winds lifting crimson leaves. Now forgotten were the lazy days of summer, as jacket collars were yanked under chins, and gloves were pulled on frosty fingers.

A sign approached on the right; Welcome to the City of Greenfeld. Four vehicles turned off varied highways to the familiar country road, following one another; a trailing rainbow of design and color. Not rushed their motors idled quietly. A sense of sadness, a sense of anticipation. They flowed around a bend to another street, near a huge acreage of slumbering field. At the top of the hill, each parked one after the other, their engines silenced. Overlooking the slope was a simple brick walk that ended at a decorative black iron entrance.

There was a rumble from the last car as the driver hopped out, slamming the door of the energy efficient vehicle. Dressed in a professional sports jacket, corduroy slacks and thick leather boots she walked a few steps to ridge of the hill, pulling the collar on her neck. She gazed over the harvested land, arranging her personalized sports cap over a short bob. She stood alone until a young man approached, slipping a paperback cookbook into his pocket. Drawing out earmuffs he secured them around his head of graying hair. They warmly embraced then gestured with excitement towards the field. A petite woman came running, careful not to trip on her velvet gown. Laughing she threw her arms around the man and woman, her lengthy multicolored scarp wrapping around them. Turning towards each other, they chatted like a brood of chickens.

One last person remained in the car. He turned off his radio and watched the commotion on the three. He was thrilled to see them but melancholy as well. So much had happened in the past years that he found little time to contact his brother and sisters. What could he say— he knew he could do better. But he was busy. He had the biggest family with a wife and five children. He worked an important job and at times didn't see his own family. Coming to visit today was crazy; long flights and longer drive. He hadn't even changed his clothes. But this time he had to show-up. He wasn't about to miss Danielle's early Thanksgiving dinner.

There was loud tapping at the window as Danielle, Paul and Natalie urged him from the car.

Out came a distinguished looking gentleman in an expensive shiny gray suit with a bold striped tie. He threw on a thick overcoat as he stepped from the car.

"Robert!"

Danielle gave her brother a strong hug. "So good to see you. My husband and son can't wait to hear about your work as a rocket scientist!"

"And you, Danielle, a famous sports manager who is also building a sports complex on our family ground. Very impressive."

Paul laughed. "Yeah, Robert is figuring other planets and Danielle is digging up the planet Earth."

Natalie grabbed both brothers and embraced them. "Hey, Paul I've heard that besides your research you've been creating incredible recipes. And that another cookbook is in the works? How do you get the time?"

"Me? How about you? You're not wearing that fancy gown to Danielle's only for our dinner? There must be something else …"

"Leave it up to you to notice. Before meeting up here, I was invited to play a few tunes for the Greenfeld Harvest concert."

"Natalie, I was glad to sneak away from the turkey basting to see you. Your performance was truly awesome. You played your violin with such grace and elegance. I'm so proud of you!"

"Always knew you were a great talent," said Robert. "Sorry, I was a jerk. I would like to hear you play."

"Well, Robert, you're in for a treat. After dinner, Natalie promised she would take out her violin. With most of our families gathered, we can all enjoy a little concert."

"I'll look forward to Natalie's fine playing. Also, I understand the twins are pushing into their early thirties and still in school completing research degrees. Are they joining us?"

"Yes, as usual William and Joseph are working hard for

their advanced degrees, but they have managed to leave the university early for Thanksgiving. Their plane was delayed but hopefully they'll be in by the time the turkey is served! But first we need to finish what we came here to do."

"Yes, Danielle, I have my letter. Does everyone else?"

All heads nodded as they dug in their pockets. The wind kicked up, blowing debris around them.

"These letters ... I always wanted to know where they came from," began Robert. "Mom gave them to us but she was never clear about details. Sometimes I think she might have written them herself."

Danielle's eyebrows raised up. Paul pulled on his salt and pepper beard.

"I can clear this up right now! It was me—I found them. Remember when William and Joseph were born and we were cleaning the house? When I was polishing the China-cabinet, I found a golden key under it, stuck in the floor molding. Prying it off, I searched the cabinet for a hidden drawer. There was one and the key opened it ..."

"Awesome! Grandma really did write them!"

"Then I pulled out a packet with red and white twine wrapped around it. Inside were all kind of envelopes. Some were family business; the most interesting were those written in grandpa and grandma's special style of writing, the stationery fragrant with berry scent. I remember wanting to look at them again in the shed, and reread my own. Then lost grandma's cards. I was very upset with myself. But I figured out mom found them when she carried me out of shed. You all know later she gave the cards to us." Natalie held her letter tight in front of her. "I'm ready to go down the hill. Are all of you?"

In single file, they went down the cobblestone path, to the decorative iron gate, the archway declaring in gold leaf, Greenfeld Cemetery. Paul eased the entrance open as they followed Danielle to an upright marble stone. Danielle, Robert, Natalie and Paul formed a crescent shape around the graveyard plot. In a bold voice, Paul read the names of those inscribed. Their full names were annunciated with pride, honor and great sadness; known to them as Grandpa, Grandma, Mom and Dad.

Danielle went to side of the grave, where a rectangular trench had been dug, a shovel placed beside it. Leaning down, she pulled up a thick plastic container with a heavy lid. And opened it.

A time capsule.

Danielle gently placed her letter, wrinkled and spotted, into the vessel. Paul was next; his letter grimy with fingerprints, folded over and over, was hastily dropped in. The letter Natalie held looked brand new, the sole telltale of time was the yellow patina. Robert was last. Stepping back, his head lowered, as he read the letter again. Then again. Fresh tears wet the envelope, as he lingered over the capsule. His lips lightly touched it as he let it go.

Danielle secured the capsule and returned it the trench. Each in turn shoved in the dark soil. With the last scoop of heavy earth, Danielle levelled the dirt with the surrounded grass, firming the plot gently with her boot.

Offering their respects, Robert, Danielle, Paul and Natalie stood close.

Robert broke the stillness. "Can we ever forget this place? What happened in that shed changed my life. I chose to become a good man."

"My life as well. I was able to move forward doing things I love … research, writing books and cooking."

"Yes, Aurora was amazing. But so was growing up with you all."

"I appreciate this place every day; soon it will encourage kids who love athletics to find excellence in their sport and in themselves."

"Yes, a special experience took place here, and perhaps is somewhere else at this very moment."

Fading crimson and burnt sienna leaves swirled in patterns dancing to the melody of the wind. The brisk air calmed, as a soft mist floated. A sense of an otherworldly presence surrounded them. Feeling in the company of their loved ones ... Grandpa's smile and Mom's nod, words unspoken ... but heard in their being, "proud of you ... continue on ... we will meet again."

On the horizon the remnants the golden sun drifted. Suddenly in the darkening sky flowed huge fluorescent pink and violet streaks as from a thick paintbrush. Sparkler bursts of rainbow color swirled and spun in the purple backdrop. Then another. And another. Until spectacular designs frolicked through the painted canvas.

In a blink, the drape of darkness fell. Pinpricks of light grew and grew into glowing crystals and brilliant diamonds.

An incredible moment ... to reach and touch a singular star.

Their hearts beating with excitement and hope, the four turned and climbed up the hill to their cars.